PRAISE FOR *HOUSE AND HOME*

"A sharply funny, nicely realized work of catharsis that will be satisfyingly familiar to anyone who has ever suffered seller's remorse." —*The New York Times*

"A highly enjoyable read . . . the house almost seems like a member of [Ellen's] family, the way it's been loved and nurtured. It's where she brought her two daughters home from the hospital, suffered a miscarriage, and raised her children. But people, and your relationship with them, are more important than bricks and mortar. This is a lesson that Ellen eventually learns, after a dramatic turn of events puts her at risk of losing everything she values most." —*Ladies' Home Journal*

"An affecting, honest story." —*Grosse Pointe Times*

"[One] of the most engrossing books this season." —*O at Home*

"*House & Home* is an extraordinary debut novel by Kathleen McCleary, who takes her fans to an all new level by introducing them to this whimsical spin on trading places. With a bit of humor and just the right amount of drama, *House & Home* is a first-rate designer's dream." —*Freshfiction.com*

"This novel is a delight. It grabs you from the opening paragraph . . . and holds you with its cathartic exploration of home and family."
— *The Oregonian*

"In McCleary's poignant, gently humorous novel, the characters seem utterly alive, and the locations are exquisitely described . . . Altogether so superior it's hard to believe that it's a debut. Readers who enjoy fine women's fiction will be delighted to discover this new author."
— *Booklist*

"McCleary's tale of real estate woe (plus a little entrepreneurship gone wrong) will resonate with unhappy homeowners, as will her portrait of a regular woman pushed to extremes trying to do the right thing for her family."
— *Publishers Weekly*

"A sparkling debut novel . . . *House & Home*'s message will resonate with anyone who has allowed a place to define who she is and how she lives. McCleary's charming, curl-up-and-read novel will strike an emotional chord with women everywhere."
— *Ijustfinished.com*

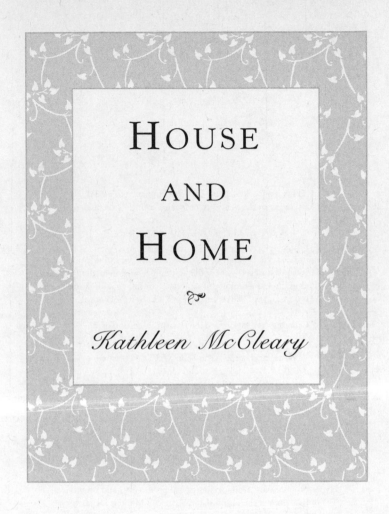

HOUSE
AND
HOME

Kathleen McCleary

voice

HYPERION

NEW YORK

Copyright © 2008 Kathleen McCleary

The Library of Congress has catalogued the hardcover edition of this book as follows:

McCleary, Kathleen
House and home / Kathleen McCleary.—1st ed.
p. cm.
ISBN-13: 978-1-4013-4073-5 (hardcover)
1. Divorced women—Fiction.   2. Dwellings—Psychological aspects—Fiction.   I. Title.
PS3613.C3577H68 2008
813'.6—dc22
2007035956

Paperback ISBN: 978-1-4013-4104-6

Hyperion books are available for special promotions and premiums.
For details contact the HarperCollins Special Markets Department
in the New York office at 212-207-7528, fax 212-207-7222,
or email spsales@harpercollins.com.

Book design by JAM design

FIRST PAPERBACK EDITION

3   5   7   9   10   8   6   4   2

To Paul,
who dragged me kicking and screaming across country,
and started it all.

ACKNOWLEDGMENTS

FIRST AND FOREMOST I have to thank my daughters, Grace and Emma Benninghoff, for their inspiration and support. Gracie allowed me to borrow liberally from her own colorful childhood in certain episodes in the book, and was a supportive first reader of the completed manuscript. Emma never wavered in her enthusiasm and absolute belief that I would not only finish, but get it published; her cards, smiles, and hugs saw me through some of my bleakest moments. I love them both with all my heart.

Thank you to the brilliant women at Voice. Ellen Archer, Pamela Dorman, Beth Gebhard, and Kathleen Carr: your warm response to my manuscript was literally beyond my wildest dreams. Ellen has been an amazing cheerleader for the book. I'm particularly grateful for the graceful direction and meticulous editing of Pamela Dorman and the sharp eye of Kathleen Carr, as well as the excellent copyediting of Susan M. S. Brown. The book is definitely richer and better for your input.

I thank Ann Rittenberg, my agent, who made me feel like I had her at hello, and has provided wonderful guidance and friendship ever since.

I would never have gotten beyond the first few chapters without

Nicole Bokat, Hildy Silverman, Rick Clay, and Bart, my first readers, at mediabistro's online novel writing course. Beyond that, Nicole and Margot Magowan were instrumental in giving me feedback and encouragement on virtually every chapter. I am very lucky to have had two such talented writers involved.

Thanks, too, to the wonderful friends whose love sees me through everything: Deborah Alfano, Wally Konrad, Fataneh Dutta, Holly Hess, Karly Condon, and Kara Ilg. I give special thanks to Laura Merrill and Lori Kositch, my first Oregon readers.

Thanks to Steve Selby, who insisted on the champagne even though I had the worst head cold of my life. You're right: You have to have at least *one* glass of champagne on the day you sell your first novel. Thank you to Stacy Hennessey, who gave me a job when I was desperate, not for money, but for human connection. Stacy's Coffee Parlor, in Falls Church, Virginia, was a great inspiration, for obvious reasons.

I also need to thank my aunt, Dorothy McCleary, whose love of books inspired me, and who always believed I had a novel in me somewhere. And my brother, Tom McCleary, whose quiet support I can always count on.

When I was in elementary school, I used to go to the library and imagine what it must be like to write one of the books on those shelves. I owe my lifelong love of reading and my appreciation for the incredible gift of a good education to my parents, Ann and Tom McCleary, whose values govern my life. Thank you.

Finally, thanks to Paul Benninghoff, my husband. He told me again and again not to worry about getting published, but just to finish writing. I did! What a long, strange trip it's been, and yet somehow we still always end up at home.

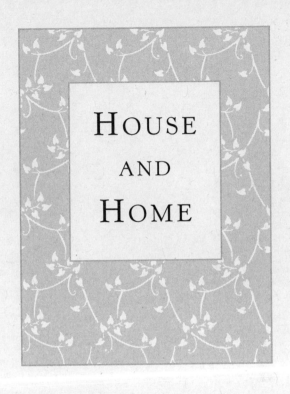

HOUSE
AND
HOME

CHAPTER ONE

THE HOUSE WAS yellow, a clapboard Cape Cod with a white picket fence and a big bay window on one side, and Ellen loved it with all her heart. She loved the way the wind from the Gorge stirred the trees to constant motion outside the windows, the cozy arc of the dormers in the girls' bedroom, the cherry red mantel with the cleanly carved dentil molding over the fireplace in the living room. She had conceived children in that house, suffered a miscarriage in that house, brought her babies home there, argued with her husband there, made love, rejoiced, despaired, sipped tea, and gossiped and sobbed and counseled and blessed her friends there, walked the halls with sick children there, and scrubbed the worn brick of the kitchen floor there at least a thousand times on her hands and knees. And it was because of all this history with the house, all the parts of her life unfolding there day after day for so many years, that Ellen decided to burn it down.

At first she thought she wouldn't have to. While she had known at every step that moving was a mistake, she could almost picture someone else in the house, perhaps a nice retired couple who would stay a few years before moving on, or a quiet bachelor who would love the garden and the big bedroom on the main floor. She was totally unprepared for Jordan, whose brisk efficiency and patronizing air of possession and pity just turned Ellen's stomach.

"I want to assure you that the house will be well-loved," Jordan told her repeatedly, after showing up unexpectedly at the back door one day, tape measure in hand. "I adore it and we have great plans for it."

Ellen was silent. She didn't want Jordan loving her house, any more than she would want Jordan loving her husband, even if he was her soon to be ex-husband. She didn't even want to meet Jordan, who had bought the house just weeks ago, with the stipulation that Ellen could rent it back until the end of May. Ellen didn't want to be able to picture the new family who would be living in her house, the other children who would make a clubhouse in the attic under the eaves and measure their growth against the doorjamb of the closet in the master bedroom. She had attended the closing last week by herself, signing the papers after Jordan and her husband had signed their part, signing away a whole life embodied by the little yellow house.

Ellen instantly mistrusted Jordan, quickly assessing her straight blond hair, cut in the usual suburban-mom bob, her small size (she stood barely five foot three, Ellen guessed), and her persistently upbeat tone of voice, and making an immediate judgment that this was someone she would never like. Jordan had a heart-shaped face, with a sharp, almost elfin chin, china blue eyes, and a spattering of pale freckles across her nose. She had probably been a cheerleader, Ellen thought, and a sorority sister. Ellen, as a petite person herself, felt strongly that small people should avoid perkiness at all costs.

"I know this must be hard for you," Jordan said. "But you

should know that I'm very good with houses. I was an art history and architecture major at U.Va. Where did you go to school?"

The question irritated Ellen. To begin with, it had been more than twenty years since she'd been in any kind of school, so she had no idea why that should be important. And it was also a question that was so completely "East Coast" as to be embarrassing. No one in Oregon ever asked—or cared—about your school affiliation.

"This is the West Coast," Ellen said, a little sharply. "You're not supposed to ask what college someone went to here."

Jordan smiled. "I need to measure the kitchen window again for my contractor," she said, putting her bag down on the tile countertop. "I'll only be a minute."

Ellen watched Jordan, standing on tiptoe in her tiny black capri pants and gray U.Va. sweatshirt, stretching the tape measure from one end of *her* windowsill to the other. Ellen felt suddenly and unreasonably enraged. And that's when she first thought of burning down the house, picturing Jordan's pert mouth in a perfect little O of astonishment when she heard the news.

Ellen didn't know what to do with the intensity of her feelings about the house. If she lost a parent, God forbid, or even a beloved pet, the outpouring of sympathy from her friends and family would be enormous and complete and sincere. But no one seemed to empathize with the huge sense of loss she had over the house, the grief that felt as real as any she had experienced. It was the death of a life, the life she and Sam and Sara and Louisa had had here and now would never have again.

To be perfectly honest, the house had its flaws. The kitchen was too small and dark and the upstairs bathroom ridiculously crowded, up under the eaves. The stairwell from the first floor to the second was so steep and narrow they couldn't even fit their queen-size box spring into the opening and had had to special-order one that was split in two. But their bedroom window looked out across the orchard next door, an overgrown tangle of espaliered apple trees, and beyond that over a row of Douglas firs to the purple and blue mounds of the Cascades in the distance. She had ripped up the carpet there herself, and stripped and sanded and polished the old oak floors until they glowed. She'd spent weeks poring over paint chips and mixing colors and painting swatches on the walls to come up with just the right shade of blue-lavender, the same color as the mountains that ribboned across the horizon outside the window. She'd stood each of the girls against the doorjamb to Sam's closet twice a year and carefully marked the date and their height and their initials. It was not just rooms, not just a house; it was an expression of Ellen herself, nurtured as carefully as the people she'd loved inside its walls.

Jordan, standing in Ellen's kitchen, tapped her little foot impatiently. Ellen noted that she was wearing Tinker Bell sneakers. Why on earth a thirty-something woman who clearly had given birth and seen something of life would want to wear a Disney character on her feet was inexplicable to Ellen.

"Ellen? You'll be out by May thirty-first, right? I really need to get my carpenters in here as soon as possible."

Carpenters. Ellen saw hammers smashing great holes in the plaster of her walls, crowbars prying loose carefully painted moldings and cupboards.

"Yes," she said. "By five on May thirty-first."

"Good." Jordan picked up her big brown handbag, overflowing with pens, blueprints (*for my house!* Ellen thought), and a sterling silver key fob attached to a ring of at least sixteen jangly keys.

"Oh, and Jordan?"

Jordan turned, running a hand possessively over the smooth ceramic countertop.

"Yes?"

"Harvard. Early decision. Magna cum laude," Ellen lied flawlessly. "See you in a few weeks."

The last day of May was little more than three weeks away. Immediately after Jordan left, Ellen poured herself a cup of tea and sat down at the computer. Of course she couldn't do anything obvious—she had two girls to raise, and no intention of spending the next twenty years in jail. She had to make sure no one was hurt. It had to be a contained fire, one that couldn't spread to the neighbors' homes or injure the firefighters. It had to be just enough to gut a room, pour thick smoke through the rest of the house, just enough to leave the house unsalvageable. Then Jordan and her carpenters could tear it down and build a perfect new house, one that wouldn't include the room where Ellen had lain in bed for five days after losing the baby, her middle child, or the rooms where Sara had taken her first step and Louisa had whispered "hot, hot"—her first word.

Ellen looked up electrical hazards. Overloaded sockets. Loose wires. Bare wires. Water near wires. The house was almost seventy years old, after all. Then again, the intricacies of electrical wiring terrified Ellen, who still had those little plastic protectors stuck in the sockets even though the girls were no longer babies, just because it made her feel better. No, she needed an accidental fire, something simple. Candles.

The screen door to the kitchen slammed, and Ellen quickly turned off the computer screen.

"Ellie?"

"Here, in the office."

Sam walked in and sat on the arm of the blue and white striped couch. His wavy, almost black hair stuck out in every direction. He was dressed in baggy tan corduroys and a navy blue Henley shirt that lay untucked over his pants. A two-day stubble of beard, black speckled with gray, covered the lean angles of his cheeks and chin. Ellen had always loved his rumpledness, even when he drove her crazy. Part of it was simply that he was so physically beautiful and didn't even know it, and clearly didn't care. With his high cheekbones, thick dark brows, and brown-black eyes, he looked almost foreign, exotic. A gifted athlete, he moved with an unthinking grace, with a complete ease and familiarity with his body that Ellen envied. She looked at him and realized that, even though she was about to divorce him, she was still attracted to him and probably always would be.

"Are the girls home? I promised I'd take them for ice cream."

"No, they're not home yet. They're staying at Joanna's for dinner," Ellen said. "But Jordan Boyce was here. She just left."

"I thought you didn't want to meet her," Sam said. He picked up Louisa's pink rubber ball from the floor and began to toss it up and down absentmindedly with one hand, catching it without even seeming to look at it.

"I didn't! She called and asked if she could come take some measurements. I told her I'd be out until six but would leave the back door unlocked. She showed up twenty minutes *after* I got home. I know she did it just so she could meet me and tell me how wonderfully she's going to take care of the house. I hate her."

"That's silly," Sam said, deftly tossing the ball above his head and catching it behind his back.

"It's not silly," Ellen said. "And stop throwing that ball."

"It's silly to hate someone you don't even know," Sam said, with some exasperation. He placed the ball down on the couch and looked at her. "You don't know Jordan Boyce. You just met her. You hate her because you hate moving."

"No," Ellen said. "I hate moving *and* I hate her."

"This is like having a conversation with a three-year-old," Sam said.

"Oh, come on, Sam. She's an idiot, with her little U.Va. sweatshirt and her fake sincerity. And the Realtor told me she's named her children Lily and Daisy and Stamen, so they all have flower names."

"She didn't name a child Stamen," said Sam. "Really?"

"She did! When she had her son, she couldn't name him Poppy or Iris or another girls' flower name, so she named him Stamen. It sounds close enough to Holden and Caden and all those other trendy boy names you hear at every preschool now. And she kept telling me again and again how the house will be so well-loved— as though I didn't love it well enough!" Ellen felt like crying again.

"Oh, come on," Sam said. "It's a *house*. It's four walls and a roof and it's been a good house for us and now our life is changing. You'll have another house."

"But it won't be *this* house," Ellen said. "That's like saying if Sara dies I can just have another child."

"It's nothing like that," Sam said. He made a disgusted *tsking* sound with his tongue that really irritated her. "That's a totally inappropriate analogy. You wanted this, remember?"

"I didn't want *this,*" Ellen said. "I never wanted to leave the house."

"Right," said Sam. He stood up in front of the couch, both hands on his hips. "You just wanted to leave *me*. It's no big deal to leave me, and to take the kids away from their father, but it's *huge* to have to give up the house."

Ellen looked at him mutely. She was forty-four, and she was tired. For the first six years of their marriage they had moved, on average, once every eighteen months. Sam was an inventor. After getting a degree in chemical engineering followed by a brilliant early career in product development for Procter & Gamble, he'd decided to start his own business, SamCan, Inc., where he created a series of wildly imaginative new products. The problem was that every new idea seemed to be accompanied by his conviction that he had to live in just the right place to launch it. They moved to Fort Worth when Sam invented the line-dancing boot, footwear that contained a small metronome that tapped out the dance beat for the rhythm-impaired. When that didn't take off (no one in Texas seemed to consider themselves rhythm-impaired), they moved on to Los Angeles, Salt Lake City, and then Brooklyn. Finally, twelve years ago, they arrived in Portland to perfect the Gutter Buddy, a motorized little broom that fit inside a gutter, chopped the pine needles and leaves into bits, then pushed them down the drainpipe.

And then Ellen simply refused to move again. After years of putting off having children, and working endless hours to get her decorating business up and running in one town after another, she was done. She wanted to buy a house and paint the walls red, not some neutral rental color. She wanted to get pregnant and have babies. She wanted to plant bulbs and know she'd be there in the spring to watch them bloom. She wanted to make friends and reminisce over shared memories that went back more than twelve months.

So they stayed. Sam took a job at Oregon Health & Science

University, working in biomedical engineering, and she opened her shop, Coffee@home, where she sold espresso drinks and home furnishings, and she had the babies and worked on the house and planted a perennial garden. She became best friends with Joanna, her next-door neighbor. They went through pregnancy and breast feeding and croup together, and their children were so close that Joanna's daughter, Emily, became known as "Three," the third child Ellen and Sam had wanted but couldn't have. After twelve years in Portland, Ellen had finally allowed herself to believe that this was it, that she had roots that were deep and strong and permanent. So when Sam came home one day and announced that he had an absolutely brilliant idea that could fly only in New York, she said, simply, "No."

The baby beeper was his best idea yet, Sam said. It was a tiny electronic beeper, the size of a pencil eraser, that could be sewed inside a onesie or a diaper cover. When the button was pushed on a remote, the beeper would go off, revealing the whereabouts of a wayward baby. Ellen had to admit that she loved the idea of the beeper. Louisa, an amazingly agile baby, had walked at ten months and taught herself to climb out of her crib at twelve months. Within a week she'd thoroughly mastered the crib escape, leaving Ellen in a complete panic when she went to wake the baby from her nap, only to find an empty mattress and a lonely stuffed Winnie the Pooh. Over the course of one memorable week she had found Louisa hiding in the cupboard under the bathroom sink, cheerfully eating a bar of vanilla-scented soap; inside the wicker toy chest, humming to the stuffed animals; and, most frightening of all, outside on the front lawn, holding out her naptime bottle to a fat robin. The idea that Louisa had managed to get out of not just the crib but the house terrified Ellen, who had spent fifteen agonizing minutes searching for her. If she'd had a baby beeper, she could have found Louisa instantly. And imagine how useful it would be in a mall or grocery store when a child darted off, Sam pointed out.

Once the idea for the baby beeper hit, Sam spent hours trying to develop a transmitter that was small enough to be easily stitched into a piece of baby clothing, yet powerful enough to send a loud signal from a good distance away. He wanted to quit work to devote himself to the baby beeper full-time. He made a few prototypes and took them to local baby clothing stores like Hanna Andersson. He drew up a marketing plan. Still there was no place in the world like New York City for obsessed parents willing to spend money on the latest baby gadget, he said, and New York was the place to be if they were really going to make the baby beeper a success.

Ellen, while impressed with the baby beeper's potential, still had her doubts and was adamant about not moving. What if the baby beeper didn't take off? she argued. What if they ended up eighteen months from now with their savings depleted and Sam out of work? They had children in school, with friends and routines and all the familiarity that years in one place finally had brought them.

And they had the house. It wasn't just four walls and a roof, as Ellen tried to explain to Sam again and again. It was the thirty-nine pages of carefully crayoned pictures of turtles that Sara and Emily had taped to the basement wall when they were four and created the Turtle Club, whose original purpose was long forgotten even while the drawings, yellowing and curled at the edges, remained. It was the faded spot in the paint on the stairwell where Louisa had tried, somewhat in vain, to scrub off the elaborate mural she had penciled there at age three. It was the view out the window of the girls' bedroom, overlooking the garden with the enormous white hydrangea, its trunk held together with duct tape ever since the ice storm six years ago.

But what to Ellen was a life beloved and well-worn, like a favorite pair of jeans, was to Sam a life of unending boredom and predictability. He craved the risk and excitement of a new entrepreneurial adventure; he didn't want to end up at fifty-five or sixty, he told her, still sitting in the same cubicle every day and mowing the same patch of lawn every weekend.

Finally, Ellen agreed to take out a second mortgage on the house so Sam could develop and sell a first round of baby beepers. The money was spent before they knew it, and then he had to borrow from their savings, and then, just as Ellen had feared, the money was all gone.

Sam had quit his job at OHSU to work on the prototypes; Ellen's shop, while it was turning a small profit, wasn't bringing in enough to cover the payments on the first and second mortgages. She was frustrated that her business, which she'd worked so hard to grow, had become their sole source of income. Coffee@home had always been a treat for Ellen—work, yes, but fun work. She loved escaping for a day or a weekend to go on buying trips to find furniture and collectibles for the shop, and then arranging it all in a way that made Coffee@home seem completely inviting. She loved working behind the counter and getting to know all the regular customers, and becoming part of their lives. She loved her little staff. Now, with the pressure to earn more and more, much of the fun was gone. She bought collectibles with an eye for profit, not passion. She pored over websites trying to figure out new ways to market the shop and started to pay for advertising in the local paper. She kept the shop open longer to squeeze a few extra dollars out of each day.

Finally she grew so angry—with herself and with Sam—that she could barely speak and spent months in a constant state of rage. In the end they agreed to separate and sell the house. Six months ago Sam had moved into a small apartment in Beaverton, about fifteen minutes away, and taken on consulting work while still commuting back and forth to New York in a persistent attempt to get the baby beeper off the ground. More than once he had asked Ellen to reconsider—for the kids, for their own relationship, which stretched back over twenty years, a living history of each of them. But for Ellen, the one wild spark in her personality that had driven her to marry someone as unconventional as Sam had been extinguished by the loss of the home and the security she had built so carefully over so many years. If she had to be the grown-up, so be it, but she was not going to be the grown-up for a forty-five-year-old man.

"We can't have that conversation again, Sam," she said finally, looking into his eyes. "You're the one who mortgaged the house for the baby beeper, and who's choosing to spend half his time three thousand miles away from his family."

"Right," he said abruptly. "I've gotta go."

She stood up and walked back to the kitchen with him.

"Sam?"

He paused at the screen door, one hand on the latch. The sadness in his face was painful to look at; she stifled the impulse to reach out and put a hand on his shoulder.

Instead she said, "Can you take the girls Friday night? I'm going to have a little party, and it would really help me out."

"Sure. What's the party for?"

"It's kind of a farewell party for the house."

"Don't you want the girls there? And I'm not invited?"

Ellen heard the edge in his voice.

"No, it's a girls' night out thing. Just Jo and Laurie and some others."

"Fine. I'll pick the kids up at six."

Ellen watched the door click behind him, stared at the pattern of filtered sunlight on the grass through the branches of the big cedar tree in the backyard.

She wondered if it was against the law to buy two hundred candles at once.

CHAPTER TWO

I T WAS ONLY 7:00 A.M., and Ellen was already hot and dirty. She could feel her hair slipping out of the big tortoiseshell clip she wore when she was working, and her T-shirt and jeans seemed to be covered in a fine layer of dust. She'd spent the early morning back in the tiny storeroom, searching for the boxes of pillar candles she had ordered last September to sell for the holidays. There had to be at least four dozen left, she thought, big, fat candles in warm shades of red and gold. They'd be perfect for her party. After almost half an hour of perching precariously on the little red stepladder and rooting through coffee filters, boxes of antique salt and pepper shakers, packets of sugar, and other miscellany, she finally found them, stashed underneath a box of Christmas lights and several unsold vintage snow globes.

She barely had time to stash the candles in the trunk of her Toyota before she had to open the store for the usual morning rush of before-work customers eager for their coffees. Cloud, the store manager, had called in sick, meaning Ellen was alone until Stacy arrived for her shift at three. Ellen tucked her hair behind her ears and began to steam milk for another latte.

The store was doing surprisingly well. Coffee@home had

started out when the house had grown too small for the treasures Ellen picked up at flea markets and estate sales and on little driving trips along the Oregon coast. She loved good furniture and quirky accessories and the often-rich history behind old things. She had a good eye for color and shape and unexpected mixes, and she loved turning the house into a home rich with comfort and beauty and memory, piece by treasured piece. She had picked up the bright red corner cupboard six years ago in Seattle, knowing it would fit perfectly in the corner of the dining room. She'd found the old carved Chinese wooden bench at a thrift store in Eugene and knew, even with her eyes closed, that it was the perfect size to fill the nook beneath the sunny bay window in the living room. When she realized that she had enough, that the house was full and felt right, she set up a booth at a local antiques mall for leftover treasures, like the duplicate pieces of milk glass and the bentwood rocker that didn't really fit in the bedroom.

When the booth did well, she rented her own space in a shopping center in West Slope anchored by a large grocery chain on one end and a framing gallery, a barbershop, an office supply store, and a gift shop on the other. Ellen's shop was next to the gift store. It was a large, square space with a wall of windows opening onto the sidewalk. She installed bead board paneling halfway up the interior walls, with a plate rail above it to hold small treasures. She painted the paneling a soft turquoise, and the walls above it a sunny yellow. The floor, a worn golden oak, she left as it was.

She filled it with the overflow from her house and her antiques booth: a mahogany dresser with drawers of golden oak and shiny brass drawer pulls; a kitchen table from the 1930s, with white painted legs and a soft green enameled top with flowers stenciled in bright yellow at the corners; a rustic armchair made of hickory branches, with an intricately woven rush seat and back. She used the plate rail to display her Fiesta ware: cobalt plates, turquoise creamers, bright orange teacups, cream-colored saucers. On the walls she hung old maps and paintings of Oregon, framed in rustic wood.

One day on a whim Ellen purchased a beautiful copper espresso machine, with a gleaming dome and a brass eagle on top. She learned how to make cappuccinos and lattes and espressos, how long to steam the milk to build up a creamy head of foam without scalding it, how to grind the beans to the right consistency so the espresso was rich but not muddy. Soon she had installed a counter and a case for scones and muffins and crisp biscotti that she bought from a local baker. She changed the name of the store, which had been simply At Home, to Coffee@home and got a black-and-white 1950s-style sign made with a big coffee cup logo and the name of the store in pink neon.

Soon she had a steady stream of customers who liked the fact that they could buy the large, comfortable armchairs they sat in every morning while they read the paper, or the Harlequin mugs that stood in a brightly colored row atop the hutch against the back wall. Every three months she held a floor sample sale and sold all the biggest pieces of furniture at a discount, before the chairs could get coffee-stained or the sofas too filled with crumbs.

Now she had a manager, a staff of five, which meant she could take weekends off and even leave on vacation once in a while, and an actual income after years of barely breaking even. And she had work that she genuinely enjoyed. Ellen loved making the drinks, the warm feel of the steaming milk in the metal jug against her hand, the grateful way people cradled their cups against their palms.

Ellen pushed her fine brown hair back inside the clip and then expertly tamped two shots of espresso grounds into the metal sieve, locked it into position in the warm copper machine, and pushed the button. Steaming water poured through the grounds, and the espresso dripped into the cup. She glanced at the customer across the counter, Mr. Tall Vanilla Latte. He'd been in almost every morning for the past two weeks now, holding his tan leather brief-case carefully in one hand while he stood in line to order. He was tall, at least six feet, Ellen guessed, and wore a three-button, charcoal gray suit. The belt of his khaki-colored trench coat was tied in a firm knot around his waist. His brown hair was closely cropped, and he had a neatly trimmed beard and mustache, with a few wiry gray hairs mixed in with the brown. He was probably a lawyer, Ellen decided, and a regular churchgoer, even here in Oregon, the most unchurched state in the Union. He was attractive in a neat and tidy kind of way, which had never really been Ellen's type. He didn't talk much, but he always smiled at Ellen shyly, so that the corners of his eyes crinkled. He often looked at her very earnestly, which Ellen found slightly disconcerting.

"That's a very unusual piece you have over there," he said, nodding his head toward the large pine carpenter's chest that served as a coffee table in the middle of the shop. The chest, which Ellen had picked up at a junk store in the tiny town of Drain, Oregon, was almost three feet tall and four feet wide, with strips of iron nailed around each corner and a beautifully carved wreath and ribbon on the front. Inside were layers of trays and drawers, filled with old planes and levels and chisels. It was one of the few pieces in the store that weren't for sale, simply because Ellen loved it and could tell it had been treasured by the carpenter who had owned it. She didn't want to break up the carefully amassed collection of tools, gathered over a lifetime and used, as she imagined, for the creation of dozens of meticulously handmade pieces of furniture. There was a date—1882—carved into one corner but no name.

"I'm sorry," she said, "that piece isn't for sale. Most everything else is, though."

"No, no, I didn't want to buy it," he said hastily, as if Ellen might have thought he was trying to take something from her she didn't want to give up. "I was just admiring it. I've never seen anything like it."

"Thank you," she said. "You should see the inside—it's loaded with old woodworking tools, and all kinds of neat little trays and drawers. I had to bring it in here because I couldn't keep my daughters out of it when I had it at home. Are you a woodworker?"

Ellen glanced at his hands, which were smooth and neatly manicured. He wore a plain gold band on the ring finger of his left hand, which made her acutely conscious of the lack of a ring on her own finger. She had taken it off just a week ago and put it in the drawer of the old walnut table next to her bed. Every day she caught herself rubbing the base of her ring finger with her thumb in an unconscious echo of her old habit of twisting her wedding ring around and around on her finger.

"No, no," he said. "I mean, I'm handy and all, but no, I'm not a woodworker." He picked up his latte and looked idly around the shop, as if uncertain whether the conversation was over or not. "Actually, I'm a gardener," he said.

Ellen raised one eyebrow quizzically, with a tilt of her head at his suit and briefcase.

"I mean, as a hobby," he said.

"You should check out the cupboard at the back," she said, pointing toward the old oak Hoosier cupboard against the back wall. Ellen had opened all the doors to the various compartments and filled them with books. "I have a great collection of old gardening books."

Mr. Tall Vanilla Latte glanced at the cupboard, at the rows of faded cloth book spines, the crumbling paper jackets. "I'll look them over," he said. "Thanks. I've been searching for an out-of-print book my mother wants for her birthday."

"Well, if it's not related to gardening, cooking, or home decorating, I don't have it," Ellen said, as she finished making two mochas for the person in line behind him. "I just buy what I like. But if you're ever going to the coast, stop at Hole in the Wall Books, in Manning. That's where I buy most of the books I get for the shop, and the owner knows how to track down anything."

"That's good to know. Thanks."

The bell by the door rang. Mr. Tall Vanilla Latte picked up his briefcase.

"You're busy," he said. "I should go."

He headed out just as Joanna walked in, dressed in a Portland Beavers sweatshirt and baggy blue plaid flannel pants that might have been pajama bottoms. She was a runner, with a lean, athletic body that she seemed for the most part to ignore, since much of her wardrobe consisted of similar sweats and pajamas. Mr. Tall Vanilla Latte stepped aside to let her pass just as she stepped in the same direction, and the two of them did an elaborate little dance until Mr. Latte, blushing and apologizing, finally darted through the door.

"Clearly, I need your biggest grande, Venti, giant cup of coffee," said Joanna, removing her baseball cap and shaking out her thick, kinky dark blond hair. She wore no makeup, as usual, and with her dark blond eyebrows and lashes and large blue eyes, she always looked, to Ellen, young, almost childlike, in spite of her crow's-feet and laugh lines. "How are you?"

"Oh, awful, Jo. The woman who bought the house stopped by yesterday. At the *house,* not the shop. Her name is Jordan Boyce. She came to tell me all her wonderful plans for transforming it into her dream home. But it's *my* dream home. I know I'm biased, but I just hated her."

"I know, I met her, too," Joanna said. "As soon as she left your house she saw me in the driveway and came over to introduce herself. If it makes you feel any better, I hated her, too. Does she really have a child named Stamen? She thinks Lily and Emily will be best friends. She also admired my red purse, right before she told me that red purses were so popular *last year.* I wanted to throw something at her."

"Oh, Jo," said Ellen, pushing her eyeglasses up on top of her head. "I can't believe I signed the papers and turned the house over to her. I should have figured something else out."

"What? The house is mortgaged up the wazoo and you can't afford the payments. What could you possibly have done?"

"I don't know," Ellen said. "Nothing. Something. Anything. It's just killing me to give it up. And it's killing Sara. She's so mad at me I can't stand it, although of course, it's not just the house, it's the separation, everything."

"Sure she's mad about everything. She has a lot to be mad about, sweetie. But she won't stay mad forever, and you're a wonderful mom. You'll get her through it. You'll get all of you through it. Oh, shit."

Joanna put her coffee down on the worn wooden counter to scramble for her cell phone, which was ringing loudly. "I'm supposed to be home so I can take a call from the president of something called the Better Sleep Council. I'm reporting a scintillating story on mattresses," she said, pushing a button and turning the cell phone off. "My glamorous life as a writer just gets better by the minute."

Ellen laughed. "Today it's mattresses, tomorrow the Pulitzer," she said. "Listen, I'm going to have a little going away party for the house on Friday. Just you and Laurie and some of the others— no kids, no spouses. Can you be there?"

"Yes," Joanna said. "What can I bring?"

"Bring some wine," Ellen said. "Oh, God, I don't know how I'm going to do this. I'm not going to be able to walk out that door for the last time on moving day."

"I'll walk with you," Joanna said, leaning forward to kiss Ellen on the cheek. "Maybe we can booby-trap the house for the she-devil before you go—hide some dead goldfish inside the curtain rods, or a dead rat inside a wall somewhere."

Ellen sighed. "I'd love to," she said. "But I don't think it would work. I think Jordan is going to take out every last curtain rod and screw, and half the walls. She *was* an art history and architecture major at U.Va., you know."

"Fuck her," said Joanna and smiled.

Joanna's regular use of four-letter words was a trait that Ellen, as a nonswearer, admired. *It must be wonderful,* Ellen thought, *to swear without thinking about it, or feeling self-conscious.*

"Yes, fuck her," said Ellen, surprising both Joanna and herself.

Ellen, for the first time in her life, felt reckless—and almost giddy with the idea that she, a very good girl who had always painstakingly followed the rules, actually could *be* reckless. Ellen was the one who always carefully walked through the house at night, closing and locking the windows and doors. She was the one who changed the batteries in the smoke detectors every April and October, when the time changed over to daylight saving time and then back again. She ate all her meat well-done, in case of *E. coli* or other dangerous bacteria, and never missed an annual physical or mammogram or Pap smear.

The riskiest, most daring thing she'd ever done in her life was to marry Sam, who was definitely *not* careful, safe, and predictable, and was prone to doing things like sitting in empty front-row seats at a baseball game, even if their tickets were for the upper bleachers. Sam drove just a tad too fast, liked to cliff-dive even now that he was in his forties, and had been known to whisk Ellen away from the shop for a day of skiing at Mount Hood or windsurfing in the Gorge or even, once, to hang out at the Pumpkin Ridge golf course because some hotshot young golfer with a strange name (Tiger?) was trying to win his third straight U.S. Amateur title. Sam's spontaneity and daring pulled her out of herself, gave her a respite from the constant sense of vigilance and responsibility that at times threatened to mummify her.

It also brought out her silly side. She made cornball jokes around Sam that she'd never make to anyone else, just to see him roll his eyes and snort, and then laugh in spite of himself.

And she, in turn, seemed to balance and steady him. When they had first gotten married, Ellen had been surprised by how much Sam loved her, and by the almost scary sense of her ability to hurt him because he loved her so deeply. "You're better than I deserve," he wrote her in one note. He loved her intellect, the fact that she was well-read and smart and funny, that she could respond to his quick wit with zingers of her own. He loved her domesticity; the soft sheets and the table set with place mats and flowers, even when it was just the two of them, no matter who cooked. She remembered things he could never seem to keep in front of his brain: his mother's birthday or the elderly neighbor in the hospital. They filled each other out.

But it wasn't enough. In the end, Ellen's vigilance wasn't enough to prevent their slow slide into debt, and her lighthearted joy with Sam wasn't enough to keep them together through the disappointment and financial hardship of one failed invention after another. Now here she was: separated, about to move out of the house she loved, with a ten-year-old daughter who was threatening either to run away or to lock herself in a closet so she wouldn't have to move. *Being a good girl for forty-some years hasn't really done much for me,* Ellen thought. *I might as well try something else.*

"Fuck her," she said again.

Joanna laughed. "I think that's the first time I've ever heard you use the word *fuck*," she said. "You *really* must not like her. Hey, who's that guy who was walking out as I came in? He's kind of cute." Joanna wiggled her eyebrows at Ellen in a hubba-hubba kind of way.

"That's Mr. Tall Vanilla Latte," Ellen said. "He's been here every morning for two weeks now. He doesn't say much. He reads *The Wall Street Journal,* he always wears a suit, his favorite color of tie is blue, and he likes the carpenter's chest over there, although he's not a woodworker. He likes to garden. He's wearing a wedding ring, and even if he weren't, he's definitely too tucked in and neatly trimmed to be my type. That's everything I know."

"What, no shoe size and literature preferences?" Joanna said. "You'd make a lousy reporter. I think he's good-looking. Too bad he's married. But maybe he's separated, like you! Grill him tomorrow when he comes in."

"Right," Ellen said. She poured a batch of coffee beans into the big grinder and clicked the switch on. *What if Mr. Tall Vanilla Latte is separated?* she thought. Maybe the new, reckless Ellen who was about to burn down a house could find passion with a new type of guy, even a charcoal-suited, neatly combed guy. That is, if she didn't end up in jail for committing arson.

The bell dinged again, and in walked Alexa, Ellen's real estate agent, a sleek-looking, late thirties brunette dressed in black pants, a black sweater, and stiletto-heeled black boots. Her thick, brassy hair was parted in the middle and hung in chic, choppy layers around her face.

"Hey, Ellen," said Alexa. "Give me a large skim latte with an extra shot. So you met Jeffrey Boyce!"

"No, I met *Jordan*. She stopped by at the house yesterday. Did she tell you? I thought you told her I really didn't want to meet her. She showed up at the back door and insisted on talking to me."

"Are you kidding?" Alexa said. She put her large brown leather handbag down on the counter and began to root through it. "I'm sorry. I told her this was all really emotional for you and you didn't want to see her. But she's just so excited about the house she can hardly stand it. She really loves it. She showed me the plans for the remodel. It's going to be lovely."

"It's lovely already, Alexa," said Joanna pointedly, giving her an evil glare even though she was wearing plaid flannel pajama bottoms and clogs versus Alexa's form-fitting fine wool trousers and high-heeled boots.

"I know, I know. Sorry," said Alexa. She fished her wallet out of her purse and handed a five-dollar bill to Ellen. "It *is* lovely. Jordan just really likes the house. So does her husband, Jeffrey. It doesn't seem to have upset you so much to meet *him*."

"I haven't met him," said Ellen. "I hope he's not as pushy as she is."

"Well, having met her, I'm sure he's quite compliant and fully pussy-whipped," said Joanna. "She couldn't be married to any other kind."

"Of course you've met him," said Alexa. "I just ran into him outside. The guy with the brown beard and trench coat."

Ellen looked at Joanna and then at Alexa. "You mean Mr. Tall Vanilla Latte is Jordan's husband? *He's* the one moving into my house?"

"Yes," said Alexa. "Didn't he tell you?"

CHAPTER THREE

"N̲O̲, ̲H̲E̲ ̲D̲I̲D̲N̲'̲T̲ tell me," said Ellen with annoyance. She felt violated, somehow, as though Mr. Tall Vanilla Latte had read her diary, or secretly slipped something precious of hers into his pocket and left. "He's been in here every day for two weeks now, and he never said anything."

"Maybe he didn't know who you were," said Alexa. "I mean, you went to the closing separately."

"Of course he knows who I am," Ellen said. "He's read the clips, and my name is all over them." She gestured to the framed newspaper articles on the wall by the front door, reviews of Coffee@home by *The Oregonian* and *Willamette Week* and the *Portland Tribune*. Mr. Tall Vanilla Latte had spent one morning carefully reading the stories while he sipped his latte and waited for a break in the downpour outside. He'd even asked Ellen what an étagère was because *The Oregonian* mentioned the antique wooden étagère by the window that Ellen used to hold the day's newspapers.

"Maybe Jordan sent him to spy on you," Joanna said.

"Why would Jordan want to spy on me? She owns the house. She's moving in in three weeks. She'll do her remodeling and get on with her well-organized life. Why would she care about me?"

"Because she knows all the neighbors love you, and everyone around here knows you because of the shop," Joanna said. "Portland is a small town. It's *three* degrees of separation between you and someone who knows you here, right? Maybe she feels some kind of competition with you. She probably thinks she has to make the house *better* than you made it. So she wanted Jeffrey to scope out what the shop is like, to figure out your style."

"Well, that's just silly," said Ellen. "I can't imagine she thinks about me at all. But Jeffrey is really strange. He's been so quiet, but he always *looks* at me, you know? These very intense looks, as though he wanted to say something but couldn't."

"Maybe he wanted to introduce himself but was afraid to, because Sam and I told him how traumatized you were about selling the house," Alexa said.

"Or maybe he just likes lattes," Joanna said.

"Well, it's good of you and Sam to paint me as some kind of psycho, so people are afraid to talk to me," Ellen said to Alexa. "I'm surprised he was brave enough to walk in here. I might have come unglued and thrown all the Fiesta ware at him."

"Well, you *have* been very intense about this whole thing," said Alexa, rooting around in her handbag for her keys. "Not that I blame you. I know you love the house. But really, Ellen, as someone who sells houses for a living, I can tell you it's a nice house, but there are better houses out there. *A lot* of them." She picked up her latte. "All right, I've got to go. I've got an open house in a few hours, and the place is a mess. If I don't see you before, I'll meet you at the house on May thirty-first, around five, okay? I want to do a walk-through so there are no issues about getting back the security deposit you gave them for renting back the house this month."

"Will Jordan be there?" Ellen said.

"She or Jeffrey will have to be there," said Alexa, "to make sure the house is in good condition before they give you back the money. Why don't you have Sam there, and you can go out for coffee or something while we walk through?"

"Fine. But I don't have to be out for good until then, right? Sam and I want to spend a little time saying farewell to the house with the girls before Jordan comes. It's really important to Sara, especially."

"Yes, the contract says five," said Alexa, turning on her stiletto heels. "Good luck with the move. See you May thirty-first. Bye, Joanna."

Joanna bundled her hair back up under her baseball cap. She was wearing just one pearl earring because, as Ellen knew, she always took the other off to talk on the phone and then forgot to put it back on. "Well, I think Mr. Tall Vanilla Latte came in because he was curious about you, and then he found you so irresistible he couldn't stop himself from coming back every day," Joanna said. "I've got to go, too. I've got to get home and finish this story."

"All right. Don't forget about my party Friday."

"I won't, sweetie. Maybe we can start planning what we'll do with your new house."

"Maybe. See you later."

Ellen sighed as the door closed behind her departing friend. She felt like a mother with postpartum depression who has no interest in her new baby. She had no interest in the new house at all. She had gone house hunting in the throes of her bitterness toward Sam, when all she could see were the chain-link fences in the backyards, the cracks in plaster ceilings, the rooms darkened by windows overgrown with ancient rhododendrons. Every house she looked at seemed strange to her, and she was completely unable to imagine herself in any one of them. Even now she could not picture the girls' twin beds in any room other than the cream-colored room with the purple trim under the eaves, could not envision the luminous Judith Cunningham painting of the Columbia River Gorge over any other living room mantel. She was blind to the beautiful bones in any other house, no matter how hard she tried not to be.

Her new house, the first house in eighteen years that she would not share with Sam, was a perfectly pleasant 1940s bungalow, small but certainly enough space for Ellen and the girls, with two large bedrooms and a big pink-and-maroon-tiled bathroom. It was in a perfectly nice neighborhood of other little one-story bungalows, with lots of azaleas and rhododendrons and big old Douglas firs. The girls would stay at Bridlemile, the local elementary school they'd attended since kindergarten. They would still be in the same district as Joanna's daughter, Emily, and they would still be within ten minutes of Ellen's shop and their favorite grocery store and the little Italian restaurant they went to most Friday nights for Italian sodas and spaghetti.

But Ellen's heart didn't leap when she turned onto the street to drive up to the new house, the way it had always lurched for her old house, especially in the spring, when the candytuft and phlox were blooming in great mounds of white and pink along the rock garden in front of the fence.

Ellen knew she could paint the rooms in the new house in a palette of colors designed to show off the arched doorways and the big picture window in the living room, could turn the kitchen with its old cabinets and tile counters into a warm and inviting haven of retro kitsch. But she just couldn't seem to drum up the energy or enthusiasm to do it. She had taken the girls to the paint store to pick out colors for their new bedroom, hoping at least to be able to muster some excitement on their behalf. Louisa had squealed and danced and grabbed dozens of paint chips in bright yellows and oranges and reds. Sara had pointed to one chip, the same wisteria purple that accented their bedroom now, and said she liked that color and didn't want a change. Ellen was overwhelmed, not knowing if it would be better to re-create their old room in the new house, as Sara wanted, or to start fresh with something new, as Louisa wanted. So she did nothing.

The phone on the counter rang. "Ellen? It's Kathleen Mahoney, at Bridlemile. Can you come get Sara? She needs to come home."

"Is she sick?"

"Nooooo," Kathleen said slowly. "She's not sick, exactly. She's just having a rough day, and we think it would be better for everyone if she came home for the afternoon."

"What's wrong? What did she do?"

"She's in Mr. Kreske's office. You can talk to him when you come."

"I'll be there as soon as I can."

"Thanks, Ellen. I'll tell Sara and Mr. K. you're on your way."

Ellen hung up the phone, feeling guilty. Sara, her older child, was such an intense and private person. She had always been serious, with large, dark eyes and a wise expression that made her seem much older. Sam and Ellen had called her their Buddha Baby, because she was such a plump and solemn infant, carefully studying their faces, her food, the books they showed her, every blade of grass she crawled across. Now, as a ten-year-old, she was still studying, keenly observing every person and situation before offering either a comment or her participation. Yet her smile, when it came, was radiant, transforming her whole face like one of Portland's "sunbreaks," a sudden, brilliant glimpse of light and warmth between the clouds.

Sara was the one who seemed the most deeply affected by the separation, pouring all her grief and anger into the move. She just didn't understand why they had to leave the house, and her best friend next door. Emily, all straight blond hair and long limbs, was Sara's counterpoint, physically and emotionally. Emily was loud where Sara was quiet, fearless where Sara was cautious, reckless where Sara was responsible. They balanced each other; they nourished each other. It was a friendship Ellen cherished for her daughter.

"I'll never see Emily after we move," Sara had cried. Of course she'd see Emily, Ellen had pointed out, at school, for playdates, for sleepovers. "But it won't be the same," Sara had said. Which was true. No more rolling out of bed and into each other's houses, no more leaning out the upstairs bathroom window to toss pebbles at Emily's window, no more spur-of-the-moment lunches and runs to the ice cream parlor.

"It's all Daddy's fault," Sara had said, darkly. At ten, she was old enough to absorb the late-night conversation from downstairs, Ellen's resentment, Sam's guilt.

"It's not all Daddy's fault," Ellen had said. "It's nobody's *fault*."

Ellen wanted to believe it herself, although her anger at Sam kept getting in the way. She understood that he wanted more. He wanted to create something revolutionary, no matter how trivial, not for the fame or money as much as for the satisfaction of knowing that he'd invented something that was in every pocket or stocked in every pantry. Inventing gave him a sense of worth and purpose, in the way that mothering gave Ellen a sense of vocation. But inventing required endless risk—financial and emotional risks that were simply incompatible with the life of stability and rootedness Ellen wanted for the girls and for herself.

And it was true that all the ups and downs, the crazy ride of the somewhat unconventional life she'd had with Sam, were something she had wanted, too. After all, she had agreed to all the moves, she had agreed to the second mortgage for the stupid baby beeper. Marrying Sam had been her big adventure, a way to ensure that her life would never follow the bland, predictable pattern of her childhood. Her children would grow up in a home bursting with creativity, invention, imagination—experiencing new places, moving from town to town, living a different kind of life.

But then, of course, she'd had a baby. And another. And her maternal instinct, which Ellen had considered just vaguely, suddenly roared forth like lava—primal, fiery, all-encompassing. She wanted a place for these children, and a circle of loving friends, and a home that was permanent and forever, a base of security to which her girls could always return. That's why the house became so important. And that's why the loss of the house, which came to seem inevitable, made it impossible to stay with Sam.

Ellen had always handled their finances—paying the bills, scraping together a little money each month to save for retirement and the girls' college, investing cautiously in a few carefully chosen stocks. But she never felt like she knew what she was doing and always worried that somehow she could be handling the money better, saving more, earning more. She complained so often about the finances that Sam repeatedly offered to take them over, but she refused to let him.

"You can't remember where you left your wallet last night," she'd say. "And you're going to remember that the mortgage is due by the sixteenth every month? I don't think so."

"Fine," he'd respond. "But if you feel stuck with the finances, it's because you're a control freak, not because I won't help you."

It was true, Ellen knew; it was also true that he probably would have a hard time remembering due dates and keeping track of all the bills. But after they took out the second mortgage on the house, Ellen couldn't stop brooding about it. Their budget was already tight; with the second mortgage, she had to dip into their savings every month to cover all their payments. Finally the day had come when the savings account balance was zero, payments on both mortgages were due, the Visa bill loomed high, and that night, Sam had brought home a new toaster.

"Look at this," he had said, coming in through the back door to find Ellen at the dining room table, poring over the checkbook. He'd made dinner earlier that night while she worked on the bills, cooking omelets with cheese and red peppers, doing magic tricks with the girls in the kitchen that involved finding eggs in their ears. Ellen, already tense, had felt unreasonably irritated by the girls' delighted screams, by Sam's fooling around. After dinner, he'd bathed them and put them to bed and then had run out to Target.

"You know how we're always putting toast in and forgetting about it?" he said. "I found this amazing toaster. Get this: Once the bread is toasted, it keeps it down and warm until you push a button to eject it! Think of all the bread and bagels we'll save."

Ellen looked up at him wearily. She had absolutely no idea how they were going to pay all they owed this month. Yet there was Sam, who'd spent the evening doing magic tricks and making wild bubble hairdos with the kids in the bath, blithely standing in the dining room talking about a toaster.

"How come you get to be the fun parent and I have to be the responsible one?" she said, looking at him over the rims of her red reading glasses.

Sam put the toaster down on the dining room table. "What are you talking about?" he said. "I bought a toaster. That doesn't exactly make me the King of Fun."

"I'm talking about you running around making eggs appear out of the air and buying new toasters while I'm trying to figure out how we can pay our bills," she said, taking off her glasses and rubbing a hand across her eyes. She looked up at him. "We don't need a new toaster."

"Come on, Ellie. It's a fifty-dollar toaster. You're telling me we can't afford to spend fifty dollars?"

"We can't afford to pay our *mortgage*," she said. She felt tears rise. How had this gotten so out of control? "We don't need a new toaster, Sam. The bread turns brown; that's all I need from my toaster. What we really need is more money coming in, and that's just not happening. Clearly the baby beeper is not a real income source for us right now, so what do you propose we do?"

Her voice was harsh, sarcastic. Sam actually flinched.

"We can borrow from our savings," he said.

"That's what you suggested last month, and the month before last," Ellen said. "Unfortunately, there's nothing magical about our savings account; it doesn't replenish itself."

Sam came around the table and pulled up a chair next to her. "Okay, so show me what's going on, and we'll figure it out," he said, leaning in under her shoulder to look at the bills spread out across the table.

Ellen stiffened. "We can't do it, Sam," she said, finally breaking down into tears. "I knew this would happen. From the stupid line-dancing boot to the baby beeper, I knew one day you'd just take this too far and we'd lose everything."

"God, Ellen, we're not going to lose everything! Calm down. Yes, we're short on the mortgage, but we can work something out."

Her tears stopped, and she felt still and cold, as though the very bones inside her skin were ice and could never be warmed. And then it came to her, with a sudden, startling clarity. "We have to sell the house," she said. "We have to sell the house and use the equity to pay off the second mortgage, then buy a new place—or rent—with whatever we have left."

"Well, that's a little extreme," Sam said, leaning back in his chair.

"There's nothing else for it, Sam," she said. "You tell me. We've even dipped into the kids' college funds; and there's not enough *there* to pay off the second mortgage. Do we cash out our retirement accounts? What happens when we're sixty-five?"

She expected him to argue with her, to come up with a plan. Of course they'd never sell the house. She had said it just for the shock value, to make him see how serious this was.

But Sam was silent. "I really believed this was the one," he said softly. "The one that would make us totally secure." He looked at her. "I just need a little more time," he said pleadingly, "for the idea to catch on. Not everyone has babies who lose themselves like Louisa. They think it's some kind of creepy 'Big Brother' thing for infants. But I'm so close on this one."

Ellen closed her eyes and shook her head. And before she knew it, the words she'd been thinking were on her lips. "I can't do this anymore, Sam."

"Okay," he said. "It's not fair you handle all the financial stuff; I'll help."

"I'm not talking about the financial stuff," she said. "I can't be married to you anymore."

There was a long silence. Sam looked down at the table, at the numbers that just wouldn't add up. He bit his lower lip. She had done it; she had used that terrible power she had always known she had to wound him. But there was no help for it, just as there was no help for selling the house. It wasn't just the house or the baby beeper or the toaster; it was all of it, all the things over all the years.

"You'd do that to the kids?" he asked.

"No," Ellen said. "*You've* done that to the kids."

"Fine!" he said, standing up so quickly that he knocked over his chair, which fell with a loud clatter against the hardwood floor. She could see the raw hurt in him, there in the still-beloved lines of his profile, the downturned eyes. All the life and laughter that his face had held just a few hours ago in the kitchen was gone now. *I want you,* she thought, *but I want you different. I want you careful and thoughtful and responsible, and that's never going to happen. I just can't do it anymore.*

That had been six months ago. Now they were formally separated and the house was sold and their ten-year-old daughter seemed to be falling apart at school. Ellen snapped herself out of her thoughts and called Stacy to come in and relieve her. Half an hour later, Ellen was in the school office, looking at the bright block prints the second-graders had drawn of lionfish and alligraffes and hippocats. Mr. Kreske, the principal, came in and shook her hand heartily. He was a jovial, big, blond man with wire-rimmed glasses who wore wide, brightly colored ties in shades of green and purple and yellow. He was about ten years younger than Ellen, which always made her feel old. Principals should always be older than she was, Ellen thought. He ushered her into his office, where Sara was sitting stiffly on a wooden chair, her face stained with tears.

Ellen sat down next to her and put her arm around her daughter's small shoulders. "What's up, sweetheart? What happened?"

"Sara got very upset about something that happened in class," Mr. Kreske said. "I certainly understand why she was upset, but she completely lost her temper. I'm afraid she yelled—and swore—at Mrs. Buckman and her classmates. I've talked to her, and I think we understand each other, but she refuses to go back to class."

Ellen looked searchingly at Sara, who sat quietly staring at Mr. Kreske with a look of pure loathing on her face. Ellen was startled by the intensity of it, the scowl that seemed to pull down all her beautiful features into an upside-down U, the blackness of her eyes.

"What happened?"

"Nothing. They laughed at me and I got mad, that's all," Sara said, not looking at her mother.

"What do you mean? Why did they laugh?"

"I don't want to talk about it. I said I was sorry."

Mr. Kreske handed Ellen a note. "I asked Sara to write a letter of apology to her teacher for disrupting the class. I told her to think about her behavior and what she was truly sorry about, and to put it down in words. Perhaps you'd like to see it."

Ellen looked down at the note, scrawled on a neatly folded piece of sky blue paper. She recognized Sara's large, loopy handwriting—even messier than usual because, Ellen guessed, she had written this in haste and in a fury.

"Dear Mrs. Buckman," the note read. "I am very sorry that you sent me to the principal's office. Sincerely, Sara Flanagan."

Ellen held back a smile. It was awful, certainly, sassy and disrespectful, but it was just so Sara. Ellen was sure that Sara truly *was* sorry that Mrs. Buckman had sent her to the office.

Ellen looked up at Mr. Kreske and thought she detected a gleam of suppressed amusement in his face, too. "I see," she said. "Well, thank you, Mr. K. I'll take Sara home for the afternoon to cool down, and we'll discuss it. I'll give you a call tonight."

She took Sara's hand, and they walked across the parking lot to the car.

"So why don't you tell me what's going on?" Ellen said after Sara was buckled in the back.

"Nothing," Sara said darkly. "I hate Mrs. Buckman and I hate Mr. K. and I hate all those stupid kids in that stupid school and I'm never going back."

"Well, that certainly covers everything," Ellen said. "Come on, sweetheart. It's not like you to lose your temper like that. What happened?"

"Nothing," Sara said again. "I just want to go home and stay there forever. *Forever*," she said loudly, meeting Ellen's eyes in the rearview mirror.

Ellen wished with all her heart that she could give Sara the chance to grow up in one house, in one neighborhood, for all her childhood. She wished she could give Sara a family that wasn't splitting apart, a father who was happy with a steady, nine-to-five job, a mother who knew how to let go and when. She wished she could find the right words, "something with wings and a heart," as Nabokov wrote, to explain it all, to reassure her too-serious daughter that it really would turn out all right. Instead she just said, "Well, I'd like to know what happened."

"Well, *I'd* like to know why Daddy's leaving and we're moving,"

Sara said. "I am *not* leaving our house and I am *not* leaving Emily and nothing will ever be the same if we move to that dumb new house."

Ellen could hear her own despair at leaving the house echoed in her daughter, even though for months she had tried to be careful, pausing before every sentence to make sure she didn't express her grief to the girls. She didn't want them to know that losing the house was a wound in her as deep and cold and blue as a crevasse in a glacier, something that felt as if it would never heal.

Joanna had not hesitated to point out what Ellen already knew: that focusing all her grief on losing the house was a way to avoid dealing with the grief over losing her marriage. Ellen still couldn't really imagine her life as just Ellen, and not Ellen-and-Sam. From the minute they had met, in college, they had shared a friendship so deep that others accused them of having their own private language. Over the past twenty-odd years, they had become so woven together that living without Sam was like living in a house without mirrors or glass, without any way to stop and truly see yourself clearly.

"Emily and Jo will be over at our new house all the time," Ellen said to Sara, trying to sound normal and optimistic, and not too cheerful or chirpy. "Emily will be able to ride the bus home with you to come play. And we'll be able to fix up the new house any way we like. I know it won't be the same, sweetie, and I wish it didn't have to be this way. But Daddy and I both love you and Louisa, and will always take care of you and that will never change."

Sara glared. "I am *not* leaving," she said. "And I will call 911 if you try to make me."

Ellen sighed. "I'm going to talk to Daddy about this. And we'll discuss it more tonight. Let's go home and get you something to eat."

At home she settled Sara at the dining room table with a bowl of cereal, her homework, and a blank piece of stationery to write a new note of apology to Mrs. Buckman. Ellen hated to see the way Sara's thin body hunched over the table, her small shoulders pulled tight.

She dialed Sam's cell phone. "Sara just got sent home from school," she told him, "for screaming and swearing at her teacher and the rest of her class."

"Why?" he asked.

"I don't know; she won't tell me," Ellen said. "But she's clearly extremely upset about the divorce and the move. I think you should spend some time with her tonight. I don't know what to do."

"I don't know what to do, either," Sam said.

"Well, it's your turn to think of something," Ellen said. "Did you really never think about what would happen if the baby beeper didn't sell? Or didn't you care, because you knew I'd be around to figure out what to do next? What a fucking mess."

Sam was silent. He was either overwhelmed by guilt, she guessed, or in shock that she had actually said the word *fucking,* or some combination of both.

"Jesus, Ellen," he said finally. "Of course I hate it that Sara is having a hard time; the difference is that I think she'll recover, just like I think she can actually be happy *in a different house.* Not everyone gets to go through life in an idyllic little bubble. I wouldn't have wished this on the kids, but I'm not pursuing it just to hurt them, or you. Did you ever think that if the baby beeper turns into something big, it could be good *for all of us*? That maybe I'd have a chance to see *something* I did become successful? And we'd have some real financial security."

"Oh, please," Ellen said. She was still feeling reckless and squashed the impulse to start saying "fuck fuck fuck fuck fuck" into the phone. "Just come and get her tonight for dinner or ice cream. You need to talk to her. And you'll have them Friday night because of my party, so maybe you can plan something special to do, take them to Oaks Park or something. She really needs a lot of extra reassurance and attention right now, particularly from you."

"I'll come at six-thirty and take her to play mini-golf," Sam said.

"Fine," said Ellen. "She'll be ready. But don't just play golf and pretend everything is okay. *Talk* to her." She hung up.

After dinner, with Sam and Sara out on their "date," Ellen made a cup of tea and sat down in the living room, on the big, honey-colored couch with its bright red pillows. She remembered when she'd lost the baby, her second pregnancy, in the fifth month. Even though by then they had Sara, a fat, healthy toddler, Ellen longed for another baby and was flattened by grief. She had lain on the couch, on this same yellow-gold couch, and Sam had done magic tricks to make her smile. He could turn quarters into pennies and then into paper roses, and tap a deck of cards and make all the cards turn into the queen of hearts. She loved his little-boy enthusiasm for it, loved the sweetness that made him want to entertain her while she felt so god-awful. And after Louisa was born, a lively baby who never seemed to sleep, Sam would do magic tricks while she gurgled in her crib, arms and legs pumping furiously as bouquets and stuffed bunnies and brightly colored silk scarves flew over her head.

Ellen looked around the living room, at the built-in bookcases with the pictures of fat-cheeked baby Louisa and big-eyed baby Sara, at the bay window overlooking the swing set where Emily and Sara and Louisa had played for hours and hours, at the burn mark on the floor from the time Louisa had stuck the cast-iron fireplace tongs into the fire and then branded the hardwood. Ellen hoped that Sara would feel better if the house did indeed burn, if she knew another little girl was *not* moving into her room, another child was *not* playing in the branches of the pink and white camellia tree outside the dining room window.

Louisa came in and climbed onto the couch, settling in next to Ellen. At five, she was small for her age, and when she sat all the way back in the deep couch, only her feet dangled over the edge. Her hair was a mop of thick dark brown waves, like Sam's. She had the fine, round shape of Sam's head, and even the hint of his high cheekbones beneath her full, still-babyish cheeks.

"Can I have a sip of your tea, Mommy?"

Ellen nodded and gave her mug to her younger daughter. "It's warm, but not too hot. Sip slowly."

Louisa leaned forward and blew hard across the tea, then sipped it in a long, slow, loud slurp.

"Needs more sugar," she said, smiling at Ellen. Her smile was Sam's, too, big and wide and with a perfect round dimple denting her left cheek.

"You think everything needs more sugar, Lulu," Ellen said wryly, using the nickname they'd given her as a baby. "Didn't you say the meat loaf last night needed more sugar?"

Louisa giggled. "Remember when Daddy put sugar in his soup?" They'd gotten up early one day last summer to drive to the beach. On the way they'd stopped for a snack, and Sam had ordered a cup of soup and some coffee. He had been folding a paper napkin into the shape of a kite and explaining the aerodynamics of kite flight to the girls when his order arrived, and he hadn't even noticed that he poured several large spoonfuls of sugar into the wrong cup, sweetening his beef vegetable soup. The girls had been in hysterics over his mistake and it had become a family joke, with one of them passing the sugar bowl to Sam every time soup was served. *Can you have family jokes once you're not a family anymore?* Ellen thought.

"Stop. There's nothing else for it," she said out loud, without meaning to.

"Stop what, Mommy?" Louisa asked.

"Nothing, sweetheart," Ellen said, tucking a stray wisp of hair behind her daughter's ear. "Silly Mommy. I was talking to myself." But it gnawed at her, an uneasy restlessness that even tea and Louisa's warm hugs couldn't dispel.

Later that night, after Sara was back from her outing with Sam, Ellen sat on top of the red and white blanket at the edge of Sara's bed and tucked it in snugly around her. Louisa was already asleep, snoring gently, her full lips parted.

"I'll tell you what happened at school today, Mommy, if you promise not to laugh," Sara said after a moment of silence.

"Of course I won't laugh, darling," said Ellen, running her fingers through Sara's hair. "You tell me."

"Well, you know how we've been studying the Oregon Trail, and all the different kinds of animals the pioneers saw? And we went on that field trip through Tryon Creek Park?"

"Sure, sweetie."

"Well, we did a bunch of little plays in class today about the Oregon Trail and the animals. And afterwards Mrs. Buckman asked each of us to talk about our favorite skit. And I was first. Only I thought she said 'scat.' Do you know what scat is, Mommy?"

Ellen nodded. "You mean poop?"

"Yeah. I said 'Coyote poop!' and then everyone laughed. Even Mrs. Buckman laughed! But I thought she said 'scat.' And then they laughed really hard and it just made me so mad. I mean, anyone could have made that mistake. So I yelled at all of them and at Mrs. Buckman and then they stopped laughing. And then I got sent to the principal's office."

"Well, it was a funny mistake. Can't you see that it's a little bit funny? Wouldn't you have laughed if Nicky or Mia had said 'coyote poop' was their favorite skit?"

Sara looked at Ellen, studying her face. "Well, maybe."

"All right. You can't yell at your classmates and your teacher, Sara. Even if you get very, very angry. You know that. Tomorrow maybe you can think about what you'd like to say in a real apology to Mrs. Buckman, and give her the note you wrote tonight. I'm sure she'll thank you and move on. You're not the first kid to lose it in her class, and I'm sure you won't be the last."

Ellen kissed her daughter on her smooth, soft forehead and stood up and turned out the light. "Sweet dreams. See you in the morning."

She was out in the hall when she heard Sara's voice, soft but steady. "And, Mommy? I know you feel bad about moving, too. But don't worry. I have a plan."

CHAPTER FOUR

ELLEN ARRIVED AT the shop later than usual on Thursday morning, after taking Sara and Louisa to school and stopping in to talk both to Mrs. Buckman and to Mr. K. It was cold and damp, one of those days in May that make Oregonians long for the hot, dry days of August. Ellen actually loved the rain. She had grown up in southern Michigan, where the sky was gray most of the winter and the snow covering the ground was gray and the lakes froze, stretching in vast ripples of gray all the way to the horizon. Ellen always had a sense of being somehow in limbo there, caught between the gray sky and ground and ice, waiting for something to happen.

When she moved to Oregon, it was like moving from black and white Kansas to a Technicolor Emerald City. Yes, the sky was gray and the rains came, but the ground was green, green all year long, and the laurels and Douglas firs and cedars were green even in winter. She loved the deep, vivid green of wet surfaces glistening under overcast skies. She was drunk on it. And she felt, finally, that with all that rich color, her life came into focus, too, that Ellen herself somehow grew more vivid and became the person she was meant to be, the one who was just a ghost in Michigan.

As much as she loved the rain, Ellen was worried about it today. If she held her party tomorrow night, she wanted it to be clear and dry, without too much wind—good weather for effectively burning down a house without setting the whole neighborhood ablaze. She made a mental note to herself to check the weather report in the paper.

Cloud, the store manager for Coffee@home, was sprinkling cocoa powder on top of a mocha latte when she walked in. He was young, just twenty-two, with thick blond hair that he wore in a loose ponytail and a blond goatee and beautiful expressive brown eyes, a dramatic combination. He was more than six feet tall, lanky and easygoing, and had a quiet friendliness that drew customers back to the store for another cup of coffee or muffin and a few minutes of conversation with Cloud.

Ellen adored Cloud; he was steady and unflappable, almost always in a good mood, and loved kids. He babysat often for her girls and showed them how to stack the plastic tops for the coffee cups, or arrange the bagels in the big, flat basket whenever they wanted to "work" at the store for a few hours. But Ellen was always conflicted about Cloud. Her maternal side wanted him to go back and finish school, use his brilliant mind and wonderful people skills in a career that was truly worthy of him. On the other hand, he was competent and trustworthy, and she'd never be able to replace him if he left.

"Busy this morning?" she asked.

"It's been steady," he said, stacking cardboard cup sleeves neatly in a wicker basket on a shelf under the counter. "Some guy came in looking for you. I told him you'd be here around nine-thirty."

Ellen glanced at the clock. It was 9:20. "Who was he?"

"The dude who always gets the tall vanilla lattes."

Ellen felt her heart pound, although she wasn't quite sure why. "With the beard? And the briefcase?"

"Yeah, that guy."

"Did he say what he wanted? Did he actually ask for me by name?"

"Naw," Cloud said, pouring a cup of coffee for the woman with short, spiky hair at the counter. "Just asked for the owner and said he'd be back later."

Ellen absorbed this information. She had thought maybe Jeffrey Boyce wouldn't come back once he'd run into Alexa outside the shop and been recognized. She wondered again what he really wanted, why he'd been coming in day after day and talking to her and looking at her with that searching gaze without introducing himself.

"You know he's the guy who bought my house," she said to Cloud. "He and his wife and their three kids."

"No way! That guy? He's been in here, like, every day for two weeks."

"I know. It just seems odd to me that he didn't say anything, you know? He never introduced himself."

"Well, you can ask him about it now," Cloud said, jerking his head toward the front of the store. "Here he comes."

Ellen turned to see Jeffrey Boyce walk in, wearing his firmly belted khaki trench coat and shaking the water off a large black umbrella with a fine tortoiseshell handle. He looked at her and blushed.

"Hello," she said, trying to be calm and not angry, although she didn't know exactly what she had to be angry about. "Tall vanilla latte, right?"

He nodded, carefully placing his umbrella in the large yellow crock painted with red and blue parrots that served as an umbrella stand by the front door. Cloud, seeing Jeffrey's red face and hearing the tightly controlled tone of Ellen's voice, disappeared toward the other end of the counter, humming a nameless tune.

"So you're Jeffrey Boyce," Ellen said, pumping three shots of vanilla syrup into a cup. "I met your wife the other day."

"I know," Jeffrey said. "She mentioned she'd stopped by. I hope she didn't upset you. Your real estate agent told me you weren't too eager to meet us."

Ellen looked at him. "It seems a little odd to me that you've been coming in here every day without ever introducing yourself. Was it just to see what I looked like?"

He blushed again, a red flush slowly climbing from just above the neat knot of his red striped tie to the top of his forehead.

"I'm, uh, sorry," he said. "I just felt really bad when the Realtor and your husband told me how painful it was for you to sell the house." He looked down at the well-polished surface of his brown wingtip shoes. "It's a wonderful house. I'm sorry you have to leave it." He looked up at her. "I guess I was just hoping I could let you know that we love it and will take good care of it."

Ellen felt the anger rise in her, like water rushing into a well during a storm, at the same time that she knew it was unreasonable. "What is it with you people? You and Jordan feel compelled to let me know you're going to love *my* house, as though that's going to make me feel better?" she said. "I don't *want* to know. *I* love my house."

And then, ridiculously, Ellen felt her eyes fill with tears. She put Jeffrey's latte down on the counter. "I'm sorry," she said. "Here. This one is on the house." And she turned and stumbled through the swinging door into the back room.

She was followed by Cloud, who had hastily put a bagel on a plate on the counter for another customer and hurried after her.

"Whoa, Ellen, calm down," he said, looking somewhat alarmed and patting her gingerly on the shoulder with one hand. "Did that guy say something to you?"

She wiped the tears from her cheeks with both hands and looked up at him. "No, of course not. It's just the house, and that man and his wife who've bought it and the whole stupid mess."

She was hugely embarrassed that she was crying, in front of Cloud, her employee, as well as in front of Jeffrey Boyce, a virtual stranger. She felt that Jeffrey and Jordan were forcing an almost unbearable intimacy on her, asking her to imagine the house with their love for it, their lives in it. She had looked at Jeffrey there at the counter and realized he was a kind man, and had suddenly imagined him in the house, whistling as he showered in the little bathroom under the eaves in the morning, eating his cereal by the big picture window in the dining room, kissing Jordan good-bye at the screen door in the kitchen. And just as suddenly she had felt a rush of complete loss, realizing that never again would she listen to Sam whistle as he shaved in the mornings, or lie in bed, her head nestled against Sam's shoulder, and watch the wind dance through the boughs of the Douglas firs that towered against the sky outside their bedroom window.

Ellen wiped a finger under each eye to make sure her mascara wasn't smudged. "Oh, God, I'm sorry, Cloud," she said, looking up into his dark eyes. "I better go out and see if I scared off all the customers." She tightened the strings of her red apron and went back into the main room of the shop, with Cloud hovering protectively behind her.

Jeffrey was still standing awkwardly by the counter, his latte in one hand. Three other customers were lined up behind him, and two more were browsing through the old books on the shelf at the back of the room. Jeffrey looked so concerned that Ellen almost wanted to laugh. She walked to the end of the counter to talk to him while Cloud started filling orders.

"Look, I'm really sorry," he said, extending his hand as though to pat Ellen's arm and then, thinking better of it, pulling his arm back by his side. "I didn't mean to upset you. Of course we'll leave you alone. But I also didn't know how to handle *this,* and thought I should show it to you."

He placed an envelope and a letter on the counter. His name and address were printed neatly in pencil on the front of the envelope, although it was clearly a child's handwriting. There was no return address. There were three stamps in the other corner, all pasted on upside down. Ellen picked up the letter, written in pencil on the crisp pink stationery she kept in her desk drawer at home. She read:

Dear Mr. And Mrs. Boyce:
There has been a mistake about the house at 2424 SW Grace Lane. We are very sorry but it is NOT for sale. Here is your money back.

Sincerely,
Ellen and Sam Flanagan

Ellen dropped the letter and looked in the envelope. There was a thick stack of bills inside, wrinkled ones and tens and fives.

"Where did you get this?" she asked. "How much money is this? Did Sara do this? How would she know your address? And where would she get all this money?"

Jeffrey carefully folded the letter and put it back inside the envelope with the money. "Well, I assumed it came from one of your daughters," he said. "I got it in the mail a couple weeks ago. I really felt bad about it. I have three kids; I mean, I know this is traumatic for your girls. I came in to show it to you and return the money, and then there always seemed to be a lot of people around or you looked kind of"—he searched for the right word—"sad or troubled, and I didn't want to add to your worries. But there it is." He handed the envelope to Ellen.

"I didn't show it to my wife," he added, somewhat shyly. "As you know, she's very excited about the house, and she's been worried all along that something would happen to keep us from getting it. She was afraid right up until the last second that you'd change your mind about signing the closing papers."

Ellen didn't tell him that she wished with all her heart she never *had* signed the closing papers, that if there were one action in her entire life she could undo, it would be that one. She didn't tell him how often she relived every moment of that day, imagining herself taking up the contract and ripping it to shreds while Sam and Alexa stared in astonishment and begged her to be reasonable. She pictured herself sitting in that gray upholstered chair and saying, "You know what? I don't want to sell the house. The deal is off," and then standing up and walking out into the rain. And since she'd met Jordan, she'd envisioned it even more often, the phone calls and frantic conversations that always ended, in Ellen's mind, with a stern, faceless lawyer telling Jordan, "I'm sorry, Mrs. Boyce, there's nothing we can do. If Mrs. Flanagan doesn't want to sell, she doesn't have to. The house is hers."

"But I don't understand," Ellen said again. "How would Sara get your address? And this much money? How much is it?" she asked, looking directly into Jeffrey Boyce's pale blue eyes.

"Quite a lot," he said. "Four hundred and fifty dollars."

"Four hundred and fifty!" Ellen's mind was racing. "She must have heard Sam and me talking about the offers on the house, and whether we thought four fifty was a good price. Of course she wouldn't know we meant four hundred and fifty *thousand*. But where did she get it?"

Cloud, who was closing the cash register drawer after ringing up another sale, cleared his throat. "Uh, well, I may know something about that."

"You!" Ellen turned in surprise. "What do you have to do with this?"

Cloud smiled a good-bye at his customer and walked down to where Ellen and Jeffrey stood. "Well, you remember that Saturday morning when you left Sara here? You and Sam had something going on with Louisa."

Ellen remembered. They'd taken Louisa in to see the child psychologist one Saturday morning to talk about the divorce, just as they'd taken Sara on her own to a similar appointment. Ellen had planned to leave Sara at Joanna's, but then Emily had come down with a fever and cough, and Ellen had decided to leave her at the store with Cloud for a few hours instead, because Sara loved going to the shop and "working."

"Yes, I remember. She was here what, three hours?"

"Well, yeah. She made this big poster in the back room about raising money for the homeless," Cloud said. "She said it was a project for her church and that you'd said it was okay if she put up the poster and a jar to collect money while she was here. She told me the whole story about this homeless family that came here from Africa and had five children and the church was trying to get them an apartment and clothes and food and stuff, and she and her Sunday school class were, like, trying to raise money to buy them toys, too."

"Oh, my God. How could she have raised four hundred and fifty dollars in one morning? That's more than we take in at the till in one morning. And then to send it through the *mail*."

"Maybe she saved money some other ways, too," Jeffrey said gently. "I know my older daughter hoards all her birthday money and chore money."

Ellen tried to think clearly. Sara had gotten twenty-five dollars from each of her grandparents for her birthday in March, so that was a hundred dollars. She had a blue plastic piggy bank in her closet into which she put every penny she found or dime she earned; Ellen had no idea how much she'd stored up there. Had Sara *stolen* money somehow? And did she now believe that she had successfully bought back the house, so they wouldn't have to move?

"Look, I'm sure you have a lot to sort out," Jeffrey said. "I'm sorry I didn't tell you about this sooner. I hope your little girl isn't too disappointed when she finds out that we still own the house."

"I honestly don't know what she'll do," Ellen said, closing her eyes tightly so the tears wouldn't come again. "She's very upset about moving and my divorce, obviously."

Jeffrey put his latte down on the counter, and Ellen realized that they'd been so busy talking he'd forgotten to drink it; it was probably cold by now. "I've got to go," he said. "Good luck with everything. I won't come in again because I understand it's hard for you, although I *am* somewhat addicted to your lattes now." He smiled at her, a shy smile full of such warmth and sympathy that Ellen wanted to reach out and pat *his* arm.

"Clearly you have a very clever and resourceful little girl," he said. "I'm sure things will work out for you."

"Thank you," Ellen said, smiling a smile that didn't reach her eyes and feeling as though she would never be able to smile with spontaneous joy again. "I'm sure it will all be fine in the end."

Jeffrey walked over to the door and picked up his umbrella, holding it between his knees while he used both hands to retie his trench coat. He still seemed somewhat hesitant, as though maybe the delivery of the letter wasn't the only thing after all, as though there was something more he wanted to say.

Ellen stood by the counter, holding the envelope in her hand, watching him. Maybe he wanted to tell her that he was willing to back out of the whole deal now that he understood how deeply it was affecting her and her girls. Maybe he wanted to turn to her and say, "You know what? Let's just rip up the contract after all. We can find another house; this one should be yours."

Ellen waited expectantly, willing him silently to turn to her. Jeffrey finished tying his belt and looked up, gazing directly at her. He opened his mouth as though to say something, then seemed to think better of it. And then he turned and pulled open the door and walked out into the rain without saying a word.

CHAPTER FIVE

THE NEXT MORNING dawned clear and bright, without too much wind, just as Ellen had hoped.

She had collected more than a hundred and fifty candles, including the fifty large pillar candles she'd found in the storeroom at Coffee@home, another fifty tapers she'd purchased on sale at Tuesday Morning, and five dozen votives she'd found at Costco. She was expecting five friends tonight, including Joanna. Sam was to pick up the girls at six and keep them until noon the following day.

Ellen spent the morning while the kids were at school cleaning the house—rubbing orange oil into the hardwood floors, wiping down the windows with glass cleaner and newspapers, dusting the sills and moldings slowly and lovingly, like someone preparing a beloved body for a funeral, which was exactly what she was doing, she thought. The windows caught the bright Oregon sun and flooded the east side of the house with soft morning light.

Ellen carefully packed overnight bags for the girls, making sure she included their most beloved toys, the ones they couldn't replace and could never live without. For Sara, it was the large stuffed buffalo that Emily had given her for her fourth birthday and that she had named, innocently, Horny, because of the small horns on his head. For Louisa, it was a doll that Ellen had made for her out of pink cotton jersey and batting when she was three, with an embroidered face and soft brown yarn hair and a pink flowered dress and red felt boots. Louisa had named her Stella Blue Moon and wouldn't sleep without her. After tonight, if the house were really and truly uninhabitable, she and the girls could stay at Jo's, Ellen figured, until their new house was available on May thirty-first.

Ellen had already packed up all the photo albums and report cards and brightly crayoned drawings and baby clothes—even her wedding dress—into several large boxes and asked Joanna to store them in her basement for safekeeping. "I just don't want to have to worry about the sentimental stuff as I'm trying to go through everything for the move," she had explained, avoiding Jo's sympathetic eyes. "This way, I'll know it's all safe with you and I can focus on the stuff I need to give to the Salvation Army or haul to the dump."

"Of course, sweetie," Jo had said. "Do you want me to do anything? I mean, I could go through all the photos and sort out the ones with Sam in them if that would help."

"Oh, no," Ellen had said. "I don't want the girls to think I've cut him out of our lives. If I can just put the boxes in your basement, it'll be help enough."

Now she went down to her own basement, with the cinderblock walls and the turtle drawings and the big rocking horse that Louisa had outgrown just last year, and removed the battery from the smoke detector. She replaced it with a dead battery from the bag they kept in the kitchen drawer for taking to the hazardous waste disposal place, only they always forgot to actually do it. She did the same thing with the smoke detectors in the kitchen, the hallway, and upstairs by the bedrooms.

She had talked to Sara last night about the money and the note she had sent to Jeffrey Boyce. They had sat on the steps on the deck overlooking the swing set, where Louisa was busily shooting Stella Blue Moon down the slide. It was a perfect Oregon May evening, cool and clear after the day's rain, scented with sweetness from the laurel blossoms that dangled over the fence.

"We can't buy the house back, sweetie," Ellen had said gently. "We've sold it and we can't undo it. I appreciate that you tried to do something to help with all your money. I know how important it is to you. But we have to move. We'll have fun fixing up our new house."

Sara had sat stiffly, silent, poking a twig into the crack between the boards in the deck.

"And what you did was wrong, honey. You lied to Cloud; you owe him an apology. And those people who gave you money thought they were helping a homeless family. Because we can't find those people to give their money back, I think we need to donate it to the homeless shelter."

"*We* are homeless," Sara had said.

"We are *not* homeless," Ellen had said, more sharply than she meant to. But even as she spoke she had felt the lack of conviction in her voice, felt her own passion for and obsession with the house murmuring beneath her words, a hypocritical countermeasure to her speech to her daughter.

Sara had maintained her silence, dropping her twig and staring stonily ahead at Louisa and Stella Blue Moon. Ellen wished she would sob or shout or melt in some way, act more like the little girl she was. She didn't know what to do with this mirror image of her own emotions, glaring furiously in front of her. Finally Sara had looked at her and said, "This house will always be our house. *Always*. I don't care who bought it."

"Yes," Ellen had said. "In some ways it will always be ours. It will always have a special place in our lives because it was our first house. Nothing will change that."

"That is *not* what I mean," Sara had said.

Now, Ellen opened the refrigerator to make sure she'd put the white wine in to chill for tonight. She'd bought seven kinds of cheeses at New Seasons, and sweet Oregon strawberries and crusty loaves of ciabatta bread. She'd made soup earlier that afternoon, a rich carrot-ginger that filled the house with a wonderful aroma. They would end the meal with a collection of fine dark chocolate truffles from Moonstruck.

The screen door squeaked open, and Louisa and Sara burst in, dropping their backpacks on the kitchen table.

"Hello, darling girls!" said Ellen, bending down to kiss Louisa's cheek and putting an arm around Sara. "How was school? Ready for your big night out with Daddy? What are you three going to do?"

"We're going to eat hot dogs!" Louisa said cheerfully, rifling through the snack drawer for a cracker. Hot dogs were forbidden items in Ellen's house and objects of great desire. "Daddy said we get two hot dogs each—but no sodas," she added, lest Ellen think Sam a reckless parent.

"Daddy makes great hot dogs," Ellen said, smiling at her youngest. Louisa had all of Sam's sunniness, a natural optimism that made both of them anticipate good things around every corner, no matter what nasty, unpleasant experience had lurked beyond the last bend. It was what made Sam get back up after every inventive disaster and move on to the next creation with the conviction that this time, he was really onto something. It was a quality so foreign to Ellen's own nature that she was constantly amazed that she could have given birth to a being as perpetually happy and hopeful as Louisa.

"I packed your favorite jammies, and Stella Blue Moon," she said. "How are you, peanut?" She turned to Sara. "What happened at school today?"

"It was good," Sara said. "We had chocolate day. We've been studying where cocoa beans grow and how chocolate gets made, and we got to taste all kinds of chocolate, even spicy fire chocolate. Gabe spit his out on the floor, and everybody thought it looked like poop."

Ellen looked at her. "Sounds like fun. Are you excited about going to Daddy's?"

"Yes. But, Mommy?" Sara looked up at her intently. "Will you be lonely?"

Ellen wrapped her in a hug. "No, darling. I'm having Jo and some of my girlfriends over, and we're going to have a little party. So I'll be having fun, too. You enjoy your night and don't worry about me. But thank you for thinking about it."

She felt Sara relax in her arms, nestle her head against her shoulder. "Now you girls run," she said, "and make sure I've packed everything you need while I check on my dinner and get dressed for my party."

Ellen listened to them stampede up the narrow staircase and thought, *This may be the last time I ever hear their feet on those steps.* Slowly she followed the girls upstairs to dress. It was just her best friends, all women in their forties, but Ellen prepared as though for a big date. The girls were busily playing pet shop in their room, so she took a long, luxurious hot shower and smoothed sesame oil into her skin. She rubbed her heels with pumice stone and smoothed them with cream, then painted her toenails—something she had not done in probably ten years. She blow-dried her hair and set it with rollers so it brushed out into shining waves of reddish brown. She put on a long black silky skirt, a black scoop-neck T-shirt, and a cardigan the color of the sky on a summer day. Around her neck, she fastened the necklace Sam had given her for their tenth wedding anniversary, a single pearl suspended on a fine leather string—elegant yet casual and exactly Ellen's style. Finally, she put on two delicate silver earrings with pearl drops and deep coppery red lipstick and looked at herself in the bathroom mirror.

She wished suddenly that Sam were there, standing in the bedroom with his rumpled hair, rifling through his dresser drawers for a clean shirt, looking up at her with a grin to say, "You look good," a statement that was, for the plainspoken Sam, quite an eloquent compliment. It always carried the underlying promise of an exciting intimacy later, and if he looked at her in a certain way as he said it, his dark eyes boring into hers, she'd get weak at the knees, like some foolish girl in a novel.

"Enough of that!" Ellen said sternly to her reflection in the mirror. "You have other things to think about tonight."

She heard the door slam downstairs and Louisa squeal, "Daddy! Daddy is here!" and feet pound on the staircase again as the girls ran down.

Ellen walked downstairs slowly, running a hand lightly along the wooden banister in a gentle caress. Sam was in the living room, with a girl clinging to either leg.

"Hey, Ellie." He looked at her intently, at the pearl necklace nestled against her collarbone, the soft folds of her skirt around her hips, the loose waves of her hair. His look alone was enough to make her blush, which irritated her no end. How could her body betray her so?

"Nice necklace," he said. "Who gave it to you?"

"You gave it to me," she said, frowning. "For our tenth anniversary, remember?"

He winked at her. "Of course," he said. "Hard to forget an anniversary that includes skinny-dipping."

"Skinny-dipping!" Sara said. "That is disgusting."

"What's skinny-dipping?" said Louisa.

"It's swimming with no clothes on, and it's totally gross," said Sara.

Their tenth anniversary had come one August just six months after Ellen had lost the baby boy in her second trimester. She had felt numb for months, moving through all the motions of all her days like an actor in a play, reading lines someone else had written. Sam, in an effort to cheer her up, had planned dinner and dessert at her favorite restaurants.

They had eaten dinner at Wildwood, buttery salmon glazed with apricot and ginger. For dessert they'd walked across the street to get warm chocolate soufflé cake at Paley's Place. It was then that Sam had given her the necklace, the pearl on the leather string. "It's the birthstone for June," he said.

"But my birthday's in November."

"It's for the baby," he said softly. "I know you've been really upset about it. I thought you could have this to remember him by."

She had looked at Sam, and all the grief she had held in for those long months—calm and composed as she worked at the shop, drove little Sara to Gymboree and the indoor playground, cooked dinner—all of it flooded over her at once. She burst into deep, wrenching sobs, right there in the restaurant.

"Oh, geez, Ellie, Ellie, don't," he said, coming around the table and sliding next to her on the banquette. He wrapped his arms around her and pressed her face to his shoulder. "It's okay, it's really okay. I just wanted you to have something." The other patrons, after looking up to see what the problem was, had gone back to their dinners and desserts and brandies.

She sniffled and wiped her nose on the shoulder of his shirt. "I feel like I let you down," she sobbed softly. "I wanted to give you another baby."

"Oh, God, no," he said. "*No*. If Sara is all we end up with, we'll still be lucky—really lucky. I mean that." He paused and squeezed her tight.

She smiled. She could see that Sam was glad his gift had touched her, even helped her, but he was also mildly embarrassed by the depth of her emotion. "I've got another surprise for you," he said. "Let's get out of here."

They paid the bill and walked out into the cool summer night, and then Sam drove her up into the hills and parked outside a huge house on Vista Drive.

"Why are we stopping here?" Ellen said.

"You know Jonathan Benning? The Intel hotshot I did some consulting work for last month? He's out of town for all of August and told me to come by whenever I want to swim in his backyard pool. He thought it would be fun for Sara."

"And you want to swim *now*?" Ellen said.

"Sure," he said.

"But we don't have bathing suits."

"That's the point," he said, grinning.

"Oh, Sam, come on," she said. "He's probably got a security guard, or those motion-detecting lights."

"There's no security guard," he said. "This is Jonathan Benning, not Bill Gates."

Ellen shook her head. "You want me to go skinny-dipping in a stranger's pool in the middle of the night. That's crazy."

"And fun."

She surprised herself and did it, sneaking silently into the backyard behind Sam, letting him unlock the gate in the big cedar fence, and then slipping her clothes off onto the concrete, sliding into the water at the deep end. She felt aroused the minute she entered the water, enveloped in its liquid warmth, with the cool night air against her face. She dived down and swam the length of the pool underwater, surfacing at the shallow end to take great gulps of fresh air. Sam glided up behind her, slippery and warm, and wrapped his arms around her, lifting the wet tangle of her hair to kiss the back of her neck. His lips were warm on her skin. She felt his hardness pressed against her, and he slipped a hand up to caress her breast . . .

"Did you really skinny-dip, Daddy?" Sara said, jolting Ellen back to the present.

"Of course not, I was kidding," Sam said, handing an overnight bag to each girl. "Here, carry these out to the car. I'll be right there."

Ellen bent and kissed both her daughters. "See you tomorrow, girls. Have fun."

She turned to him after the girls were gone. "You really should watch what you say around them, Sam. Sara picks up everything."

"I know, I know. I'm sorry, okay?" He looked around the room again, at the polished wood of the floors, the cheery red paint on the trim, the dent in the plaster ceiling where he'd stuck the Christmas tree that was just a few inches too tall for the living room. "The house looks good, Ellie," he said. "Remember what it looked like when we bought it? All the plaid wallpaper and horse themes in every room?"

"Of course I remember," she said.

"You know I'm going to miss it, too," he said. "This is the house where we became a family."

It was such an uncharacteristically sentimental thing for Sam to say that it caught Ellen off guard. So it wasn't just four walls and a roof, even to Sam. Reflexively, she put a hand on his arm, but then found herself saying, "I don't want to talk about this. Either I'll get really angry again or I'll cry and destroy all the work that went into caking on this makeup and trying to look good."

He looked at her, his brown eyes straight into hers. "You do look good," he said.

Ellen felt a rush of desire throughout her body and suddenly put a hand on either side of his head and pulled his face down to kiss him. He kissed her back, urgently. His mouth pulled fiercely at her lips, her tongue. His hands gripped her hips, pulled her tight against him.

She broke away. "Stop. I'm sorry," she said. "It's just too easy and too familiar, and when you mentioned becoming a family here, it just got to me. I'm sorry, Sam."

He walked across the room, toward the kitchen and back door, toward the driveway where their daughters waited, and then turned to look at her again. "Don't be sorry, Ellie," he said, smiling and cocking an eyebrow at her. "Next time, just follow through." And he was gone.

Ellen felt like a fool, furious with herself for giving in to her emotions, and furious with Sam for even suggesting that there might be a next time. They were in the midst of a separation; he had no right to look at her like that. And he was distracting her from the business at hand, which was tonight and all that would come after.

Now she needed to focus. Her friends would be here soon, and she wanted everything ready. She took out the long wooden matches from the old tin box on the top shelf of the bookshelf and started to light the candles, six along the mantel, another half dozen on the table in the front window, more scattered on the coffee table and end tables. She felt languorous, trancelike, as she moved slowly through the rooms, lighting the candles that would, she hoped, become a funeral pyre for her house. She almost understood, with an awful, gripping clarity, how those women in the news headlines who murdered their children could do something so terrible and yet still believe it was an act of love.

Her children were safe, Sam was safe, Stella Blue Moon and Ellen's wedding gown and the birthday pictures were all safe. It was just a house, and she was going to burn it down.

JOANNA APPEARED IN the doorway to the living room, dressed in blue jeans and a flowing top embellished with blue glass beads. Her thick, curly hair was knotted on top of her head in a careless bun. She wore one bright blue topaz stud in her right ear.

"Jesus Christ, Ellie! Is this a séance or a funeral?" she asked, looking from the mantel to the table to the bookshelf.

Ellen smiled. "I wanted to do something special," she said. "It's my farewell party. Although I guess it's kind of a funeral, too. A funeral for my marriage, a funeral for our life in this house—"

"Oh, shit. Me and my big mouth. Stop, sweetie. Everything looks lovely," Jo said, moving closer to put an arm around Ellen. "Really. Please, let's make this fun. My God, think of what you're leaving behind! The fence that's constantly in need of painting and repair. The Crazy Cat Lady neighbor with her all-pink outfits and foliage phobia. Not to mention the furnace that you know is going to fall apart any day now and cost three thousand dollars to replace. And you haven't even met your neighbors in the new house yet. I bet one of them is a single, gorgeous, well-organized, financially stable guy who's just been waiting for the right short brunette to come along."

"Yeah, I'm sure of it," Ellen said drily. "Listen, I did want to ask you a favor, though."

"Anything."

"Could I sleep in your guest room tonight?" Ellen asked. "I don't know, it's only the second time Sam has taken the girls overnight since we split up, and I just don't want to be here all alone."

Joanna hugged her. "Of course! Bed's all made up, since Pete's mom is coming next week. And it's yours any time you want it. Any time."

"Thanks. If you just leave the back door unlocked after you go home tonight, I'll come over once I'm done cleaning up after the party. I really appreciate it, Jo."

"It's nothing. Now, do you need any help?"

"Food's all ready. Come talk to me in the kitchen while I warm up the soup," Ellen said, glancing around the living room at the flickering shadows cast by the candles. "I'm hoping it will be a party we'll never forget."

An hour later they were all there, sitting in a circle on the living room floor and picking at the cheese and fruit, well into their third bottle of wine. Molly, who sat next to Ellen, was the mother of Sara's best friend from kindergarten. A native Oregonian, Molly was slightly self-conscious about the fact that she'd never gone to college, even though she was the smartest person Ellen knew, and the most kindhearted. Laurie, on the other side of Molly, lived just up the hill from Ellen and Jo on Grace Lane. No-nonsense, maternal, she'd nursed Ellen through her miscarriage, bringing her iron-fortified muffins and spinach quiches, and stopping by with movies and books "guaranteed to get your mind off it." Karly, who sat next to Jo, owned the gift shop next door to Coffee@home; she and Ellen had been friends for eight years. And tall, lanky Debbie, who lay on the floor in front of the fireplace, had played first base on the women's softball team that Ellen had joined when she first moved to Portland, in the years B.K. (Before Kids).

"Molly owes me twenty dollars," Laurie said, laughing and staring meaningfully at Molly, who rolled her eyes.

"For what?" Ellen asked.

"She bet me you'd never actually leave the house," Laurie said. "And I said you would: Common sense would prevail."

"It's not that I thought you *couldn't* do it," Molly said, somewhat sheepishly. "I just thought you *wouldn't*. You're so clever; I thought you'd figure out a way to keep it."

"Cleverness has nothing to do with it," said Karly. "Ellie's tough. I think Ellie should stand at the door with a shotgun when Jordan comes to move in. I can just see her, our Ellen, all five foot two of her, defending her house to her last drop of blood."

"God, you make me sound like Granny on *The Beverly Hillbillies*," Ellen said with a laugh.

"Yes!" shrieked Jo. "That's it! 'Git off my property!' It's the role of a lifetime for you, Ellie. Get that shotgun loaded."

"No, that's not Ellie," said Molly, putting an arm around Ellen and hugging her. "She's going to go gentle into that new house."

"I don't know," Ellen said ruefully, leaning against Molly. "I feel more like I'm going to 'burn and rave' and 'rage, rage.' Although

I've done enough of that already, God knows. Maybe I'm ready to go gentle now."

Ellen, flushed and logy with the meal and the wine, felt her tension and sorrow melt in the warmth of her friends' affection and support. These women were perpetually on her side; they knew her inside out, loved her even though she worried too much and was hyperresponsible, and they would do anything to help her or her kids. She knew that if she dropped dead the next day, they'd step in, keeping her memory alive for her children, reinforcing the values she tried hardest to live. As long as she had these women, she could get through anything.

"Can we talk about my dog now?" asked Debbie. She sat up to refill her wineglass from the bottle on the coffee table. "So the dog has gotten so attached to me that he won't let Jim in the bed," she said. "Last night I was in bed reading, and Buster was lying next to me, and Jim came in and started undressing. Well, Buster began to growl, and every time Jim came near the bed, he'd bark at him and bare his teeth."

"That's a problem," Molly said.

"It's only a problem if you really *want* Jim in your bed," said Jo, smiling.

"Well, that's the thing," Debbie said. "Jim threw a fit and said the dog has to go. And frankly, the dog is the family member who treats me the best, so I'm not so sure I want to get rid of him. I mean, Buster doesn't ask much of me, never complains, never criticizes, loves what's served for dinner, and is always thrilled when I walk into a room. If it comes down to it, I'd be hard-pressed to pick Jim over Buster right now."

The women laughed. Ellen smiled. But she was thinking about Sam, about the hungry way he'd kissed her earlier that evening, about the eagerness he'd always had to get into *her* bed. When her friends made jokes over the years about how their sex lives had become low priority, almost a chore, Ellen had always remained silent. Throughout their marriage, she had wanted Sam as much as she had the day they'd met, and he had matched her interest and eagerness. They made love in the shower early in the morning, before the girls were awake, on the floor in front of the fireplace late at night, even in the kitchen, with Ellen pressed against the counter, moaning as Sam thrust into her from behind. Ironic that *her* marriage, the one in which the sexual fire had never even flickered, was the one that didn't last. *If only it were enough,* she thought. *If only being wildly attracted to someone were enough . . .*

"Maybe you just need a bigger bed," Molly said.

"Or a dog whisperer," said Laurie. "You know, to teach Buster that Jim is the leader of the pack."

"But Jim's *not* the leader of the pack, and Buster knows it," Ellen said, with a wink at Debbie.

"Exactly," Debbie said. "That's what Jim is *really* upset about. He wants to be leader. It's bad enough that the kids view me as the ultimate authority; now the dog does, too."

They all laughed again. They talked for hours more, draining the last bottle of wine, carefully slicing up and sharing the last chocolate truffle. Finally, just after eleven, after they'd gone through the house one last time and marveled at how it looked, and picked up all the dishes and washed the wineglasses, and hugged Ellen hard, they left and Ellen was alone in the house.

She walked carefully from room to room, saying a silent goodbye to each space. Then she picked up the candle snuffer and walked back through the living room and dining room. She couldn't leave every candle blazing; that would be too stupid, too obvious.

She had to put out all but a few, easily overlooked tapers—the kind of oversight anyone might make, especially after drinking a few glasses of wine. Slowly she extinguished the candles on the mantel, then the votives on the coffee table and end tables. She looked carefully around the room and finally decided to leave three candles burning: one on the table in the front window, right next to the curtain; one on the wooden bookshelf, where the heat of the flame had already blackened a dark circle on the shelf above it; and one in the dining room, on the very old and very dry wood of the corner cupboard.

She turned out the last of the lights. Ellen took one long, final look around the room, imprinting every detail one last time into memory. The candles flared, their flames streaming upward. Then she turned and walked through the kitchen and out the back door, closing and locking it firmly behind her.

CHAPTER SIX

ELLEN WAS WIDE awake; definitely too wide awake to slip into Joanna's guest room and try to sleep. Not that she'd sleep at all tonight, she thought. She was slightly drunk from all the wine, and also keyed up and restless and in desperate need of a cup of tea and some quiet. She figured it would take several hours for the candles to burn down to pools of wax, to sear the wood of the bookshelf or the corner cupboard, or for flaming curtains to heat the wooden lathe beneath the plaster walls. She wanted to be at Joanna's to keep watch through the night, but surely she had time to grab some tea at the shop and calm herself down a little.

Cloud was just closing up as she arrived. He had a red bandanna tied around his head and was wearing a blue Mount Bachelor T-shirt, wide-wale corduroy slacks, and leather sandals—with socks. The sandals-with-socks look was something it had taken Ellen years to get used to after she moved to Oregon. In Michigan, people wore sandals in the summer and shoes in the winter. Here, people wore sandals year-round. They just added thick athletic socks in the cold months.

"I did the drawer already," he said. "We had a good day. The sun comes out for a few minutes in the afternoon, and suddenly everyone wants iced lattes." He looked at her. "You look really nice, Ellen," he said. "Hope you had a good evening."

She smiled at him. "I did. Thanks, Cloud. I'm just not ready to sleep, though, so I thought I'd sit here for a few minutes and have a cup of tea."

"You're in luck," he said, nodding toward the back counter. "Just made a pot."

Ellen and Cloud shared a love of good tea, in spite of the fact that they both spent much of their time making exquisite coffee drinks. Ellen had never liked the bitterness of coffee, not even when it was diluted with cream and a generous bit of sugar, as Sam always drank it, or with steamed milk and flavored syrups, as she made it for most of the customers in the shop. But tea—Ellen found comfort in the very process of measuring out the leaves, boiling the water, steeping it just long enough, and inhaling the rich aroma, different for every kind of tea. She loved the light, jasmine scent of white tea; the rich, citrusy scent of Earl Grey; the smoky aroma of oolong. In Cloud she had found a fellow fanatic. He pored over websites searching for new tea suppliers and ordered in different varieties every month. Ellen kept a white stoneware teapot in the back, just for the two of them, and they both made sure it was always filled and hot.

Ellen slipped off her sandals. She padded barefoot across the wood floor—not sticky, she noted, so Cloud had done his usual thorough cleaning job—and found a clean mug on the counter. Cloud poured a steaming trail of hot tea into the mug. She cupped her hands around it and breathed in the aroma.

"Lady Grey?" She looked at Cloud.

"Yeah," he said. "Don't put maple syrup in it, please."

Ellen smiled. When she was feeling blue or craving something sweet, she loved to put cream and maple syrup in her tea—a crime to a true tea aficionado, since the syrup and cream distorted the delicate flavor of the freshly brewed leaves.

"No, no, no, I wouldn't dare," she said. "Just milk."

She sank back into the big, overstuffed blue and white checked armchair in the center of the store and put her feet up on the carpenter's chest.

"So it was a good day?" she asked, sipping her tea as Cloud finished wiping down the espresso machine.

"Yeah. We sold that kitchen table, the one with the green top. Hey, Ellen, is Sara okay? I felt kind of bad about the whole money thing, you know, her trying to buy the house back."

"Oh, Cloud, I'm sorry she lied to you," Ellen said, feeling suddenly weary. "She's going to apologize. I don't know how to make this all easier for her. She's so upset and so angry and so adamant that she'll never move. I honestly don't know what to say to her. Her parents are splitting up and she's moving to another house and those are hard things. I can't pretend they're not."

"You know, my parents split when I was a kid, and I turned out okay."

"You turned out better than okay, Cloud," Ellen said, gazing at him over the rim of her turquoise mug. "You'll have to tell me your secrets. Because I look at Sara and all I can think is that we're wounding her in some deep and permanent way with all this. We're not just divorcing; we're also taking away her *home*."

Cloud stopped stacking cups and looked at Ellen. "Sara has it better than I did, Ellen, because you're so good at making a nice home. The house isn't that important—it's all the stuff you do to it. You know, the way you painted that red color on the mantel, and that picture you framed that Louisa painted of Sam, and that quilt you hung on the wall in the girls' bedroom. It just makes it feel like home."

Ellen was silent. She knew that Cloud's parents had divorced when he was six, and that he had spent his somewhat erratic childhood in a succession of communes, VW buses, and even a teepee. But he was so easygoing that she hadn't spent too much time considering what it might have meant to him not to have a real house, with a room of his own and a bookshelf for his rock collection and a closet full of stuffed animals and baseballs and Legos. Cloud didn't feel particularly sorry for himself because he hadn't had all that, but clearly he valued it or he wouldn't have noticed the details of her own home. With a flash she realized that what attracted Cloud to his job was the fact that it was a home of sorts, a place filled with wooden chairs polished to a satiny patina from years of wear and brightly colored, mismatched mugs and paintings on the wall in solid mahogany frames—things that had substance and age and stability to them.

"Well, thanks for saying that, but I don't know. I feel as though I could make that house a home because I loved it so."

"It's not the house, Ellen, it's you," Cloud said, almost stubbornly. "You're the home."

Ellen studied him, his expressive brown eyes, the lanky gracefulness of his long arms and legs and lean torso. She knew he was right, but the problem was that she didn't *want* to be the home. She was too bereft to know how to make a home for her now altered family; she didn't know how to build a nest in this barren new landscape.

She stood up and walked over to the counter to pour herself more tea.

"Here," she said gently, taking the dishrag from his hand. "I'll finish closing. You head home."

"You sure?"

"Yes. It's Friday night. Get out of here."

"Great," said Cloud, leaning into the back room to grab the messenger bag he carried everywhere. "I'm meeting some friends at Norse Hall."

Ellen grinned. Cloud, with his long blond ponytail and clunky sandals, was an amazingly graceful dancer and spent many of his evenings haunting the dance floors of old refurbished clubs in Portland, including Nocturnal and Norse Hall. He could salsa and tango and jitterbug and waltz and cha-cha. When he babysat for Ellen he taught both her girls how to do a basic two-step. Louisa would stand on the arm of the sofa, one chubby hand around Cloud's neck, the other holding his hand, while he danced her side to side and twirled her around, ending with a final dip, Louisa leaning back in his arms, one leg in the air, toe pointed, just as he'd taught her.

"Have a great time, Cloud. Thanks for everything. I'll see you tomorrow."

"See you tomorrow, Ellen." He grabbed his sweatshirt from the coatrack by the front door and stopped. "You know, you should come dancing with me sometime. You're small; I could do some amazing lifts with you."

Ellen laughed. "For my fiftieth birthday," she said. "November twentieth, 2014. It's a date."

She locked the door behind Cloud and walked to the big armchair. She sat down, leaned back against the soft fabric, and closed her eyes. All at once she felt tired in a way she had never experienced before, a weariness that was packed into her bones and sucked the life and warmth and energy out of her eyes, her skin, her mind. She put her elbow on the armrest and rested her forehead against her palm.

She remembered San Juan Island, and a long weekend she'd spent there with the girls last year. They'd seen whales spouting in the harbor, and the red-barked madrona trees, and an eagle flying in great soaring circles above their ferry. Sometimes she thought about just disappearing, withdrawing all the cash she could find and taking a bus and then a ferry and starting a new life on San Juan Island, working as a barista, living in a little room above a shop, where she could be somebody completely new. It was a lovely fantasy, which of course she would never carry out because she would never in a million years leave her kids. But sometimes it was so wonderful to think about it, just walking away from the inventory and the bills at the shop, and Sam's hurt and guilt, and Jordan's greedy lust for the house, and the inevitable wrenching grief that was going to come with moving day and finalizing her divorce.

Ellen heard a tap at the front door. It was well after 11:00 P.M. and she had already flipped the old painted wooden sign around to read "Closed." Probably someone who had just finished dinner at the Italian restaurant next door and wanted a decaf cappuccino, *please*. She squinted through the half dark and saw a man peering through the glass, a man with a familiar outline—trench coat, neatly trimmed beard. Oh, God.

Ellen got up and walked to the door and unlocked it. Jeffrey Boyce stood there, hands in the pockets of his trench coat, looking somewhat naked without his usual briefcase.

"I'm really sorry to bother you," he said. "I just needed to talk to you about one more thing, and when I called your home and you didn't answer, I thought you might be here. I didn't realize you closed at eleven."

She looked up at him. "I have to warn you that I'm just exhausted," she said. "But come on in."

She opened the door all the way to let him in, then dropped back into the armchair.

"Listen," he said, standing across from her. "I've been thinking about the house. I have to be honest with you; I really didn't want to make this move."

Ellen shifted in her chair, feeling suddenly more alert.

"What do you mean?"

"I mean I really love our *old* house. We haven't even sold it yet because Jordan loved yours so much she just kind of jumped when she saw it and made the offer. But this whole move—it kind of snowballed."

"You mean *you* don't want to move?" Ellen asked.

"Well, not really. I like our house," he said, sitting down opposite her on an Adirondack twig chair. "It's nothing fancy, but it's got a great flat yard for the swing set and a big wide driveway for the kids to Rollerblade in, and I just like it. I like to garden and I've spent years working on my garden there. I've got a climbing hydrangea that I've trained all the way up the front of the house and across the portico. I built a playhouse with a tower for the kids in the backyard, but it's so big we could never take it apart and move it."

Ellen wanted to empathize—she, of all people, understood not wanting to leave a home you had loved and nurtured—but she didn't have time right now for climbing hydrangeas and playhouse towers. She needed him to get to the point. "But then why are you moving?"

Jeffrey smiled, a small, sad smile there in the half dark. "Well, Jordan wants to join the Multnomah Athletic Club, and she thought a Portland address would be more upscale than a Beaverton one; our house now is your basic Beaverton daylight basement. I think she wanted something a little showier. She felt it was time for us to get out of our 'starter' house and into our 'move up' house. She kind of has a grand plan for everything, and this is the next step in the plan."

The whole thing seemed ridiculous to Ellen, who paid so little attention to status symbols that it took her weeks to figure out why Karly had given her a key chain with the initials LV embossed in the brown leather when her own initials were EF. ("You really need to read *Vogue* more often," Jo had said, laughing and explaining about Louis Vuitton leather accessories.) Beaverton was a perfectly pleasant suburb just fifteen minutes from downtown Portland, with a mix of new and older homes on well-kept lots. It was true that West Slope, where Ellen lived, was a part of Portland itself, and closer in, with more towering old trees and some quaint older homes. But they were still mostly modest houses, nothing like the big, grand houses in Portland Heights or Westover, with their panoramic views of the city and the mountains.

Ellen leaped up from her chair, heart pounding. She paced from the chair to the counter and back. *I have to get out of here,* she thought, *before the house burns down.* She rubbed her palms nervously, still pacing. "I don't mean to get too personal, but didn't you discuss this?" she asked. "I assume you talked about it and agreed to look at houses and then to buy mine."

Jeffrey ran both his hands through his cropped hair and then rubbed the back of his neck. "It's hard to explain because you don't know Jordan," he said finally. "She has a very forceful personality."

He sat up straighter. "Which is a good thing," he said hurriedly, as though he wanted to make it clear that he was in no way criticizing or being disloyal to his wife. "Her plan got us from nothing to saving enough to buy the house we're in now, and to being able to buy your house. It's just that we talked about it and I thought we were still talking about it, but she was already on to the next step. When she saw your house, she called our real estate agent to write the offer, then came home and told me we were going to buy it. It just happened so fast."

"So what are you saying?" asked Ellen, desperate to get to the heart of it and equally desperate to leave. "Are you trying to tell me that you don't want to buy my house after all?"

Her heart leaped with hope and a sense of joy, as well as a wild terror that she was going to be too late if she didn't get home immediately. Getting the house back would give her a center, a purpose, a way to knit her life together again even when she did finally get divorced. It would mean that Sara and Emily could continue to hoot their secret barn owl signals out their bedroom windows to each other at night, that Louisa could once again check herself against those marks scratched in the doorjamb of Sam's closet to see if she was the same height Sara had been at the same age. It would mean a host of things, all of them beloved to Ellen.

Of course there was the issue of the money, the whole reason they'd had to sell in the first place. But in these desperate weeks since she'd signed the papers, as she'd lain awake at night reliving it again and again, Ellen had decided that she needed the house even more than she needed Coffee@home. At the time she and Sam had split up, she'd been more concerned about supporting herself and the girls long term, particularly if Sam's vaunted baby beeper continued to fade into oblivion. Sure, he was willing to pay child support, but who knew if he'd actually have any money? But now that she'd actually experienced what it meant to give up the house, it seemed much easier to contemplate giving up the business. Not all of it, of course. Ellen, ever practical, knew she couldn't throw away her only source of income. But if she sold roughly half the company, she could pay off the second mortgage and continue to work to make monthly payments on the first mortgage. There was still the matter of giving Sam his share of their equity in the house, but since he was the one who had taken out the second mortgage for the stupid baby beeper, he could jolly well wait a while for his money.

"Look, I'm premature in even bringing this up with you," Jeffrey said. "I just really felt badly yesterday about your daughter, and when you were crying—"

"Oh, God," Ellen said, stopping her pacing to sit back down in the armchair opposite him. "Please don't bring that up. I really am not the kind of woman who cries very easily, and I'm certainly not the kind who cries to get her way. I'm embarrassed about the whole thing."

"I know, I know," Jeffrey said, holding up his hand to silence her. "I mean, it's just you and your daughter seem to feel so strongly about leaving your house, and I feel so strongly about leaving my house, it seems as though we should be able to work something out."

"Of course we can work something out!" Ellen said. *And if I'm lucky there is still a house there to be sold back and forth between us,* she thought.

"Listen," she said, standing up quickly and looking for her sandals. "I'm sorry. I've got to go. But I'm so grateful you came. You have no idea what this means to us."

"Well," he began. "I can't—"

"We can discuss the details tomorrow," Ellen said. "But I *really* have to go. I just remembered something, and it's urgent."

She slipped on her sandals and felt around on the counter for the key to the shop. Jeffrey stood up, too, his hands in the pockets of his khaki coat, watching her. "Jordan—" he said, but Ellen cut him off.

"I understand she was really excited about the house," she said. "I know it must be a real disappointment to her to give it up. But your house sounds perfect for you all. And God knows, there are other houses and other neighborhoods that are much more prestigious for MAC club members than mine. I swear I'll call you first thing in the morning. Please thank Jordan for me."

Ellen stopped her hurried fumbling with her mug and the keys and the Closed sign to turn to Jeffrey. She reached out a hand and put it on his arm. He jumped as if startled, and she pulled her hand back. "Thank you so much, for everything, being so kind about Sara's note and all." She looked into his blue eyes. "Really. I hope you will come back to the shop once all this is over. The tall vanilla lattes will be on me."

She held the door open for Jeffrey, then followed him out, quickly locking the door behind her. She ran down the sidewalk to her car, throwing a "good-bye" over her shoulder as she went. Starting up the car, she shifted into reverse so quickly that she almost banged her head on the steering wheel. "Steady," she said to herself. "It's all right." She drove carefully out of the parking lot and down the street, turned right on Seventy-eighth and then right on Canyon Road.

She was almost all the way to Grace Lane when she heard the sirens.

CHAPTER SEVEN

THERE WERE TWO fire trucks parked in front of her house, red lights flashing. She could see Alfred and Marybelle standing in front of their house across the street, huddled in their bathrobes. Alfred, without his trademark glasses and red cap, looked surprised and a little lost, with strands of gray hair sticking up wildly around his bald spot. *Oh, God, oh, God, oh, God.* Ellen looked frantically for smoke or flames as she pulled up behind the second truck.

She leaped from the car and ran up the front steps, through the gate, which was already open, and toward the front door, which stood ajar. A strong hand grabbed her firmly by the elbow.

Ellen turned to face a young fireman, with blue eyes and a shock of thick brown hair, dressed in his regulation coat and boots with a mask hanging from his neck and an oxygen tank strapped to his back. "Please, it's my house," she said, gasping for breath. Her heart was hammering at her ribs like an angry toddler banging on a table.

"Is there anyone in there?" the fireman asked suddenly, urgently. "Is someone inside?"

"No, no, oh, God, no," Ellen said. "I just left a few minutes ago and the house was empty. I locked it when I left. Is there really a fire?"

"We're checking it out," he said. "One of your neighbors called and said they smelled smoke."

Ellen glanced wildly across the street at Alfred and Marybelle. Had they smelled smoke all the way over there? Could the fire have started so quickly and burned so fiercely already?

Suddenly Joanna, barefoot and wearing flannel pajamas and a sweater, came around the corner of the house in the company of another fireman. She stopped when she saw Ellen, eyes wide, then ran up and enveloped her in a ferocious hug. After a few seconds, she pushed her away and glared.

"Jesus Christ, Ellie, I don't know whether to hug you or slap you! You scared me to death! Where the hell have you been?"

"At the shop. I wasn't tired, so I drove over to make a cup of tea and sit for a while. What happened?"

"I woke up and poked my head in the guest room and you weren't there," Joanna said. She was wearing her husband's large blue cardigan over her pajamas, and she pulled it close against the chill of the May night. "So I popped over to see if I could help you finish cleaning up. The back door was locked, so I used the key under the mat to get in. I couldn't find you, but I smelled smoke, and then I saw some of the candles were still burning—one was really close to the curtains in the living room. So I put the candles out, but I still smelled something. There was a big black mark on the bookshelf where the candle had burned the wood, and then I started thinking about those fires where something gets hot and just smolders for hours before breaking out into huge flames and I got kind of creeped out so I called the fire department."

Joanna looked at Ellen. "The house could have burned down," she said. "This was close."

No, this was Providence, thought Ellen, surely a sign that the house was meant to be hers forever.

"I tried calling your cell phone," Joanna added, "but it was sitting on the kitchen counter."

"I'm sorry, Jo. Thanks so much." Ellen reached out and squeezed her arm. "I mean, my God, you saved everything."

The fireman standing next to Joanna held out his hand toward Ellen, palm up. It contained three rectangular batteries.

"All the batteries in your smoke detectors were dead," he said. He gave her a hard look. "And there were candles all over the house. None of them were lit, but still— The bookshelf was burned, and we had to chop into it and spray foam to make sure the whole thing didn't ignite at some point. I don't know what you were thinking. A bunch of candles and dead batteries is a nightmare scenario, ma'am," he said, shaking his head. "This could have been really bad."

"I'm sorry," Ellen said, wishing he wouldn't call her ma'am. It made her feel like she was about eighty-five. "I tried to be careful with the candles, but I must have forgotten one or two. And the batteries— I'm getting divorced and I'm moving and things have been a little crazy. Usually I always replace them when the time changes, but I must have forgotten in April."

"You were lucky," he said, slipping the batteries, the evidence of Ellen's folly, into his pocket. "You've got kids—I saw their room upstairs. You can't take chances like this."

"I know," Ellen said. "Really, I do. I know. I'm usually very careful. I'm sorry."

"I've got to file a report," the fireman said. He walked over to the truck and rummaged in the front seat, pulling out a clipboard, then walked back to where Ellen stood with Jo, by the white gate with the chipped paint just outside the front door.

"This is your house, right?" he said, looking at Ellen.

"Yes," she said, and then, "Well, no. I mean, it *was* my house, but I sold it and I'm renting it back, but I think I'm going to buy it back now from the people I sold it to."

Jo looked at Ellen in surprise. The fireman stopped scribbling on his clipboard and gave her an exasperated look. "So, *who* owns the house right now?"

"Well, right now it's owned by the Boyces. Jordan and Jeffrey Boyce. They live in Beaverton. But I've lived here for the past ten years."

"Okay," he said. "Can you spell that last name for me?"

"B-O-Y-C-E," Ellen said. God, was he going to call Jeffrey and Jordan and tell them that she had almost burned down the house? That would really tick Jordan off exactly at the moment that Ellen least wanted to make her angry. On the other hand, maybe it would make Jordan even happier to be getting rid of the house, now that it was damaged goods. Maybe she'd feel that stupid, careless Ellen and her smoky house deserved each other.

"The station has probably already called the owners," he said. "I'll check. Wait here a second, will you?" He walked back to the truck, his rubber boots squeaking on the dry grass.

"Ellie, what is going on? You can't buy the house back," Joanna said. "It's too late for that."

"No, it's not! Jeffrey Boyce came by the shop while I was there tonight. *He* doesn't want to move. He likes his house, and he'd rather stay there. He said he'd be willing to sell the house back to me."

Jo looked at her sympathetically. "Ellen, you can't afford it, baby. I know how hard this all is, but you've got to let it go."

"Jo, seriously. He wants to sell the house back to me. I've been thinking about this like crazy for weeks, you know I have. Anyway, the shop is doing great. I can sell part of the business and make enough to pay off the second mortgage. Sam just has to agree to wait awhile for his share of the equity. I can't imagine he'd give me a hard time about that after all we've been through."

"You'd sell Coffee@home for the house? That's your future, sweetie. That's what's going to support you and the girls."

"Jo." Ellen looked at her, her brown eyes staring deep into Joanna's blue ones. "Jo, it's my *house*. And I'll still have part of the business."

A dark green SUV with a University of Virginia bumper sticker pulled up in front of the white picket fence. Jordan hopped out, dressed in a T-shirt and jeans, with an expensive-looking camel-colored raincoat slung over her shoulders. She looked at Ellen and Joanna, a look that expressed dislike and—was it fear?—then swept past them to the fire truck, addressing herself to the fireman with the clipboard.

"Hello? I'm Jordan Boyce, the home's owner," she said, extending a hand. "What's happened? How bad is the damage?" Her voice was urgent, intent.

"A little smoke damage and a splintered bookcase," the fireman said. "It could have been worse. If you hang on, I can give you information for your insurance company."

Jordan turned to Ellen and Joanna, taking in Ellen's flowing skirt and jewelry, so different from her usual jeans and T-shirt. "The fire department called me about twenty minutes ago," she said. "It's lucky no one was in the house. I'm just *shocked*. Do you want to tell me what happened? The fireman said candles were *left burning*." Jordan pulled the collar of her coat together around her neck with one hand and compressed her lips into a thin line. "Really, Ellen, this is quite serious. I don't plan to have this affect our homeowner's insurance. I hope you're covered as a renter."

Insurance. It figured Jordan's neat, logical mind would jump immediately to that, Ellen thought. She felt like a teenager whose parents arrive home unexpectedly in the midst of a wild party they weren't supposed to know about. First the baby-faced fireman had lectured her about the batteries, and now Jordan, in a very grown-up designer raincoat, was going to give her another lecture. Ellen felt almost giddy for a moment that she—careful, responsible, by-the-book Ellen—was being tut-tutted over by the fire department and a social-climbing suburban mom five years her junior. She shook off a smile and tried to suppress the irritation that seemed to seep out her pores whenever she encountered Jordan. She was getting the house back, and that was all that mattered.

"Of course I have renter's insurance, and once we get all the sale papers sorted out again, I'm sure we can even get my homeowner's insurance to cover it—maybe they'll cover it retroactively once the new sale goes through."

Jordan looked at her blankly. "The new sale?" she said. "What are you talking about?"

"I talked to Jeffrey tonight," she said. "About buying the house back. He told me how much he loves the house you're in now, and how hard he's worked on the garden, and how great the yard is for the kids and all. He said you guys were willing to sell the house back to me."

Jordan raised her well-waxed eyebrows. She looked stunned, and even more, slightly afraid. This time there was no mistaking it. *Is she afraid of* me? Ellen thought. Jordan squeezed her eyes shut tightly and then shook her head, as if trying to clear it. "Jeffrey said *what?* I have no idea what you're talking about."

Ellen suddenly felt cold all over, and tight, breathless. *Please don't make me beg,* she thought. "Jeffrey stopped by my store tonight. He said you were reconsidering about the house. He said—"

"He misunderstood." The words were hard, terse. *There is something odd between them,* Ellen thought, *between Jeffrey and Jordan. She knows they're not on the same page about the house, and she doesn't know what to do.*

Jordan shook her head again, pulled herself together, and smiled at Ellen, an artificial, sorority-girl smile that stretched across her face like plastic wrap. "*You* must have misunderstood, Ellen. Jeffrey and I love this house and are thrilled to be moving in. Our architect has already drawn up the plans for the remodeling. Of course we're not going to sell it back."

Ellen stared at her. Now that she had even a glimmer of hope about the house, she wasn't about to let it go. "Jordan, this house doesn't really mean anything to you," she said softly. She tried to keep her voice neutral, even, so she didn't sound pleading or, worse, possessive. "And it means everything to my kids and me. I'd really like to buy it back, and I'm willing to pay for anything you've had to pay for, like the inspection or the closing. Jeffrey said he was willing, and he seemed to think you were, too. He seems really attached to your house in Beaverton."

Jordan sucked in a deep breath and turned away from Ellen, gazing toward the house, where the fireman stood with his clipboard. "I don't need you to tell me what my husband is attached to," she said finally. "We have no interest at all in selling the house back to you. You really need to let this go."

Joanna materialized from the front stoop, where she'd been sitting talking to one of the firemen. She put an arm around Ellen, who was standing, frozen in place.

"It's really late, and we've all had way too much excitement tonight," she said, talking to Jordan but with her eyes on Ellen. "Maybe you guys could discuss this tomorrow with Jeffrey there, so everyone's on the same page. Really. The house will be fine, no one got hurt. We all need to count our blessings and get some sleep."

"There's nothing to discuss," Jordan said. "You need to be out by May thirty-first, as we agreed. My contractor is coming the next day to start the remodel. And, Ellen, I really don't want to talk about the house again. This is my house; you are a renter, and as of the end of May you won't even be that. You decided to sell it, you put it on the market, you signed the papers. I bought it. End of story."

Ellen realized, with a sudden, final clarity, that Jordan was absolutely right. It *was* Jordan's house. All at once Ellen saw that Jordan had a vision for her life and her family, a vision that now included—at least for the next few years—this house. The Christmases, the birthdays, the long afternoons on the deck, were unfolding before Jordan like a movie reel, day after day, month after month, here, in Jordan's new house. It was just that Ellen couldn't imagine how her own life was going to unfold now, without the house, without Sam. Would she be alone on Christmas morning while the girls squealed and opened gifts at Sam's place? What would things be like when the girls went off to college and she was alone—without Sam, and without Jo next door and Laurie up the block? Her life didn't look anything like the vision she'd held of it just a year ago.

Jordan walked back to the fire truck, where she pulled aside one of the firemen and began talking. She pointed at the house several times, and the fireman nodded. Finally he walked over with Jordan in tow.

"I'm just going to walk the owner through to see the damage," he said to Ellen. "We'll be out of your way soon."

Ellen stood, hugging herself, trying to absorb the roller-coaster ride of the last few hours, from the loving farewell to the house through the wild hope of her conversation with Jeffrey to the heart-thumping fear when she heard the sirens. It seemed possible that it was all a dream. Maybe she'd wake up in her bed tomorrow to find that she had never agreed to sell the house, that the whole thing, from meeting Jordan in her kitchen up to this moment, was just her mind working overtime, trying to process the whole idea of so much change. And while the dream seemed to go on and on, when she woke up it would have been just a few hours, and she'd realize that her dream was telling her *not* to sign the contract, to hang on to the house however she could.

"Well, if ever anyone was in need of some tea and a Valium, it's you," said Joanna, wrapping an arm around her. "Come on, this has been a crazy evening and you must be completely wiped out. Let's go home. We can deal with all the insurance stuff and the smoke damage tomorrow. I'll get you in bed and come back and lock up once Jordan and the firemen are done."

"Okay," Ellen said. "All right."

"Hang on a minute here. I'm just going to check how long they'll be."

Joanna disappeared inside the front door. Ellen could hear

murmuring in the living room. She sat down on the cool bricks of the front stoop and wrapped her arms around her knees. Looking up, she saw the familiar outline of the Doug firs across the street against the night sky, and the three stars of Orion's belt, tilted toward the tip of the tallest fir.

The house was really and truly lost to her. She couldn't burn it down now. One fire was an accident; a second fire would clearly be the work of a deranged middle-aged woman desperately trying to hold on to something that was no longer hers. She hugged herself more tightly and buried her face in her knees.

Through all the years with Sam, all the unpredictability and uncertainty, she had wondered: *How long can I do this?* She had tried to love the adventure of it all but couldn't squelch her craving for order, for security, for reassurance. The house had given her the rootedness that Sam couldn't, and with the loss of the house, the weak threads in her relationship, the kind that rent at every marriage, had become great, gaping tears that couldn't be fixed. It was a mess, and she felt acutely her own failures. If only she had been more flexible with Sam, or firmer in her own convictions. If only she'd refused the second mortgage, or been less critical, so he hadn't felt such a need to prove himself over and over again with these inventions. She couldn't imagine her future now. *Who am I without the house? Without that life?*

Joanna came out the door then, followed by Jordan and the fireman.

"Come on, Ellie, let's go."

"It's a nice place," she heard the fireman say as they walked away.

"Oh, it's wonderful," Jordan said. "And it'll be even better when I'm done with it. I just can't believe it's *mine*."

With those words echoing in her head, Ellen followed Joanna around the yellow house, through the gate on the other side, and up the street to Joanna's door, where she let Jo give her a cup of chamomile tea and a Valium and put her to bed, still wearing her flowing skirt and her sky blue sweater.

CHAPTER EIGHT

Ellen woke after a night of fitful sleep. She lay in bed and stared out the window of Joanna's guest room at the fir trees swaying in the wind. Her head hurt, although she couldn't tell if the ache came from the wine, the faint acrid smell of smoke on her clothes, or just the events of last night. She rolled over and buried her face in the pillow.

What is wrong with me? she agonized. Here she was in her forties, a time when she was supposed to have figured out who she was, what she wanted out of life, and how to get it—at least according to the magazine articles she read. This was the age when she was really supposed to come into her own—confident in her abilities, accepting of her weaknesses, indifferent to popular opinion, passionately on her own side. She was supposed to be reveling in her hard-earned laugh lines and exploring new facets of her shamelessly confident middle-aged self. She was most definitely not supposed to be lying in bed, a would-be arsonist with her face in a pillow, feeling completely lost and inadequate.

She turned her head, opened one eye, and stared at the bedside table. Jo had several books stacked there as well as the two latest *O* magazines, with lots of advice on how to "live your best life."

What if I've already lived my best life? Ellen thought. *What if I'm moving on to my worst life now?*

Well, Oprah had nothing to say about that, of course, because Oprah was never going to be forced to sell her beloved house to an obnoxious woman with Tinker Bell sneakers.

Ellen sat up and felt her head throb. She would never drink wine again. Well, maybe she'd drink wine again, but she'd never drink wine and then stand near a smoky house again, she vowed, and then she smiled in spite of herself. She got out of bed, tried to shake the wrinkles from her skirt, and ran her fingers through her hair.

Jo poked her head in the door. "Sam's called about six times. Jordan called him about the fire, and he wanted to be sure you're okay. No, no, sweetie, don't worry," she added quickly, seeing the sudden alarm on Ellen's face. "He didn't mention it to the kids."

"Jordan called him? What a pain in the neck she is!" Ellen said. "Was she 'telling' on me to my husband because I almost burned the house down?"

"Of course Sam was going to find out about it," Jo said. "Anyway, he just wants to talk to you. He's worried about you, Ellie."

Ellen rolled her eyes at Joanna. "Don't give me that poor Sam look, Jo. Really."

Ellen leaned over to peer out the window toward the back door of her own house. The morning light glowed above the roofline, leaving the back of the house in shadow. The wind rippled through the cedar boughs in the backyard, and a bushtit darted into the rhododendron by the deck. It was such a peaceful, achingly familiar scene. There was no smoke, not even a fireman's muddy footprint to indicate anything of what had happened the night before.

"My head is killing me," Ellen said, turning back to Joanna. "And I made a fool of myself in front of Jordan. What was Jeffrey thinking? I could kill him for getting my hopes up like that."

"I definitely missed something last night," Joanna said. "Did he really tell you he was ready to sell the house back?"

"Yes, and I think he just felt so badly about Sara and everything that he kind of jumped the gun and told me before he'd cleared it with Jordan. He seemed so sure, and so nostalgic for his own house, that I felt like he really understood what this meant to me. I just can't believe he hadn't talked to Jordan about it."

Ellen rubbed both eyes, which were caked with sleepy dust and last night's mascara. "God, I feel like hell," she said.

"Did he tell you that Jordan had agreed?" Joanna asked. "Did he actually say, 'We want to sell the house back to you, for sure'?"

"Well, not exactly," Ellen said slowly. "It was more like he didn't really want to leave *his* house and was hoping we could work something out." She closed her eyes. "God, I was an idiot. I mean, I just jumped all over what he said and assumed . . ." She trailed off. Everything. She had assumed everything.

"Seems you and Jordan are even," Jo said drily, coming over to pull up the pink comforter on the bed and giving a good shake to each of the pillows. "She told Sam about you almost burning the house down, and you told her about Jeffrey not really wanting to buy it."

"Well, yes, but I didn't mean to," said Ellen, gazing out the window again at the yellow house. It was riveting; she couldn't tear her eyes away from it. "I thought she already knew. Did you see the look on her face? Something's not right in Denmark, as Shakespeare would say."

"I'm sure something's not right in Beaverton," Jo said. "Imagine being at *their* breakfast table this morning. She's probably reading him the riot act for about the fifteenth time since she got home last night."

Ellen sighed. "That's one comforting thought. Now I really need tea."

She followed Jo into her kitchen and sat down, resting both elbows on the white Formica-topped table she'd found at a flea market in Gresham and given to her friend years ago. It was vintage 1950s—just right for Jo's kitchen, with the kitschy fruit wallpaper and the black and white linoleum floor and the white chenille curtains.

Jo's husband, Pete, stood at the stove in his sweatpants and tattered UCLA T-shirt, watching a large pancake sizzle on the griddle. Pete was tall and lean and had a thatch of bright red hair. He looked almost exactly like Bill Walton, who had played for the Portland Trail Blazers in the late 1970s. After years of insisting to yet more disbelieving Trail Blazers fans that he was not Bill Walton, Pete had taken to saying sure, he was Bill Walton, and yes, he'd be happy to autograph something and yeah, of course he still loved the Dead.

"Hell of a night you had, Ellie," he said with a grin. "A hen party with lots of alcohol and a house fire. Doesn't get much better than that."

"Thanks, Pete," Ellen said. "Could you put the kettle on for me? Yes, it was quite a night. Did Jo tell you everything?"

"Yeah," he said, looking at her sympathetically. "I'm sorry."

"Oh, God. Just don't tell Sam about the whole buying the house back thing, okay?" she asked. Sam and Pete played basketball together every Thursday night with a group of other fortysomething guys. "Sam already thinks I'm crazy about the house."

"You *are* crazy when it comes to the house," Pete said. "But you have many other fine qualities."

"Thanks," Ellen said. "Is that pancake for me?"

"Nope. Emily. We've got a tent outside, and we're eating pancakes in the tent this morning. Want to join us?"

"I'm afraid that, after my hell of a night, pancakes in a tent is a little more than I can handle," Ellen said. "I think I'll stay here with Jo."

"So where are Sam's little cloning experiments this morning?" asked Pete, as he slid a spatula under the bubbling pancake and flipped it over. Sara and Louisa, with their dark eyes, thick hair, and wide cheekbones, looked so much like Sam that Pete loved to tease Ellen about it. Pete had been witness to Ellen's awful miscarriage, then the long, cautious months in bed before Louisa was born, and he thought it a great cosmic irony that, after all that tribulation and perseverance, the girls looked so much like their father they could have sprung fully formed from his chest without any involvement from Ellen.

"With Sam. I don't know what I'll tell them about the house. They're traumatized enough without worrying about house fires."

"Send them over here, and we'll hunt for salamanders in the woodpile. That should be a good distraction."

Ellen looked at him. She loved Pete. He was careful and practical and all the things that Joanna was not—in many ways, he was a lot like Ellen. Yet he didn't take life as seriously as she did, and he was always happy to bring the kids to find giant slugs in Forest Park or to ride the roller coaster at Oaks Park, things that Ellen hated to do.

"Hey. If you change your mind about pancakes, you know where to find us," Pete said. He expertly flipped the pancake onto a tin plate, tucked a plastic syrup bottle under one arm, and grabbed a mug of orange juice. He kicked the screen door open and maneuvered his way through, humming all the while. It wasn't until after the door slammed behind him that Ellen realized he had been humming "Burning Down the House."

"Funny, very funny!" she called after him.

A few minutes later, Ellen and Jo were sitting at the table with their mugs. Jo stirred her coffee, moving the spoon around in slow circles until a little whirlpool formed in the middle of her mug. "So," she said finally, looking up to meet Ellen's eyes. "Was that really an accident last night?"

Ellen's heart thumped hard against her chest. "Jo!" she said, hoping she sounded surprised, and perhaps even slightly indignant.

Joanna looked at her. "Oh, Ellie. I don't mean to accuse you, and to tell you the truth, the only reason it even occurred to me is because *I thought of it, too.* I mean, ever since you signed the papers and Jordan came over that day I've been thinking, *What if a tree fell on the house so she just couldn't have it?* Sometimes I feel like I'd rather have a black hole there than your house without you in it. Emily grew up in that house as much as your girls did. I just can't imagine it without all of you. I know I'm going to run through that gate a million times to tell you something before I stop and remember you don't live there anymore. And I'm going to be looking for Sara's face at the back door every day."

"Well, if the house did burn down, I'd certainly feel relieved," Ellen said carefully, avoiding Jo's eyes. Would it make her best friend an accessory somehow if she told her that the candles had not been an oversight? "I know it's crazy. It's the if-I-can't-have-it-no-one-else-can-either that you feel when you're six. Only I'm not six, and it's totally irrational, and I don't know what to do with all this *feeling* I have about it. I don't wish Jordan ill, I really don't. I just don't want her to have my house. I think it would be easier if it were somebody who was older, or single, or had no kids. It's just Jordan . . ." Ellen trailed off.

"Is living your life," Joanna said gently. "She's having the life you were supposed to have, living there in that house with her kids and her husband."

"Oh, yes, Jo, yes. That's it exactly!" Ellen looked directly into her friend's blue eyes. She paused for a minute. Then, "I planned the party very carefully," she said evenly.

Joanna's eyes searched Ellen's face. She took a deep breath. "Okay," she said. "Okay. What's next?"

Ellen looked at her in amazement. "Jo," she said. "I can't. We can't. This was my one shot."

Joanna played absentmindedly with her spoon, pushing her finger down and spinning it on the smooth surface of the table. "I'm not saying we should do anything to destroy the house," she said. "But things happen all the time that make houses unlivable—or simply bad deals, and then buyers back out. They find out there's a huge water problem, or an environmental hazard or—"

"They can't back out, Jo. The sale has gone through. They own it now," Ellen said. "I've thought about this over and over again," she continued, wrapping her hands around the warm mug. "There's nothing I can do. I keep thinking if I had a million dollars I could make them some outrageous offer and buy the house back no matter what the cost. Even Jordan would give it up if she could sell it and move to Dunthorpe or Portland Heights—now *those* are real MAC club addresses, not Grace Lane."

"Right," Jo said. "You need to hit the lottery, or rob a bank."

"No. What if I franchised the business, tried to get the numbers to be really impressive, so I could sell it? Then I might have enough."

"Ellen," Jo said quietly. "That's a pretty tall order. And once Jordan gets into the house and starts knocking down walls and painting and creating her perfect little vision, she's not going to want to leave."

"I know," Ellen said. She looked out the window at the thick trunks of the Doug firs, with Emily's bright blue tent pitched between them. She was silent a long time. She thought about all the hours she had spent gazing at those trees, either from here or from the windows of her own house. She thought about Jordan taking over that view, and Jeffrey, with his quiet smile, digging a new garden in her yard. While she was frustrated with Jeffrey—and angry at herself—for getting her hopes up about the house, she couldn't help but feel a kinship with him, another overly attached being somehow propelled along an unexpected path. She thought of his blue eyes, and the way he'd leaped when she'd touched his arm.

"You know, I think Jeffrey is attracted to me," Ellen said.

Jo looked at Ellen carefully. "He's also *married*."

"I know, I know. I'm not going to *do* anything about it," Ellen said quickly. "And he's never said or done anything out of line. He's way too honest and straitlaced for that."

"He probably likes you because you have normal eyebrows," Jo said. "Jordan's eyebrows are so overwaxed she looks constantly surprised."

"Well, I've always counted on my eyebrows to get me through," Ellen said wryly. "Really, Jo. I have this strange connection with Jeffrey. He definitely empathizes with me—it's as though he's the only one who understands what the house means to me and why it's so hard to leave it."

"Oh, please," said Joanna, rolling her eyes. " 'He's the only one who understands me,' " she mimicked. "If you want to try to justify having an affair with Jeffrey Boyce, you're going to have to do much better than that."

"I'm not having an affair with Jeffrey Boyce and I don't plan to," Ellen said. "Although *that* would be a hell of a way to get the house back, wouldn't it?"

They both laughed, but then Joanna grew serious. "You have two weeks, sweetie," she said. "Let's think. Does Jordan know we're in an earthquake zone?"

"All of Portland is in an earthquake zone," Ellen said.

"Yes, but we're in the hills, we're on a fault here. If she's earthquake phobic—"

"Oh, God, and if she's afraid of snakes we could fill the basement with them and then invite her down," Ellen said. "Come on, Jo. It's a lost cause."

Ellen rested her forehead against her palm. Her head still ached. Maybe she needed a piece of good dark chocolate.

"I need to research this," Joanna said thoughtfully, getting up to pour herself a second cup of coffee. "I know there are certain issues that can void the contract. When we bought our first house, there was a horrific mistake about a week after the closing—the mortgage company thought Pete had gotten laid off and called in our loan. Wanted us to pay off the entire hundred thousand. It was a mess to sort out—someone in the HR department at Pete's work had confused his name with some other guy who had been fired. But, Lord, the bank was all over us." She scratched her nose. "What if Jeffrey lost his job, or quit? Jordan doesn't work, so they'd have to sell."

"I don't know, Jo," said Ellen, getting up to root around in the pantry for something to eat. "I don't see how we can get Jeffrey fired, and anyway, I don't want to ruin his life; I just don't want him to live in my house."

"What about doing a search to see if there are any claims against the title?" Joanna said. "I know there have to be ways to invalidate a contract after closing. I'm going to check this out today."

"You do that," said Ellen, absentmindedly munching on an oatmeal cookie she'd found in Jo's mouse-shaped cookie jar. "I think I'm going to go out to the coast Monday on a buying trip. I need more stuff for the shop, and I just have to stop thinking about all this for a day—or an hour."

She drank the last of her tea and put her mug down on the counter. "Yuck. I guess it's time to go pay the piper now. I've got to shower, and see the mess in my house, and pick up the kids and explain it to them, and face Sam. I *really* wish you had some chocolate here."

"I'll come over to help with the mess," Jo said. "The kids can play upstairs while we deal with the living room. You know, Pete may be able to repair that bookcase for you."

She hugged Ellen hard. "Now you go home and get cleaned up and stop thinking about the house and Jordan and Jeffrey, okay? You're right; just block it out for now. We're going to get through this."

"That would be a relief," Ellen said. "So okay, I promise, I'll stop thinking about it all."

All but Jeffrey, that is, she thought. *I'm not ready to give up thinking about Jeffrey yet.* But she didn't say it aloud, not even to dearest Jo.

CHAPTER NINE

ELLEN PICKED UP the stiff plastic brush and scrubbed hard at the soot stain on the living room wall. Clearly she was going to have to paint over it; half an hour of hard labor had done little other than get the wall thoroughly wet. Jordan had called twice already with instructions on how the damage was to be handled. She wanted to send her own carpenter, at Ellen's expense, to fix the built-in bookshelves, and her contractor to repair the wall. Ellen, too tired to argue, had agreed to everything and then decided to try to clean the wall herself, hoping to avoid paying money to anyone hired by Jordan. Now she'd stopped answering the phone because she knew she couldn't talk to Jordan again without completely losing her temper.

"Ellie?" Sam came straight into the house without knocking and followed the sound of her scrub brush into the living room. "Ellie? Why didn't you call me?"

Ellen put the brush down in the bucket and sat back on her heels. She was wearing gray sweatpants cut off at the knee and a faded pink V-neck T-shirt she'd bought almost six years ago at Target. Her hair, which she'd washed and carelessly twisted into a knot behind her head, was escaping its clip and hanging in damp strands around her face. She could feel the bags under her eyes. God, why hadn't she spent more time appreciating all those years when she could roll of out bed with no makeup and still somehow look fresh and lovely? In Ellen's opinion, the supposed wisdom that came with being forty-something really didn't make up for the enormous pain in the ass of having to apply undereye concealer before being seen in public.

"Are the kids with you?" she asked.

"No, they're at Jo's. Emily saw us drive up, and Jo said she'd take them for a while. Now what happened?"

"Look, I'm sorry," she said, trying vainly to push her unruly hair back into the clip. "Everything happened so fast last night. Nobody was hurt; the house is fine. I just didn't see any reason to call in the middle of the night and wake you up. I was going to call you this morning and explain everything."

"Jordan called me in the middle of the night and said you'd almost burned the house down. I was really worried."

"It's ridiculous that she called you. You see why I hate her? It's like she's telling on me and you're my father or something. It's none of her business."

"It *is* her business if something happens to the house; she owns it. And it's certainly my business if something happens to you."

"Sam." She looked at him. Somehow since their separation he had grown more protective of her, as though he saw the strands that connected them as impossibly fragile, like spun glass stretched taut and ready to crack with the slightest movement.

Sam had always been independent. He didn't need reassurances of love or anniversary gifts or birthday cards to know that Ellen cared; he assumed she felt the same about him, year after year, as he always felt about her. He didn't call home much when he traveled; he knew that she could manage and that she'd call if one of the kids got sick or anything else went wrong. He went about his days immersed in his work and his lunchtime basketball game at the gym and picking up the salmon at the Wednesday farmers' market for dinner. He liked to tinker in his shop in the basement, making funny little songbird sculptures out of old wires and nuts and bolts. His life was one of immediacy, whereas Ellen's was one of thinking and planning and analyzing and rethinking.

Once, earlier in their marriage, he'd been away on a research trip. On the fifth night he'd been gone, she had lain awake sleepless, worried that, after three months of trying, she still wasn't pregnant. Finally she'd called him. "I can't sleep," she said. "I can't stop thinking about it. What if I can't have kids? What if it's not just that I'm infertile but that I have some terrible disease, like in *Love Story*? What if I'm dead before Christmas?"

"I wish I were there," he said.

"Why?" she asked. "What could you do? It's me; I can't stop thinking."

"I'd rip your clothes off and give you something else to think about," he said.

That was Sam. But now he hovered more. Since their separation, he'd taken to calling every evening to talk to the girls and then making them put Ellen on the phone. He suddenly wanted to know about things he'd never paid attention to before, like when the kids' annual physicals were and if she'd had the oil in the car changed recently.

For Ellen, it was too little too late. After more than a decade of being hyperresponsible for every aspect of their lives together, she didn't need Sam suddenly stepping in and trying to fix things.

"Listen, we just have to get through getting moved out of the house, okay?" she said.

"Okay," he said. "But you still haven't told me what actually happened last night."

"I had a party, I forgot to put out all the candles, there was some smoke, and Jo called the fire department. It was a dumb mistake."

"But all the batteries in the smoke detectors were dead? That's not like you, Ellie."

"Well, it's certainly like *you*. When was the last time you changed the batteries, or even thought of it? You really can't give me a hard time about this, Sam. You're not exactly Mr. Responsible."

"God, Ellen, I'm not trying to pick a fight. You've just been so angry and intense about the house, I—"

Ellen stood up. "Angry and intense? You bet. Most women whose husbands mortgaged their homes for a baby beeper would be calm and detached, right? Sam, I made a home for us here. It was our whole world, and now it's all gone."

"It's not all gone, Ellie."

"I know." She felt sheepish, even in the midst of her rage. She *was* grateful for her strong, healthy children, for the work that made it possible for her to buy another house, for her own sturdy health. She knew all that, but she also knew that this was her fatal flaw: to love things too much, and to find it too hard to let them go. Losses haunted her, gnawed away at her present joys instead of sweetening them.

"But all the most important things in my life happened here," she said quietly, stubbornly. "Getting pregnant with the girls and bringing them home here as babies, and losing the other baby . . ."

She trailed off. When she had been five months pregnant with their second child, she had gone in for a routine prenatal visit.

The doctor had asked after Sara, laughed over the story of how she had stuffed a large piece of playground chalk into the Thanksgiving turkey, taken Ellen's blood pressure, then put his stethoscope to her abdomen. He'd moved it around a few times, then his face had changed.

"What?" Ellen said, her heart suddenly lurching.

"I'm sure it's nothing," the doctor said with a reassuring smile. "I'm just having a little trouble finding the baby's heartbeat."

Ellen felt a cold sense of dread, and in that instant, she knew. The doctor brought in the ultrasound machine, spread the warm jelly on her abdomen, and they both stared at the screen, at the little fetus there, one tiny hand still clenched into a fist, so perfectly formed and so perfectly still. There was no heartbeat; her baby floated dead inside her.

"I'm so sorry," the doctor said, turning off the machine and putting a hand on her shoulder.

She'd had to have a procedure to remove the dead fetus, a boy, from her body, and had lain in bed in their room upstairs for a week afterward, mired in grief. Sam had brought flowers, and taken care of Sara, and cooked little meals for her, but he hadn't grieved in the same way Ellen did, and it was his grief she had craved. The baby had been an idea, a hope, to Sam; to Ellen it had already been a person who wiggled and kicked and hiccuped. She was the only one who had known the little creature moving inside her, and she was the only one to miss him once he was gone. In leaving the house, she was leaving that baby, the boy she'd dreamed about while planting sweet woodruff under the hydrangeas, whose name she'd pondered gazing out the window above the kitchen sink, whose place at the dining room table had already been firmly established in her mind.

Sam was silent. He looked out the bay window at the swing set, the one that was usually in motion with Sara and Emily and Louisa swinging simultaneously. He rubbed a hand through his hair. "Just so you know, I had to tell the kids about the fire. I told them Mommy forgot to put out a candle and there was a little smoke but everything was fine. They really weren't that concerned once they knew you were all right and their toys were all right."

He walked over to her and picked up the brush from the bucket. "I can finish cleaning this," he said. "You're right; I never changed the batteries. I always knew you'd take care of it."

The phone rang, and Sam stepped into the kitchen and answered it reflexively. "Hello? Hi. Oh, okay. Good. Thanks for letting us know. Yeah, that's fine."

He hung up and turned to Ellen. "That was Jordan," he said. "She said she talked to her decorator and they're going to be painting the walls chocolate brown or something anyway. So we don't have to scrub the walls."

"What?"

"Jordan said she's going to paint the walls chocolate brown, so don't worry about scrubbing out the soot stains."

"I heard you," Ellen said irritably. She looked around the living room at the rich cream-colored walls, dotted with bright patches of sunlight from the bay window. She tried to imagine it all dark brown; then she tried to imagine it without the carved bench in the bay window, or the rug by the fireplace that Sam had found in Turkey, or Sara's sculpture of a penguin, lovingly glazed in purple, that rested on the mantel. Her imagination failed her.

"Brown will look awful in this room," she said.

"Ellen, I'm sorry," Sam said. He stood there by the window, holding the scrub brush. His dark hair had grown long and curled around the nape of his neck in a way Ellen had always loved. He was wearing a navy Hoodoo sweatshirt and baggy cargo shorts that couldn't completely conceal his athlete's body. She knew he was sorry; she knew if he could undo all the actions that had brought them to this point he would. But she was just sick of the whole thing.

So she did the only thing she could think to do: She picked a fight with him.

"You have absolutely no right to lecture me about this, Sam," she said, returning to the conversation they'd been having before Jordan's phone call. "Just tell me the last time you changed the batteries in the smoke detector, or paid a bill on time. God, it's a good thing we *didn't* have another baby, because I've spent the past ten years being responsible for three kids as it is."

"If you want to talk about being immature," Sam said, in the loud voice he used only when he was really angry, "let's talk about giving up on eighteen years of marriage because you can't have the house you want." He paused. "Ellen, it's a fucking *house*," he said and turned and walked out, slamming the screen door behind him.

Ellen put the bucket and scrub brush away in the basement and made lunch. After lunch she was going to start packing up the books and paintings in the family room, something she'd been putting off because she knew the empty shelves and walls would make the impending move so tangible, so real.

She sat on the deck and ate her sandwich, flicking the crumbs from her lap onto the grass for the birds. She loved this spot, with the sun-warmed wood of the deck underneath her and the sound of the birds in the laurel hedge and the filbert trees. Directly across from her, she could see the little sculpture of a cherub, reclining amid the violets and sweet woodruff, which Sara had chosen at the nursery one day. The cherub had since become a grave marker, with several generations of goldfish buried beneath it. Ellen couldn't help but smile thinking of the fish—Dottie Whitefin, Dottie Blackfin, and the incongruously named Lindsay Warmnose. She didn't want to leave the cherub here but couldn't bear to move it, either.

The phone rang in the kitchen, and Ellen ignored it. If it was Jordan, she definitely didn't want to talk to her, and Sam would still be way too mad to call. The kids were with Jo, so she knew it had nothing to do with them. She listened to the phone ring and ring and then stop. A few seconds later, Jo leaned out her kitchen window.

"There you are! Pick up the damn phone, will you? I want to talk to you."

"I can just come over," Ellen said, standing up and tossing the last of her crumbs into the yard. "What's up?"

"No, don't come over," Jo shouted. "Little pitchers have big ears, if you know what I mean, and if you're here they'll all come running. I'm going to call you." She disappeared, and the phone rang again immediately.

Ellen ran into the kitchen and picked up. "Okay, I'm here."

"Well, I found out a few things," said Jo. "Mostly, that it's pretty impossible for a seller to get a house back after closing. Most lawsuits seem to have to do with buyer's remorse, not seller's remorse. I mean, you might be able to sue Jordan and Jeffrey if you could prove that they fraudulently induced you to sell the house, but since you put it on the market and signed the contract, that would be pretty tough."

"I know," Ellen said. "It's impossible."

"Oh, Ellie. Don't sound so hopeless. I'm still rooting for Jeffrey either to quit his job or to show a little backbone and tell Jordan he doesn't want to move."

"Right. I'm sure Jordan will be really open to that now that she's found out he talked to me about selling the house back. She's probably more determined than ever to hang on to it."

"Then maybe he'll see the light and divorce her," Jo said.

Ellen laughed. "Yeah, I'll count on that. Thanks, Jo. I know you'd do anything to help me, but I think we have to give up now. Really."

"The opera ain't over until the fat lady sings," Jo said.

"Fine," Ellen said. "But I can hear her humming."

ON MONDAY MORNING, she left home just before ten, once the girls were off at school and she'd cleaned up the kitchen. She headed west on Highway 26, past the farms of Helvetia and the trailer homes in the foothills of the coast range. She planned to spend the day in Astoria, poking around antiques shops to find new inventory for Coffee@home, with a stop on the way at her favorite used bookstore in Manning.

The overnight rain had stopped, and the sun streamed through the clouds in broken shafts. The pavement sparkled; along the sides of the road the boughs of the firs, heavy with rain, glistened with thousands of tiny droplets, and water dripped from the needles into the dirt at the side of the road. As she crested one rise, she could spot the round, snow globe–shaped dome of Mount Saint Helens off to the north. Ellen was thrilled to have the temporary distraction of this trip.

Thirty minutes later she pulled into the parking lot of Hole in the Wall Books. The store was literally in the middle of nowhere. From the road, it looked like an expanded fishing shack, with weather-beaten cedar boards, a crooked front porch, and a blue tarp covering a small upstairs window that had been blown out in a windstorm and boarded up. Inside, the floorboards were uneven, but the shelves were arranged in neat rows and everything was spotlessly clean. Ellen's favorite spot had always been the corner with a love seat, two green velvet armchairs, and a giant floor lamp with a fringed shade, where you could sit and read.

She stepped inside, savoring the slightly musty aroma and the sunlight that slanted across the old pine floors. Dottie Murphy, the owner, was behind the counter, busy ringing up the purchases of someone in a blue jacket.

"Hey, Dottie!" Ellen called. "I'm heading out to Astoria today for a buying trip and wanted to be sure I got to see you."

Dottie looked up and smiled. She had a strong Irish face, bright blue eyes, and soft brown hair fading to gray that she kept pinned up in a loose bun at the back of her head. "Good to see you, Ellen. I think I got more Miss Read in—Thrush Green."

Ellen smiled. Miss Read was a prolific British author who had written a series of novels about life in a small village in the Cotswolds. There was nothing remarkable about the stories—a widow figuring out how to live after her husband dies, a lonely schoolteacher falling in love with a stray cat. Ellen had read them over and over, and was amassing a collection of everything Miss Read had ever written. It was pure escapism. *God, a few good Thrush Green novels would really ease the pain of the move,* she thought.

After ten years of patronizing Dottie's shop, she knew just where to find Miss Read. A woman after Ellen's own heart, Dottie believed that authors, both fiction and nonfiction, were profoundly influenced by place, so all books were arranged by geography. Some authors were shelved according to where they were actually from, such as IRELAND for James Joyce; other were shelved according to the locales where their significant work took place, such as AFRICA for Isak Dinesen. Sometimes you really had to hunt, or give in and ask Dottie. Miss Read, of course, was set squarely in the middle of ENGLAND.

Ellen was completely lost in reading the back cover of *Return to Thrush Green* when the door opened again. "Joan and Edward Young have to face an illness in the family," Ellen read, "while crabby old Albert Piggott is rapidly going downhill without his wife, Nelly, and the Curdles' family fair is making a loss." Most of the denizens of Thrush Green seemed to live in their cozy cottages without ever having to move, Ellen thought. Now, if she lived in Thrush Green, she'd have a whitewashed cottage with a thatched roof and a garden full of hollyhocks. She'd grow gooseberries and drink jasmine tea. She was so engrossed in her daydreams that she didn't even look up when the bells hanging from the door jingled, but then she heard a familiar voice.

"Excuse me," said the voice that Ellen recognized at once. "I'm looking for a book called *Markings*, by Dag Hammarskjöld. Do you have a copy?"

What on earth was Jeffrey Boyce doing in Manning at 10:30 on a Monday morning? Ellen stood rooted to her spot in the stacks, stunned, holding *Return to Thrush Green* in one hand and frantically trying to figure out where to hide. She remembered mentioning Hole in the Wall to him in her shop, back when he was Mr. Tall Vanilla Latte, but she hadn't expected him to appear there less than a week later.

"Ah, Dag Hammarskjöld," she heard Dottie say. "One of my favorites. 'Do not look back. And do not dream about the future, either. It will neither give you back the past, nor satisfy your other daydreams. Your duty, your reward—your destiny—are *here* and *now*.' Great man. We don't get a lot of requests for him."

Ellen heard the rustle of Dottie's corduroy slacks as she bustled out from behind the counter. No matter what Dag had to say, Ellen most desperately did not want to meet her destiny here and now. Dottie's wooden clogs clacked against the floorboards.

"Let's see, he's Swedish. So he's probably in SCANDINAVIA. That's right across the aisle from ENGLAND. Makes sense, you see. After all, the real Scandinavia is right across the North Sea from Britain, right?"

Ellen was standing between two large rows of floor-to-ceiling bookshelves. The aisle ended at a wall with a framed print of a woman in a yellow dress reading a book. Ellen was trapped. She hadn't seen or spoken to Jeffrey in the three days since her candle party, and she didn't want to see him and couldn't imagine that he would want to see her. She was sure Jordan had drawn an absolute line in the sand about visiting Coffee@home for vanilla lattes, and just the sound of his voice called up such a hurricane of anger and compassion and even—was it desire?—that Ellen felt as if she were about thirteen.

So she did what any thirteen-year-old would do in similar circumstances; she pulled the hood of her red rain parka down over her head and face, turned her back to the approaching footsteps of Dottie and Jeffrey, and tried to make herself invisible.

CHAPTER TEN

LLEN CLUTCHED HER book to her chest and squeezed her
eyes shut. *My God, this is so ridiculous*, she thought. She heard
Dottie and Jeffrey round the corner into the aisle while Dottie
kept up a stream of patter about Dag Hammarskjöld.

"He died in a plane crash, you know? Quite a Christian mystic.
And of course you know he won the Nobel Peace Prize. Have you
read his book before? If you like it, I have other authors who
might be right up your alley."

Jeffrey was silent. Ellen could hear the squeak of his shoes, wet
from the puddles in the parking lot, against the dry floorboards.

"Oh, Ellen," Dottie said brightly. Ellen felt a ball of lead drop
from her throat into her stomach. "Did you find the Thrush
Green books?"

Ellen turned, shaking the hood of her parka back from her
head. Jeffrey froze. He stared at her wordlessly for a moment and
then blushed. She expected him to make a stumbling excuse and
leave. And indeed, his eyes darted to the dead end of the row of
shelves and then around, as though looking for an escape. But then
he turned and looked at Ellen straight on, with those blue eyes that
crinkled at the corners. She liked his little laugh lines. Jeffrey had

laughed so seldom in her presence that she found them almost mysterious, a clue that he did indeed laugh, although *at what* remained unknown.

"Hello, Ellen," he said.

Dottie, who had been crouched on the floor searching for Dag Hammarskjöld, looked up. "You two know each other? Figures, doesn't it. That's Portland for you. What's that they say? It's three degrees of separation between you and someone you both know here."

"Yes," Ellen said. "Three degrees."

Jeffrey continued to look at her, so long and persistently that she didn't want to look at him anymore.

She held out the book in her hands. "I found it, Dottie. It looks great."

"And here's *Markings*," Dottie said, pulling a book with a yellowed paper jacket from the bottom shelf. "You'll really like this. Very thought-provoking. Have you ever read St. John of the Cross? Or Kierkegaard's *Fear and Trembling*?"

Jeffrey looked at Dottie and smiled. "I'm afraid you've mistaken me for an actual intellectual," he said. "My mother wanted *Markings,* and it's her birthday next week. I don't really read much anymore; I never seem to have the time."

Dottie grinned. "But at least you have time to shop. If we can't have readers, we'll take shoppers who are related to readers. Next best thing."

She turned to Ellen. Suddenly Ellen wanted to giggle over the absurdity of it all, running into Jeffrey in Hole in the Wall Books of all places, and hiding from him inside her rain hood. But she simply held her book more tightly and said, "I've read this one twice, Dottie, but I don't have a copy of my own. I'm so glad to find it."

"Good," Dottie said briskly. "I've got more there, too, so take your time and poke around. I've got to get back to the register. Glad we had what you needed, Mr. Nonintellectual." She winked at Jeffrey and headed back down the aisle toward the front of the store.

"Ellen, I owe you an apology," he said once Dottie had disappeared. "I'm so sorry I got your hopes up about the house."

For three days now, ever since the night of her failed attempt to burn down the house, Ellen had revisited her conversation with Jeffrey again and again. Why on earth had he implied that they were willing to sell the house back to her when he hadn't cleared it with Jordan? It seemed almost cruel, but she knew, by the way he'd been so concerned about Sara's letter and her own tears that day in the shop, that he wasn't a cruel man. Looking at him now, she realized he simply had wanted it to be true, he had wanted to sell the house back to her so he could keep his beloved garden and the play tower he had painstakingly built for his children, and the familiar, quiet life he had there with his family. Ellen also had wanted it to be true, so when Jeffrey had thrown out a thin thread of hope that night, she had clutched it foolishly, as though it could be a real lifeline.

It also seemed to her that perhaps Jeffrey was one of those people who are exquisitely tuned in to the feelings of others, and that he had seen in her the cold, blue wound of losing her house and history and husband, and felt a genuine empathy. Her despair and regret were as subtle as the fireworks on the Fourth of July, she knew, but it softened her to think that Jeffrey, a stranger really, seemed so concerned. And now his wife was furious with him, Ellen was sure, and he was going to have to move and leave the world he had so happily made for his children, just as she was.

Ellen knew that if Jo were here she would read Jeffrey a riot act laced with choice swearwords. But Ellen wasn't Jo, and she felt such a connection with Jeffrey that she said only "It's all right. It really is. I have to let it go."

They were both silent for a minute.

"What are you reading?" he asked cautiously.

Ellen looked down at the book in her hands, with its homey illustration of an old-fashioned wood stove with a kettle on the burner and a dog curled up on a rug by the hearth. "Oh, it's the literary equivalent of comfort food. My all-time favorite author. A series of novels about life in an English village."

The silence covered them again, and Ellen felt suddenly, chokingly claustrophobic, trapped in this aisle in this bookstore with this man who was going to live a life in her house.

"I have to go," she said, pulling her parka close around her. "I'm actually working today—on a buying trip. I shouldn't even be here."

She turned sideways to edge past him in the narrow aisle, and he stepped back. He was wearing another charcoal gray three-button suit, only this time he had on a dark green hooded parka instead of the usual trench coat, and wore thick-soled oxfords instead of wingtips. A few drops of rain, from the hanging boughs of the cedars in the parking lot, glistened in his hair. He smiled an awkward, small smile at her as she passed.

"I'm sorry about the fire and everything," she said. "Good luck with the house. I know you'll take care of it."

Ellen was close enough to Jeffrey to see the lapels of his suit rise and fall with his breath. He smelled like cedar. She felt an urge to lean against him, to say that she knew he understood her, that they were just alike. After all the months of fighting with Sam about the money and splitting up and selling the house, she wanted nothing so much as to be able to lay her head down on a comforting shoulder and not have to make decisions anymore. She wanted to feel that someone else would take care of figuring out how to sort through ten years of a life lived in one place and box it all up and move it. She wanted someone else to handle the kids on the last day in the house, walking with them through the strange, empty rooms. Actually, she'd be thrilled if someone else would just figure out what to cook for dinner that night.

She cleared her throat. "If you have any questions about the house or garden once you move in, you can call me," she said. "I'll leave a can of the exterior paint in the garage so you'll know the color if you need touch-ups. I know you'll be changing everything inside, so—"

"Look, Ellen, don't," Jeffrey said suddenly. "I feel terrible about what happened. I hate to move into the house knowing that there's bad feeling between us—between our families, I mean. Couldn't I take you out to lunch? We don't have to talk about the house. I'd like to talk books with you, since you seem to be a regular here."

Ellen's heart thumped once, a frantic rabbit leap in her chest. She looked at him in surprise. "Lunch? What are you even doing here? Don't you work downtown?"

"Yes, at Merrill Cole. But I have a meeting with a client out in Astoria at two, and I came early so I could stop here, and in Cannon Beach to buy kites for the kids. I'd ask you to get a cup of coffee, but I figured maybe you get enough coffee in your life as it is." And he smiled again, a genuine smile this time that did reach his eyes.

"I'm headed to Astoria, too," she said. "But I guess I could take time for lunch. Maybe we could drive on from here and meet in Cannon Beach." *I'm not having an affair,* Ellen said firmly to the voice of Joanna in her head. *It's just lunch.*

"Do you want to ride with me?" he asked. "If we're both going to Astoria . . ."

"Oh, no, no," she said. "I'm going to a bunch of little antiques stores and resale shops, so I'm hopping from place to place. I really need my car."

"Well, maybe I could ride with you," he said. "I'm just going to one meeting. Seems silly to take two cars when we're both going to the same town."

Ellen looked at him, thinking hard. Did she really want to spend the next few hours with Jeffrey Boyce? Was it wrong, because he was married and she was (almost) single? Probably not, except for the fact that she felt so strangely attracted to him, strangely because, with his short hair and neatly trimmed beard and general tucked-inness, he was definitely not her physical type. She had always been drawn to men like Sam, with tousled hair and five o'clock shadow and carefree (or was it careless?) attitudes—bad boys. Jeffrey was most definitely not a bad boy. He was the kind of guy she should have married, if she had married for predictability and security and all the things that seemed so much more appealing to her now than they had when she was twenty-five. The only other thing that made lunch with Jeffrey feel slightly illicit was the fact that she disliked his wife so much.

"I guess that would work," she said slowly. "Do you know the Lazy Susan, in Cannon Beach? We could have lunch there and then get on to Astoria. I have to be home by six-thirty, so I'll need to bring you back here to Dottie's to get your car by five-thirty."

"That's fine," he said with a smile. "That's good. Let's pay for our books."

He reached out to put a protective hand on her elbow as they turned to make their way down the narrow aisle but then drew it back, as though he was unsure whether the gentlemanly gesture might be misinterpreted. She liked his reticence. He seemed to Ellen to be considerate, a refreshing change from let's-all-do-our-own-thing Sam.

They walked to the front of the store, past the aisles marked CANADA and SOUTH AMERICA and ANTARCTICA. *Are there authors from Antarctica?* Ellen thought wildly. Dottie was leaning over the counter at the front, her tortoiseshell glasses at the end of her nose, paging through a publisher's catalog. She looked up.

"All set? Come on, Ellen, just one Miss Read?"

"I'll be back, Dottie. You know I'm moving in two weeks, so I'll be lucky if I find time to read this one."

"Moving? You're not leaving Portland?"

Damn. Ellen hadn't seen Dottie in months, so of course she didn't know about the split from Sam and selling the house. The last thing Ellen wanted was to go into long explanations, especially in front of Jeffrey.

"Oh, no, no, no," she said vaguely, waving her hand. "Just moving to a different house."

Dottie looked at her over the rims of her glasses. "I'm a little surprised, Ellen. I thought you adored your house. It's old, right?"

"Yes, a 1938 Cape Cod. I just need something a little bigger now that the girls are getting older," Ellen said. "Anyway, I've got to get going. I'll stop by again on my way home this afternoon. I'd love to catch up more."

She quickly paid for her book while Dottie rang up Jeffrey's purchase, carefully wrapped it in tissue paper, and put it in a paper bag. They walked to the front of the shop, where Jeffrey pulled open the old oak door with its crooked wrought-iron handle and held it for Ellen. She smiled in appreciation and walked past him into the parking lot, stepping carefully around the puddles in the gravel. Jeffrey walked next to her. She glanced at him sideways. She felt the way she had in high school when she and her boyfriend had skipped class one sunny afternoon and driven to Tiger Stadium to watch the Detroit team play—daring and reckless.

"The Toyota's mine," she said, pointing across the parking lot to her silver car. "If we go straight to Cannon Beach, we'll be there before the Lazy Susan opens, so you should still have time to buy those kites."

They tossed their purchases in the backseat and climbed in. Ellen pulled the car through the wet gravel and out onto Highway 26. The sky was overcast again, with thick, low gray clouds that intensified the vivid green of the ferns and trillium leaves in the forest on either side of the road.

They were both silent for a few minutes. "So how long have you lived in Portland?" Ellen asked finally.

"Four years," he said. "We moved out from Washington, D.C."

"Ah, the *other* Washington," Ellen said. "It kind of drives me crazy that all the East Coast–based papers—you know, *The New York Times* and *The Wall Street Journal* and *USA Today*—assume that 'Washington' *must* mean D.C. It never even occurs to them that some of us think of Washington State first."

Jeffrey nodded, considering. "True enough, although I hadn't really thought about it before. And how long have you been in Portland?"

"More than ten years," Ellen said. "It just feels like home to me now. I grew up in Michigan."

"The land of Nick Adams."

Ellen turned her head briefly to look at him. "So you *are* a reader."

"I used to be," he said. "I used to read a lot. But working full-time, and having three young kids, and a house . . ."

"I know," Ellen said. "I used to read a lot more than I do now."

They were both silent again. They passed the sign for The World's Tallest Sitka Spruce, with its crooked arrow, and a farm stand with old mason jars filled with spring flowers and a sign that read "Bouquets: $5. Honor system."

"Ellen," Jeffrey said tentatively. "I don't mean to pry, but why did you sell the house? I know you're getting divorced, but it seems to mean so much to you. Surely you and your husband could have found some way to keep it. You could have made some arrangement to pay off his share of the equity . . ."

Ellen looked at the road. "The million-dollar question," she said. "My husband is an inventor, and we took out a second mortgage to finance one of his inventions. It didn't fly, and we didn't have the money to pay both mortgages. So we had to sell."

"What was your husband's invention?" Jeffrey asked.

"A baby beeper," Ellen said. "It's a little transmitter you sew inside the baby's clothes that beeps when you push a button, so you can find the baby."

"Hmm, really," said Jeffrey. "That's interesting."

"It's not interesting. It's completely ridiculous," Ellen said. "I mean, a baby beeper! How many people are constantly losing their babies? Or want anyone else to think they're always losing their babies? My husband is very creative, and he's a great father, but he's never been good at planning and organizing and anticipating. That's always been my department. I really blame myself for this mess. I should have known not to agree to the second mortgage. I'm the responsible one."

Jeffrey smiled. "I've always been very responsible, too," he said. "Sometimes I wish it was easier for me to take risks."

"Well," Ellen said drily. "Watch what you wish for. I felt the same way. That's why I married Sam. He's not afraid of anything and never worries and always takes risks, whether it's skiing off a cliff or mortgaging the house for the baby beeper. Marrying him was the one great risk I've taken in my life, and it doesn't seem to have turned out very well."

Jeffrey stared pensively at the crest of the ridge of mountains in front of them. "I did just the opposite," he said. "Jordan is even more responsible than I am. I make a to-do list once a week; she has lists of everything—all the places she needs to see before she dies, all the books she has to read. You should see our pantry: all the spices and lentils and flour are in Tupperware containers with labels that she hand-lettered. She is unbelievably organized."

"But why did you pick someone who is so like you?" Ellen asked. She was really curious. She could not imagine being married to someone who had the same need she did to balance the checkbook every week and buy extra life insurance. It would be a constant battle for control.

"Jordan was so responsible that I thought, *Finally, I can relax. Here's someone even more responsible than I am,*" Jeffrey said. "It just seemed like it would make my life easier to know someone else was being vigilant, too."

Ellen looked at him in amazement and for a moment almost

forgot she was driving. She had to swerve when she looked back at the road and realized she was drifting across the yellow line. What a concept! For her entire life she had been convinced that opposites attract, and that the best relationships were those like hers, or Jo's— ones that involved two radically different people. But Jeffrey was brilliant, she thought. He was completely right. Constant vigilance was exhausting. Ellen had spent all the years of her marriage double-checking the locks on the doors at night and consulting with a financial planner to make sure they were saving enough for retirement and reading all the handwritten prescriptions from the doctor before getting them filled to make sure the pharmacist didn't make a mistake. Imagine if she had been able to just hand off some of those things to Sam and never had to think about them again!

"And has it?" she asked intently. "Made your life easier, I mean?"

Jeffrey smiled a little and cocked his head thoughtfully. "I don't know. In some ways, yes. In other ways, it's been more difficult. I guess that's like all marriages."

Ellen was quiet for a few minutes, considering. "I guess I thought if I married someone like me, we'd fight all the time because we'd both want to be in charge of everything. You know, '*I'll* balance the checkbook.' 'No, let *me* balance the checkbook.'"

"Jordan and I don't really fight," Jeffrey said. "She likes to run things a certain way, and she's very good at it. So I let her run things, because I know she does everything as carefully as I would."

But then do you only do what she wants? Ellen thought. *Do you ever want to just say, "The ski report is fantastic this morning, let's skip pressure-washing the deck and head out to Mount Hood?"* She was completely intrigued to consider what her life might have been like had she made the choice Jeffrey had, to marry someone who would have handled things while she devoted more time to her garden, or to visiting Scandinavia, or to *anything* other than worrying and trying to remember everything she was supposed to get done. But she also saw just a glimmer, like a faint light shining from beneath a closed door, of what Sam's spontaneity had added to her life. She filed this away in her mind to think about later.

"And don't you ever want to run things?" she finally asked, trying to make the question sound as she meant it—curious and not judgmental.

"Hmm. It's not so much that I want to be in charge," Jeffrey said. "It's just that sometimes I'd like to live without the lists. Go back to the same vacation spot year after year, or reread a favorite book, like you do with that British author you were talking about. Jordan's even got a reading list for me, books that everyone must read before they die. Certain things are more important to her, like joining the MAC or belonging to the Junior League.

"Actually," he continued, looking out the passenger window, away from Ellen, "this whole push Jordan has made to move, and 'move up,' has been very difficult for me. It's made me question a lot of things."

"What things?" Ellen asked, a little uncertainly.

He turned and looked at her again. "My job. I was a good student, went straight to college, then on to law school, then immediately got married and went to work for a firm. Then I took the job at Merrill Cole, on track to make partner. I just feel sometimes as if I'd like to do something completely different—own a vineyard maybe. I'd love to do something that let me work outside, in the dirt."

Jeffrey ran his hand absentmindedly back and forth along the cloth-covered armrest on the car door. "I think I told you that Jordan is eager to move into a 'better' house; that's why we bought yours. And in a few years I know she'll want to move to Portland Heights, or Dunthorpe. It's just that I feel a little trapped sometimes. You know, I've got to keep working and earning and working and earning so we can have all these *things*. I know it's a cliché. Middle-aged man begins to ask, 'What do I really want to do with my life?' It's easy to start to question everything."

Ellen was silent, listening. She knew what it was like to feel trapped. At the same time, her mind couldn't help leaping to the thought that, if only he'd had this impending midlife crisis a few weeks ago and, say, quit his job, he might never have bought her house, or qualified for the loan to buy her house even if Jordan wanted it. What was it Jo had said? Their lender had tried to call in the mortgage a few weeks after the sale because they thought Pete had lost his job. Something like that.

"You know," Jeffrey said, turning toward her as if he'd been reading her mind, "I'm thinking about quitting my job."

CHAPTER ELEVEN

ELLEN WAS SO distracted by the idea that Jeffrey wanted to quit working that she almost missed the turn to Cannon Beach. As far as she knew, Jordan was a full-time mom, which would mean that, if Jeffrey gave up his job, they'd have to sell the house. Hadn't he told her that night at Coffee@home that they still hadn't sold their old house? Surely they couldn't afford *two* mortgages, if he stopped working, particularly the more expensive one on her house. Ellen knew from the closing that Jeffrey and Jordan had put just 5 percent down, so their monthly payments had to be pretty significant. God, maybe Jeffrey really would quit and they'd be begging *her* to buy the house back.

"You can't quit," she said, trying to switch lanes. She pulled the car into the next opening in the flow of traffic and gently braked as they rounded the curve of the turn onto Highway 101. "You just bought a house."

"I know," he said with a rueful smile. "Ironic, isn't it? I just bought a house I don't really want, and you really want a house you just sold."

"Ironic?" Ellen said. "It's awful. Couldn't we just trade lives?

You take over the coffee shop and fulfill yourself with some hands-on work; I'll take my house."

Jeffrey gave a small, mirthless laugh. "Now there's an interesting idea," he said.

Ellen took her eyes off the road for a second to look at him. He was leaning at a slight angle, knees toward her, so he could look at her as they talked. He seemed more relaxed than she'd seen him before. Maybe it was because he was wearing a parka instead of his usual trench coat, Ellen thought. She tried to imagine him behind the counter at Coffee@home, with a red apron tied over his three-button suit, steaming milk and chatting up the customers about Fiesta ware, and the image was at once so improbable and silly that she couldn't help but laugh.

"What's so funny?" he asked.

"I don't know," she said. "You wearing an apron and working at Coffee@home. The fact that you and I both want something we can't have. Just the whole thing."

Jeffrey smiled at her, at the great cosmic joke of their mutual longing and loss. There was a poignancy in his smile that touched Ellen. His empathy threatened to erode the mountainlike steadiness she had carefully built over the painful last six months. She had held Sara night after night as she'd cried about the divorce and moving, and wiped her tears and snuggled her to sleep. She'd played endless games of dollhouse with Louisa, just as they'd always played it, with Mommy and Daddy and the two baby dolls. She had arranged for all the repairs to the house so they could put it on the market, decommissioning the old oil tank, patching the rotten beam outside the back door, repairing the leak in the roof over the bay window. She had handled it all; she was a rock.

But what she really wanted was to melt like the Wicked Witch of the West, a puddle on the floor, to be down, lower than down. For a long time, the thing that had kept her from dissolving into nothingness was the house, the tangible proof that she had created a home that meant something, that nurtured them all.

When she was young, living a perfectly ordinary life in a perfectly manicured Detroit suburb, she had thought that adventure would make her happy. She'd wanted to be Ernest Shackleton or Isak Dinesen, facing a future full of the unknown, a present full of constant challenges that would lift her out of herself.

When she met Sam, she did start to have adventures—flying in a tiny plane over the mountains of southeast Alaska to see the glaciers, dancing at Grateful Dead concerts, rafting down the churning waters of the Deschutes River. But after several adventures, Ellen started to realize that her favorite part was the return home, the enveloping warmth of the soft cotton sheets on the bed, the cup of tea at the dining room table, poring over a novel. Sam always said to her, "You don't have to go. I knew when we got together that you didn't like doing stuff like this. And I married you anyway. That's not really what's important to me."

Finally it had begun to sink in. She was a homebody, and she was good at it, and she was happy. Sam loved her. She didn't have to leap off cliffs to be different, to live a worthwhile life. She was who she was.

And who she was became clearer to her—and richer, fuller—because of Sam. Left to her own devices, she might have become a hermit, she thought sometimes, her adventures confined to wild flights of the mind through the novels she devoured, or exotic combinations of colors in designing a room. Sam pulled her out into the world. And when she worried—second-guessing the doctor who said the mole on Louisa's knee was nothing to worry about, spending endless hours envisioning what she'd wear to her child's funeral—Sam balanced her, calmed her. He was the one who helped her escape from the crazy Ferris wheel in her brain.

But now Sam's closet was empty and his baseball caps and catalogs of magic tricks and used coffee mugs no longer cluttered the coffee table and hallways, and no matter how many games of dollhouse she played with Louisa, there was no way to hide that emptiness. And when Jeffrey smiled at her in sympathy over their shared losses and desires, she realized that part of her wanted not just the house but also all that it represented—someone to love and understand and accept her.

Suddenly Ellen felt tears well up in her eyes. She could not cry again in front of Jeffrey. She blinked hard.

"What does Jordan think about your proposed job change?" she asked, trying to keep her voice neutral, normal.

"Jordan doesn't know I want to quit," Jeffrey said quietly, turning again to look out his window. "It's a pipe dream. I can't quit. It's just that I've always had this interest in owning a vineyard, and there's a small one for sale right now in Dundee. I keep thinking about what that would be like, to give up lawyering and move down there and live on the vineyard and run it. It's not a big place, about twenty acres, mostly Pinots and Gewürztraminer. The kids could go to the little county school. But Jordan would be bored silly in a small town like that."

"It's your escape fantasy," Ellen said. "I thought only middle-aged women had escape fantasies."

"Is that what you call it?" Jeffrey said. "I thought it was a midlife crisis."

"A midlife crisis is when you change the spouse or the car," Ellen said. "An escape fantasy is when you change the place. Although a true escape fantasy, at least the female, forty-something version, usually involves escaping absolutely alone. No spouse, no kids, not even a lover or a pet. It's all about not having to be responsible for anybody."

Jeffrey contemplated this for a while. "I haven't told Jordan about the winery that's for sale, either," he said. "Of course she knows I've always been interested in good wines, and gardening, but I've never told her that I might like to own a winery someday. That's a little far off the plan."

"But why can't you talk to Jordan about this stuff?" Ellen asked. "Now *I'm* the one trying not to pry, but it seems so important."

Jeffrey sighed. He stared out the windshield at the road curving before them beneath the towering trees on either side.

"It's complicated, I guess," he said finally. "When we moved here, four years ago, it was hard on Jordan. She hated leaving the East Coast; all her friends and family were there. And while Portland is small and friendly, sometimes it's *surface* friendly. It took her a really long time to break in, to make friends. She grew up in D.C. and went to private school there and then to U.Va. It's just a different culture. It drove her nuts that people here don't dress up to go out to eat, or to go to church, or that they don't know the difference between Wesleyan and Williams. In D.C., small talk is all about where you went to school and what you do. She felt like she was speaking a foreign language here."

Jeffrey paused and cleared his throat. He was quiet for a moment. "Then, right after we moved here, Jordan had a miscarriage," he continued. "We already had Lily and Daisy, but she was almost twelve weeks along when she lost the baby, and we didn't know anyone here yet, and her family was all back East. I guess it's pretty common; women have miscarriages all the time, but it got to her. I felt really guilty. I thought maybe it was the stress of the move that caused it. The doctor said that had nothing to do with it, but . . ." His voice trailed off, and he stared down at his knee.

He lifted his head. "Anyway, I'm afraid that if I start talking about quitting my job and moving again, it will really upset her. She's been pretty happy over the past year or so. Besides, she's moved once for me. It's a lot to ask her to do it again, especially for something that might not even work out."

Ellen felt an unexpected stab of sympathy for Jordan. She had lost a baby, too, an experience she wouldn't wish on anyone. And she hated moving, too. If she hadn't moved next door to Joanna when she first arrived in Portland, it might have taken her years to feel rooted. All those long months from October until March or April—when it rained all the time—made it difficult to just run into someone, to get to know her and chat outside the grocery store or in the front yard. People joked about it, but it was true: You saw your neighbors for the "last mow" of the lawn in late September, then didn't see them again until April. It was easy to feel isolated, particularly if you were trapped in your house, prisoner to the needs and routines of small children.

Jeffrey turned to her with a smile. "So now you know my deep dark secret," he said. "What's yours?"

"That I'm obsessed with my house," Ellen said, "although I guess that's hardly a secret."

He laughed. "Hardly."

No, Ellen thought, *my secret is that I am not a rock, and I need someone to lean on.* But she said, "Actually, my secret is that I have an escape fantasy, too. Mine is to live on San Juan Island, homeschool the kids, and learn how to hook rugs and let my hair go gray. I love the idea of waking with the whales and working with my hands."

"And you want to live on an island," Jeffrey said. "I'm sure that's very significant, somehow."

Ellen laughed. They were getting close to Cannon Beach now. The sky beyond the fir trees was clear and blue, ocean sky. *Even when you can't actually see the ocean,* Ellen thought, *you can always sense it's there because the sky over water has such a different feel to it—a wider sky, with a different light.* White clouds scudded across the horizon.

They drove into town past the cedar-shingled cottages and the kite shops and art galleries, and the small front gardens overflowing with deep purple iris that always seemed to grow larger here than anyplace else. It's the sea air and the cool nights, Jeffrey said when Ellen commented on it, that, and the six months of rain each year. Ellen pulled into a parking spot on Hemlock Street near the Lazy Susan.

"I think the best kite shop is over on Spruce Street," she said.

They got out and walked down the block. The sidewalks were almost empty, and many of the shops were closed because it was a Monday and May, and the busy summer season hadn't officially begun. The air was cool and damp, salty, and the late morning mist left a fine sheen on Ellen's skin. She felt shy, almost schoolgirlish, walking down the sidewalk next to Jeffrey, their shoulders close but not touching.

"So how did you and Jordan meet?" she asked.

Jeffrey smiled. "At U.Va.," he said. "I was at law school there; she was an undergrad. I had a law school friend who was really into theater and dragged me along to a play the drama department was doing, and then to a party afterward. Jordan was the set designer. She was just so involved; you know, connected to all these people, so confident. I've always fallen more on the introvert side—"

Ellen lifted her eyebrows in mock amazement, and Jeffrey smiled.

"I was really drawn to her energy," he continued. "She had this big circle of friends and acquaintances, and seemed to have her hand in everything. I was leading this almost hermetic life in law school, just grinding it out. I wanted to be in that circle."

"So you asked her out?"

"No, God, no," he said. "Way too shy for that. Believe it or not, she was interested in me after we chatted for a while at that party. So she called and asked *me* out. I was really surprised, and really flattered. Then we started dating, and that was it. We got married the week after I graduated from law school."

Ellen was quiet for a minute. She watched the gulls wheeling against the sky. They were almost at the kite shop now, a bright blue shingled building with a peaked roof and the words "Once Upon a Breeze" cut out in white wood against a dark cedar board above the front door.

"How did you meet Sam?" Jeffrey asked.

Ellen blushed. She had been skiing, on a spring break outing in Vermont during college. Her friend Sally, who went to Middlebury College, had a share in a ski house in Waitsfield; Sam, who was also at Middlebury, had a share, too. Ellen had been standing with Sally at the bottom of the mountain when Sally had pointed up the slope to a figure in black almost floating down the steep incline in quick, graceful turns. Ellen watched him, struck by the sheer athletic beauty of the way he moved. As he swooped down the end of the trail, he caught sight of Sally and glided over to them. As soon as Ellen saw him up close—his dark eyes, his easy and casual elegance on his skis—she wanted him, in a purely animal way. She wanted the body that moved in such a graceful and effortless rhythm down the mountain to move inside her in a similar rhythm. She was shocked by the intensity of her physical attraction to him, and a little frightened by it. As a result, she was stiff with him, awkward, almost cold.

But then, as she watched him over the weekend, she grew more interested in *him*, and not just his body. He was passionate about skiing, up early to be at the lifts when they opened, on the mountain until the last run at three. His enthusiasm extended to everyone in their little group. He skied down the bunny hill over and over with Sally's young niece between his legs, showing her how to turn, and accompanied Ellen and Sally on their first, tentative forays on some of the harder runs. He was kind; when they ran across a teenager who'd fallen and lost what seemed like every possible piece of ski gear, Sam stopped and helped collect his stuff, then got him back into his skis, all the while telling tales of his own incredible wipeouts to restore the boy's wounded pride.

Ellen and Sam had danced around each other all weekend, exchanging jokes and glances, brushing past each other in the kitchen of the small house. On Sunday night, as they were about to leave, he had cornered her in the mudroom as she was collecting her gear and kissed her, fiercely, urgently.

She responded with all the pent-up desire she had contained over the last two days, kissing him just as urgently, her hands pulling at his thick hair, her body pressed against his. He finally pulled his mouth away first, his arms still wrapped around her, his face hot against her neck.

"I have a plane to catch," she murmured. "I have to get back to Ann Arbor."

"Or," he said, kissing her ear, "you could miss your plane and spend the night here, in this house that's about to be empty of everybody except you and me."

She was elated; she was appalled. She didn't miss planes and skip classes; it was unthinkable. But leaving was equally unthinkable now, and her body's insistent need was stronger than her thinking brain, her rapid calculations about airfare and timing and her Psychology of Religion seminar. She stayed.

They spent the night on the floor of the cabin, in front of the fire, on a pile of quilts and comforters and sleeping bags scrounged from the bedrooms. They made love all night long, in the orange glow of the fire. For Ellen it was a night in which all her senses were heightened. She was aware of the sharp, cold air just beyond the fire's reach, the smooth, soft wood of the pine floors, the musky, warm scents of balsam and damp wool and sweat, and her own exquisite sensitivity to Sam's touch.

After she returned to school the next day, Sam called her immediately, and the day after that and the day after that. But she was scared by the emotion he called up in her, the physical desire that seemed to be literally out of her control. She was in a fury of indecision about getting together with him again. Sam, in turn, hated talking on the phone, and just wanted to see her. He couldn't understand her reluctance when his own desire was so straightforward. He thought she was playing hard-to-get, and he hated games. After a month he stopped calling, and their night in Vermont became a memory of what Ellen thought of as a highly uncharacteristic moment, the only "one-night stand" she'd ever had.

Three years later she was living in New York, taking a year to study interior design at the Parsons School, when she bumped into Sam, who was in the city while visiting family and friends on Long Island. She was coming out of the subway at Fourteenth Street, and there he was, standing with two other men, laughing, his dark hair long and curling around the nape of his neck, his face wind-burned and covered in a two-day stubble. She took one look at him, recognized him immediately, and thought, *I'm going to sleep with him again.* He turned and saw her, grinned with delight, and they chatted and had a beer with his friends before going back to her place. They were married a few years later.

"We met on a ski trip in college," Ellen said finally in answer to Jeffrey's question. She didn't want to elaborate. She didn't want to think about Sam right now.

Jeffrey reached forward and held the door open for Ellen, and she stepped inside. The shop was a riot of color, with brightly colored kites hanging from the ceiling, stacked on shelves, leaning against the walls. Kites in the shape of sharks, orcas, and dragons fluttered against one wall, while on another wall rainbows, suns, teddy bears, cats, and puppies waved gaily from diamond-shaped kites that hung in rows all the way to the ceiling. Ellen felt giddy, almost drunk, on the sensory overload of the ocean air and now all the colors, as well as the strange sense of freedom she had at being alone with Jeffrey.

She walked up to a purple and red box kite and fingered the smooth nylon fabric. The kite was huge, almost six feet across.

"That's bigger than all three kids put together," Jeffrey said with a smile. "I'm looking for something a little smaller."

"Do you—what's the word?—*kite* often?" Ellen asked.

"When we can," Jeffrey said. "The kids love it. It was something we never did before we moved to Oregon. Then, our first year here, Lily was turning five. We didn't know that many people, but Jordan called everyone from Lily's preschool class and invited all the kids and parents to a big kite party at the beach. It was really wild—sixteen preschoolers and several siblings and at least twenty adults, all flying kites. That's the great thing about Jordan;

I would never have had the guts to call people I barely knew and organize something like that."

Ellen was quiet, trying to imagine Jordan, her hair mussed by the wind, running barefoot through the sand with a kite streaming behind her. It seemed completely out of character with her image of Jordan, the neatly coiffed perfectionist.

"And did Jordan fly a kite?" Ellen asked. She was too curious; she had to know.

Jeffrey laughed. "The biggest kite on the beach. She took it as a personal challenge."

It's amazing she wasn't lifted off the ground and blown to Nebraska, Ellen thought, picturing the petite Jordan hanging on for dear life to a giant box kite like the one in front of her.

"She wasn't trying to show off," he said a minute later, as if he was almost afraid that Ellen would think poorly of Jordan. "It was for Lily. She wanted Lily to be able to hold the biggest kite."

Jeffrey bought three kites, a big one with a dragon face and a twenty-five-foot tail for flying on the beach, and two small Tiny Dancer kites for his daughters to attach to the backs of their bikes. They stashed the kites in the trunk of Ellen's car, then walked to the Lazy Susan.

The restaurant had just opened, and they had their pick of tables. Ellen sat on a wooden chair with her back against the wall in a corner, while Jeffrey sat opposite her. They ordered omelets and fresh juice and strong black coffee (for Jeffrey) and Earl Grey (for Ellen).

They talked about Ellen's business and love of antiques, about Jeffrey's favorite wineries in the Willamette Valley, and finally, about their kids. Jeffrey's two girls, Lily and Daisy, were nine and six; his son, Stamen, was three. Ellen told him about bringing Louisa and Sara to Cannon Beach for a day trip a few years ago.

Louisa, a chubby three-year-old in a blue gingham bathing suit with a fat ruffle across her behind, had toddled toward the waves and then stopped as the cold water hit her toes. She had stood stock-still for several minutes, letting the water lap at her feet, then squatted down and put her tongue out to lick the next wave. Watching her, Ellen had had an almost out-of-body experience, feeling the salt shock her own tongue as Louisa licked the water. She wanted to tell Jeffrey that she remembered that incident as a spiritual moment of grace, witnessing the miracle that was her child encounter the miracle of the ocean for the first time, but thought it might be too silly—or too intimate—a remark. He seemed to understand, though; he told his own story, about a young Lily standing barefoot in their garden one night with a plastic beach pail full of water and a cup, carefully offering up a drink of water to the full moon.

"Jordan actually drew a picture of that for Lily's scrapbook," Jeffrey said, smiling at the memory. "She's made these amazing scrapbooks for each kid, with photos and all kinds of stuff she puts together. A little square of fabric from Stamen's baby blanket, or the ticket stub from the time we took Daisy to Disney On Ice for her birthday. She's got a whole series of scrapbooks for each of them, one for each year. I don't know how she finds time to do it with everything else she does. She volunteers at their school, she volunteers at our church. That's what I mean about when I met her, she's just the kind of person who takes care of things."

Ellen shifted uncomfortably. Jordan sounded passionately involved and maternal. Ellen would have loved to have scrapbooks marking each year of her children's lives, only she could never find the time to sit down and organize all the boxes of mementos she had collected, let alone arrange them artfully on pages. "I'm too busy living my life to document it," she had remarked crabbily to Jo once, after receiving yet another invitation to yet another home scrapbooking party. But here was Jordan, with her lists and schedules and labels, accomplishing something Ellen would really love to do. It was easier just to hate Jordan, to think of her brisk efficiency and life lists as silly, almost cartoonish.

"It's great she gets so much done," Ellen said finally, trying not to think of all the things Jordan would be getting done in *her* house, the remodeling and painting, the removing of all traces of Ellen and her life there.

"Yeah, she's pretty amazing," Jeffrey said. He pushed the remains of his hash browns around on his plate with his fork.

He looked up at Ellen. "So," he said. "We should probably get going." He insisted on paying the bill and took Ellen's elbow as they walked out, guiding her between the now-crowded tables. Outside, they'd started down the street toward Ellen's car, when she suddenly stopped and reached for Jeffrey's arm.

"Wait a minute," she said. "We've got to stop at the candy store."

"Candy store?" he asked.

"Oh, yes," she said. "Don't tell me you've never eaten taffy from Bruce's."

Jeffrey grinned—a big, genuine, wide smile. "Well, if it's taffy," he said.

They walked up Hemlock Street to the pink and white striped building that held Bruce's Candy Kitchen, a Cannon Beach institution for more than forty years. Inside, a small basket by the door proffered free samples of taffy, and glass-fronted cabinets held even more, as well as assorted chocolates, licorice, gummies, and Swedish fish.

Ellen was surprised at how quickly she had fallen into an easy rapport with Jeffrey, at how light-spirited she felt after these long, heavy, despairing months. She couldn't help but compare him with Sam. Jeffrey, at least, didn't seem to have Sam's ridiculous ignorance of the realities of life, the bills and repairs and door locks. Being with Sam *was* like having a third child. And Jeffrey was sweet, buying his children kites, telling the story about Lily and the moon. Although Ellen had to admit that there was an ineffable sweetness about Sam, too; he would piggyback the girls upstairs at night and lie on the floor between their beds, telling crazy stories about guys named One-Eyed Joe and Blondie Openshirt. Was Jeffrey passionate about things the way Sam was? she wondered. Sam had such intense and infectious enthusiasm for the things he loved—skiing, inventing, baseball, sex— *Stop*, Ellen told herself. *Don't think about that.* Jeffrey was still a mystery to her.

They paid for their candy—a pound of assorted taffy each— got back in the car, and headed north to Astoria. Ellen dropped Jeffrey at his meeting, in an old blue and purple painted Victorian house, now converted to offices. Then she spent the next two hours browsing in a variety of antiques stores and thrift shops, where she found some great items for Coffee@home, including a hand-carved Scandinavian cuckoo clock and a complete set of 1950s state glasses, from Alabama through Wyoming. It was a wonderful distraction to paw through piles of old linens and postcards, and to study the dovetailing on the drawers of an old dresser. For a while, Ellen even forgot about the move. But then she'd run across something—a small, old print of Crater Lake in a rustic wood frame that would just fit into the spot above the clock in her kitchen—and she'd suddenly remember that she had to think about her *new* house, the one that still seemed like a borrowed dress that would never really fit.

Her cell phone rang; it was Jeffrey, calling to say his meeting had ended. "Are you done shopping?" he asked. "Because I have a brief-case full of papers. I can sit here and read if you need more time."

"No, no, it's fine," Ellen said. "I have to get back home to fix dinner for the kids anyway. Sam's dropping them off at six-thirty. I'll be by to pick you up in about ten minutes."

An hour later they were back on Highway 26, and then driving east, past thick forests interspersed with open scars of clear-cutting. They were both quiet, but it was a companionable silence. Some-thing about Jeffrey felt restful to Ellen. She liked his shyness, his gra-cious manners, the way he observed things, like the bright orange undersides of the wings of the northern flicker that darted from tree to tree just above the road. After all the roiling intensity of her relationship with Sam, it was nice to just be quiet with someone.

Before she knew it, they were within sight of Dottie's bookshop, where Jeffrey had left his car. Ellen pulled into the parking lot, tires scrunching across the gravel, and turned off the engine.

They were both quiet for a minute.

"It's been a really nice day, Jeffrey," she said finally. "Thanks for lunch. I'm glad I ran into you." Her words sounded flat. She wanted to say something to let him know that the day had been an unexpected gift for her, a respite from so many things. But it seemed too forward, too intimate.

"I wish there was something I could do to help you, Ellen," he said, leaning back against the car door to look at her. "I really do. About the house, I mean."

"Oh, it's all right," she said. "Two years from now it will seem crazy to me that I was ever so obsessed, right?"

He was quiet. *At least he's not agreeing that I'm crazy, like Sam does,* Ellen thought.

"Maybe *I* should sell Coffee@home and buy that vineyard in Dundee," she said finally, to break the silence. "I'd probably like picking grapes and drinking wine. Working in a wine-tasting room has got to be a lot like working in a coffee shop."

Jeffrey had his hand on the handle of the car door but didn't open it. He looked at Ellen, then looked out the front window, and sighed.

"I wish—" he began, but then stopped, his hand still on the door handle. He didn't move. "Well," he said finally, turning to look at her again. "Maybe I'll see you at the coffee shop."

"Yes, sure, that would be great," Ellen said, feeling oddly bereft. She put the key ring on her index finger and spun the keys around and around absentmindedly. It seemed as though there should be something else to say, but she couldn't think of anything. Suddenly the keys flew off her finger and landed at Jeffrey's feet.

"I'm sorry," she said, feeling foolish, and leaned over to grab them at the same time that he leaned forward to retrieve them for her. They bumped heads lightly, and Ellen turned to look at him and apologize, but before she knew what was happening, he had put an arm around her shoulders and pulled her closer to him and was kissing her, hard, on the mouth.

She was shocked at the feel of his lips, the unfamiliar bristle of his mustache and beard. She hadn't kissed a man other than Sam in twenty-some years. Jeffrey's tongue parted her lips, met her own tongue, and she was kissing him back. She put her hand around his neck and pulled him to her, feeling the strange, soft crop of his hair, so different from Sam's thick curls. Her body—celibate for more than six months now—responded with a rush, and she was flooded with the desire to rip her clothes off and have sex with him right there in the car.

"Oh, God, stop," she said finally, pulling away. "I can't do this. You're married. And to tell the truth, I really don't like your wife, but I still can't do this."

"I am so sorry," Jeffrey said, slumping against the car door. "I've never done anything like that before. Ellen, I—"

Her cell phone rang, and, grateful for the distraction, she picked it up without thinking and snapped it open.

"Hello?" she said, trying to make her voice sound normal and not breathless, amazed. "Hello, it's Ellen."

"Oh, Ellen, I'm glad I reached you," said the voice at the other end. "It's Jordan Boyce."

CHAPTER TWELVE

"JORDAN?" ELLEN SAID.

She was stunned. She was instantly overcome with guilt and the insane but terrifying notion that Jordan was standing in the parking lot watching them. At the same time, she felt intensely annoyed that Jordan had somehow gotten hold of her cell phone number. Would the woman never leave her alone?

Jeffrey, at hearing Ellen say Jordan's name, had gone completely white. He was frozen like a trapped animal in the passenger seat, pressed up against the hard gray vinyl of the car door.

"Alexa gave me your number," Jordan continued. "I've been trying to reach you all day. It turns out that the measurements we have for the kitchen are wrong, and I need to get into the house to-day to take new measurements for the window. The contractor is leaving town and wants to go over the plans tonight. Alexa didn't have a key, and we couldn't reach your husband. Don't you leave a spare key with the neighbors?"

Of course Jo had a key, Ellen thought, but it would be a cold day in hell before she'd give it to Jordan or let her into the house.

"You need to get into the house," Ellen said, still too shocked to do anything other than restate the obvious. Jeffrey, at hearing this, relaxed visibly. It seemed he too had envisioned his wife, armed with binoculars, standing somewhere nearby and watching them make out like teenagers in the car.

"Yes," Jordan said impatiently. "That's what I said. Can you meet me at the house sometime this evening?"

"I'm, I'm not at home right now," Ellen said. "I should be home around six. You couldn't reach Sam?"

"No," Jordan said. "You know, Ellen, as owner I really should have a key. Most landlords do, I believe, and I'm juggling a lot of deadlines here with the architect and contractors to get everything going when you move out. I need to be able to get access to the house more easily."

God, Ellen thought, *she is so annoying.* "Jordan, we have a contract. I'm living there with my kids for two more weeks. It's fine if you need to get in once in a while when we're not home, but I can't have you or your contractors coming in and out all the time. It's too disruptive for the kids."

"It wouldn't be *all the time,* Ellen," Jordan said. "Anyway, I need to get in tonight to take these measurements. You'll be home by seven?"

Yes, and getting dinner for my kids and trying to figure out what the hell happened to me today, Ellen thought. *I can't see you.*

"Seven won't work, Jordan," she said. "I'll try Sam again and see if he could meet you over there now. I'll have him call you." She snapped the phone shut before Jordan could say anything else.

Ellen and Jeffrey were both silent for a minute.

"Well, *that* was certainly unexpected," Jeffrey said finally. Ellen couldn't tell if he meant Jordan's call, or their kiss, or both.

Jeffrey stared out the windshield. Ellen knew without being told that she was the first woman other than his wife he'd kissed since he'd been married, and she felt his guilt. Conscientious, highly responsible Jeffrey had just impulsively—and passionately—kissed her. He looked so overcome that she couldn't stand it.

She reached out and put a hand on his arm. "Jeffrey," she said, holding his arm so he would look at her. "Don't feel badly about this; we both just gave in to an impulse, and no one will ever know. It just happened and it's not a big deal. I had a lovely day with you."

He turned his head and looked at her, his eyes moving from her eyes to the tendrils of hair around her ears to her mouth and back to her eyes. "So does this mean I'm moving from escape fantasy into full-fledged midlife crisis?" he asked with a halfhearted smile.

She laughed. "No! We shared a kiss, but no one is getting divorced over it. At least you're not. And my divorce certainly isn't about this."

She took her hand from his arm and looked ahead, out the windshield, at the tangle of Oregon grape and salal and blackberry vines ringing the parking lot. She didn't know what else to say. She wanted to see him again; she was appalled that she'd kissed a married man with three children. She felt oddly and unexpectedly attracted to him, yet kissing him felt like a betrayal of Sam. She felt she desperately needed some time on her own to sort out her conflicted feelings about her marriage, yet she was lonely, and Jeffrey, who was so like her, seemed to understand her in a way that even Joanna did not. She wanted him; she never wanted to see him again.

Oh, shit, she thought. *I* am *thirteen*.

"I've got to go, Ellen," Jeffrey said, looking at her.

He opened the car door and stepped out, closing the door behind him. He stood there for a moment, looking at her through the window; then he turned and walked quickly across the parking lot to his car, straight through the puddles, with the muddy water splashing over his thick-soled shoes and onto the cuffs of his neatly pressed wool trousers. He didn't pause and didn't look back, and once he was in his car he pulled out quickly. Before Ellen knew it, he had disappeared onto the highway.

Her cell phone rang again, but this time she looked carefully to see who it was before she answered. It was Sam.

"Hey," he said. "Jordan just called me. She wants to get into the house today to take measurements or something. Is that okay with you?"

"Yes, that's fine," she said. "She just called me. She said she hadn't been able to reach you. Can you meet her there to let her in, though? I really don't want to have to see her again."

"Sure," Sam said. "Where are you?"

"I'm at Dottie Murphy's bookstore," she said. "I should be home in an hour. How are the girls?"

"They're great. I picked them up at school and took them to the batting cage," Sam said. "I guess that's why Jordan couldn't reach me. Louisa really nailed a few shots."

"They were slow pitches, Mommy, but I hit them really hard!" Louisa yelled from the background.

"Tell her I said 'fantastic' and she can show me her swing when I get home," Ellen said. "How about Sara?"

"She's fine. She wasn't quite as excited about the batting cage as Lulu, but we went to Starbucks afterward and got big scones, so she was happy."

"Starbucks?" Ellen said archly. As the owner of an independent coffee shop, she was an avid antagonist of big chains.

"I'm sorry," Sam said. "Starbucks is two minutes from the batting cage and I didn't have time to drive twenty minutes to take them to Coffee@home, okay?"

"You're overreacting, Sam," she said. "It was a joke."

"Okay," he said. "I guess I just don't expect jokes from you anymore."

How did this happen? Ellen wondered. *How did we go from reading each other's minds and finishing each other's sentences to snapping at every remark?*

"Well, never mind," she said with a sigh. "If you could let Jordan in before I get home, I'd really appreciate it."

"That's fine," he said. "I'll go over now and stay with the girls until you get there. You know, the move is coming up pretty fast. I guess we need to talk about dividing up some of the furniture. I've been sleeping on an air mattress in my apartment and eating standing up at the kitchen sink."

Dividing the furniture? Ellen's mind had not made the leap from Sam's moving out to both of them really setting up homes of their own—separate homes. She'd been so focused on the house and not losing it that anything beyond that had seemed simply unimaginable. She tried to picture it. The little pine shelf she'd bought to complement the corner cupboard in the dining room, the blue porcelain candlesticks that looked so good in their bedroom with the blue-green painting of the Willamette Valley, the pair of Hitchcock chairs with the rush seats that sat on either side of the bay window— would they all be split up willy-nilly, tossed here and there to fill out a room? Who would take the photo albums? Who would get the beautiful black and white portrait of six-month-old baby Louisa, grinning impishly with her dimpled fingers stuffed in her mouth? Who would get the blue and white quilt that covered their bed?

"Um, okay," she said slowly. "Obviously we're not going to do that in front of the kids."

"Yeah. We'll figure it out later. We just need to get it done."

Ellen said good-bye and snapped the phone closed. She rested her forehead against the warm vinyl of the steering wheel for a minute. She was suddenly, overwhelmingly tired. Finally she put the key back in the ignition and headed home. She drove in sunlight that was just beginning to fade, a radiant brightness that made the pavement sparkle even though it was after five—the start of the long, long summer days that were among the million things she loved about Oregon. The sun was a brilliant light in her rearview mirror all the way back.

She kept thinking about Jeffrey, about the strange, soft feel of his mustache and beard against her face, about the pressure of his lips and his tongue, so insistent, and the way she had responded. She was surprised. She had always been so profoundly attracted to Sam that she didn't even fantasize about other men, yet here was another man who clearly called up something in her. She suddenly wondered if Sam had kissed another woman since their separation. The thought disturbed her. While she was angry with Sam and disappointed by Sam and just fed up with Sam, she still believed he loved her, and even more, she realized, she *wanted* him to love her, even if she wasn't sure that she loved him anymore.

I can't think about this, she thought. *I'm going to make myself crazy.* "I'll think about it tomorrow," she said out loud, in her best imitation of Scarlett O'Hara.

When she got home, Sam was in the kitchen, unscrewing the switch plate for the light switch next to the back door.

"What are you doing?" she asked.

"This switch plate is cracked," he said. "I thought I'd just replace it with one that isn't broken."

"You're replacing switch plates for Jordan?"

"Well, I guess I didn't think of it that way. It just needed to be fixed."

Ellen didn't want to pick another fight, so all she said was "Did Jordan come by?"

"Yeah, she's been here and gone. The kids ran over to see Emily when we got back, so they weren't here when she was. She wasn't that bad, Ellie, really," he said, holding the new switch plate in place and carefully inserting the first screw into the tiny hole.

"She just really annoys me," Ellen said.

"Her husband seems nice enough," Sam said.

Ellen felt herself blushing and turned quickly to hide her face.

"I met him at the closing," Sam continued. "Quiet guy, kind of buttoned up. But friendly. I think he's a lawyer. You'd probably like him. He's not as abrasive as she is."

"I don't really need to have anything to do with either one of them," she said tartly.

"Okay, okay, fine," he said. "So since the kids aren't here, can we talk about some of the furniture? I need to get my place set up. The kids will be sleeping there, too, you know, and it should feel a little like home."

"Well, what do you want?" Ellen asked. She rummaged in the cupboard for her large pasta pot and filled it with cold water, then set it on the stove to heat. She was trying to sound calm, neutral, but her emotions were churning.

"I've been thinking about it," Sam said. He put the screwdriver down on the counter and then turned and opened the refrigerator. "I'd love a beer," he said.

"I don't have any," she said. "I'm sorry. I haven't bought it since you moved out."

He stood up with a sigh, running a hand through his hair. "Right. Anyway, I don't want to take the living room sofa or anything major that's going to make things seem too different to the kids. I just need some chairs, a table, a couple dishes and pots and pans—that kind of stuff."

The screen door flew open, and the girls ran in with Emily in tow.

"Where's some paper, Mommy?" Sara said. She was wearing knee-length boys' shorts and a red shirt, and had her brown curls pulled back in a careless ponytail. Louisa was wearing the only thing she would wear most days, a blue gingham dress with a big yellow bow in the back. "We're going to play post office and we need paper and pens and envelopes and scissors."

"It's all in the den, in the usual place," Ellen said. "Second drawer on the right. Why do you need scissors?" she asked suspiciously. Sara had once cut Louisa's hair and put all the tendrils into an envelope, "so you'll have something to remember her by, Mommy."

"For cutting the paper for small letters," Sara said. She picked up the screwdriver from the counter where Sam had left it. "Hey, Daddy, can we use your screwdriver?"

"For what?" Sam said.

"For screwing and unscrewing things," she said, beaming at him.

"Very funny, missy. What 'things' do you need to unscrew?"

Sara looked around the kitchen, at the table by the door piled with permission slips and reminders of PTA meetings, the pot simmering on the stove, the clean white ceramic countertops.

Her eye fell on the discarded switch plate that Sam had just removed.

"That!" she said. "We need to fix all those light switch holders, okay?"

"Not okay," Sam said, gently taking the screwdriver from her. "Go play post office."

"Fine! Come on, guys, let's go." They trooped past Ellen into the hallway, Sara, then Emily, then Louisa, with Louisa's giant yellow bow trailing along behind them.

Jo appeared at the back door, in jeans and sandals and a long, loose green tunic, her curls bound under a red bandanna.

"Hey, look at you," she said, eyeing the screwdriver in Sam's hand. "It's Mr. Fix-It. I didn't know you had it in you, Sam."

"Very funny," Sam said, grinning at her. "Actually, if you give me a beer, I'll fix something for you."

"I'll give you a beer if you promise *not* to fix something for me," Joanna said. "Mirror Pond. They're in the fridge. Pete's there; he'll probably have one with you."

"Sold." Sam put the screwdriver down and turned to look at Ellen. "We'll have to finish figuring out the furniture stuff later," he said. "Okay? Why don't you think about it and let me know what you're willing to give up?"

"All right," she said.

"I'll be back to say good-bye to the kids," he said. "See you in a minute." He disappeared out the screen door.

"The furniture?" Jo asked, raising her eyebrows at Ellen. "Sheesh. That's like getting into the nitty-gritty divorce stuff. Yuck."

"Yuck is right," Ellen said with a sigh, reaching up to get some spaghetti from the cupboard to drop into the now-boiling water.

"It's all starting to get very real. I mean, we'll be moved out *in less than two weeks,* Jo. We'll be gone. Two weeks from today this kitchen probably won't even *be here* anymore. I think it's the first thing Jordan is going to rip apart."

Ellen poured a jar of marinara sauce into a saucepan and lit the burner beneath it. She was silent for a minute. Finally she said, "I ran into Jeffrey today. On the coast. We actually had lunch together."

"Are you kidding?" Joanna sat down on the stool by the back door and looked at Ellen expectantly. "What was he doing there?"

"I stopped at Dottie Murphy's bookstore on my way to Astoria, and he stopped there, too. We started talking, and then he asked me to have lunch. So we went to Cannon Beach."

"Like a *date?*" Jo said. "My God, I was *joking* about your having an affair with him. I never in a million years—"

"It wasn't a date," Ellen said, burying herself in the refrigerator so she didn't have to look at her friend.

"Then what was it?"

"I don't know; it was like we were friends. He really is a nice man." Ellen opened the crisper and pulled out a head of lettuce and a red pepper.

"And?"

"I was sure I had a tomato in here. And nothing, Jo. We had lunch. We talked. I probably won't see him again, unless I run into him in the neighborhood when we're at your house sometime."

"But what did you talk about?" Jo said, leaning forward. "Are you sure you're not attracted to him at all?"

"Attracted to whom?" said Sam, pulling open the screen door and stepping into the kitchen, beer in hand.

Ellen was so startled she stood up and banged her head on the top shelf of the refrigerator.

"Ow! Don't you knock?" she said. "Attracted to nobody. Geez." She rubbed the top of her head gingerly.

Sam looked at her, his brown eyes wide and dark, not moving. "Jo said, 'Are you sure you're not attracted to him?' It must be somebody."

Joanna looked at Sam, at the stubborn intensity in his face. "I think I hear Pete calling," she said. "I'll see you guys later." She escaped out the door.

Ellen turned to face her husband. "It was just girl talk, Sam. It was stupid."

He picked up his car keys and cell phone, which he'd left on the counter, and shoved them in his pocket.

"Okay, fine. I guess it's really none of my business now anyway." He walked to the door and stood for a moment, his hand on the knob. "It just reinforces what I've been thinking lately."

"What do you mean?" Ellen asked.

Sam turned his head and looked out the screen door, at the familiar view of the cedar tree and the deck and the garden cherub in the backyard. He paused for a moment, then turned back to look at her. "I think we need to stop living in limbo," he said. "It's time just to go ahead and get divorced."

CHAPTER THIRTEEN

ELLEN ARRIVED AT the store on Thursday morning exhausted from yet another sleepless night. *Everyone tells you about not sleeping when you have babies,* she thought, *but no one tells you that once you're in your forties and the "babies" are finally sleeping like rocks, you still won't be able to sleep, because you can't turn off your mind, not to mention whatever the hell is going on with your hormones.*

She had tossed and turned every night since spending Monday at the coast with Jeffrey. Sam and the house and her divorce and moving and Jeffrey were all tangled up in her mind and emotions like fishing line spun crazily off the reel. Maybe they'd be wildly busy today and she wouldn't have time to think, she thought. Thank God for work.

Cloud was already at the shop and had hot tea brewing in the white stoneware pot. He wore a faded blue and green plaid button-down shirt and baggy striped pants with dark shades of brown and orange.

"No offense, Cloud, but you look a little like bad TV reception today," Ellen said. "The plaid, the stripes, the colors—"

"Sorry." He rolled his eyes. "I've been busy and didn't do laundry. I was hoping you wouldn't notice."

"Lord, these poor people haven't even had their morning coffee yet and they've got to look at you. Here, at least wear this." Ellen tossed him an apron.

"All right, boss." He smiled.

They had a steady stream of customers all day. Ellen made endless lattes and cappuccinos, gave a pep talk to the writer who'd just received his fifteenth rejection, empathized with the mom of three who'd just found out she was pregnant with twins, and teasingly scolded the regular customer she'd spotted at Starbucks the week before. She also cleared out space in the main room for the things she'd bought in Astoria and spent an hour on her cell phone ordering new inventory. She didn't have to think.

She was actually starting to relax, staring out the front window of the shop while she waited for a fresh pot of coffee to brew, when she noticed a man striding across the parking lot with dark hair and a relaxed, athletic walk. *God, here comes an attractive guy*, she thought, idly noting his broad shoulders and lean hips, the casual, comfortable way he moved in his body. As the man drew nearer, she realized with a shock that it was Sam.

He looked quickly to the left and right before crossing the parking lane in front of the shop and pushing open the glass door. "Hey," he said.

"Hey," she said finally, trying not to look at him. "So what's up?"

"Coffee," he said.

"Medium mocha?"

"Yeah, that would be great. Make it a triple."

He stood awkwardly at the counter, picking up the little packets of honey-roasted almonds and mints and then putting them back down.

"We really need to talk about the divorce stuff," he said at last. "The furniture, what the time frame is for finalizing all this."

"Okay," Ellen said slowly, pouring steamed milk over the chocolate syrup and espresso shots in the cup. "I just— Oh, I had hoped we could wait to do all this until after the move." She sighed.

"It would make more sense to know where the furniture's going now, instead of moving it all to your place and then moving some of it from there to my place," Sam said. He took a long sip of his drink. "If we figure it out now, I can move out the stuff that I'm going to keep before you move."

"Your place," "my place." The words stung Ellen. She took a deep breath.

"All right. I can't talk now, obviously," she said, nodding at the main room of the shop. Cloud was busily stacking the state glasses Ellen had bought on a bookshelf in the corner, while six other customers sat reading newspapers and sipping drinks.

"Yeah, I know," Sam said. "And you'll have the kids around tonight. Maybe we should just get a sitter and we can talk at my house, or grab a bite for dinner some night."

I don't want to do this, Ellen thought. *Can't I just pretend a little longer that everything isn't changing all at once?* If only the house had burned down, the house and everything in it. Then there would be the refreshing sense of starting over and moving on, not all this unbearable heaviness of sorting through the past, splitting it up, and dragging it forever forward like some Sisyphean boulder.

"Let's just get this over with," she said aloud, to herself as much as to Sam. She looked at him. "Let's just do it tonight."

"Hey, Cloud!" She called to him across the room. "Could you watch the girls tonight for an hour or two while Sam and I get together?"

"Lemme think." He straightened up, stared at the ceiling for a moment, then said, "Sure, Ellen. I don't have plans tonight."

She turned to Sam. "So where do you want to meet?"

"Next door?" he said. A few doors down from Coffee@home was La Prima Trattoria, a little Italian restaurant that they went to all the time. The girls always got the same thing, spaghetti and exotically flavored Italian sodas. Ellen and Sam usually shared a bottle of wine and grilled salmon with a side of pasta and salad.

"All right," she said. "Can we make it eight? I want to feed the kids and get them through homework."

"Fine," he said. "See you then."

Ellen stared after him as he walked out, still somewhat stunned that, when it came to Sam, her body seemed to be on a different wavelength than her mind. She took a clean rag and wiped the moisture from the steamer, then wiped down the counter by the cash register. She untied her apron and hung it on the hook by the storeroom door.

"I'm heading home," she said to Cloud. "I'll see you after your shift. You're welcome to have some dinner at my house. Probably high-end organic mac and cheese, if you can stomach it. I'm not meeting Sam until eight."

"Sounds good," Cloud said with a wave. "I'll see you tonight."

Ellen picked the girls up at school and headed home. They were ecstatic to hear that Cloud was going to babysit.

"We can play hot lava!" Louisa squealed from the backseat. "And we can play it all night!"

"Hot lava?" Ellen asked.

"It's where everything is hot lava except the furniture and pillows," Sara explained. "So you have to jump around from the couch to the coffee table, or throw pillows on the floor to walk on so you don't get burned. Cloud taught us, and he always plays it with us."

"Sounds like fun," Ellen said. "I'll just be gone for a couple hours. Cloud will tuck you in, okay?"

"Where are you going?" asked Sara.

"To have a late dinner."

"With who?"

What do I do? Ellen thought. *Do I tell them I'm meeting Sam? Will they think it's a date? I need to go the library to get a manual on how to handle all this. It's like being dropped into a foreign country and not speaking the language.*

"With Daddy," she said cautiously, turning in to their driveway. "We just need to talk about a few things."

"What things?" Sara persisted.

Ellen looked at her in the rearview mirror. Her older daughter's dark eyes—so like Sam's—were intent, focused. She was looking at Ellen, too, straight into the mirror.

"Just things about the move, sweetie," Ellen said, meeting her glance. "We need to make sure Daddy has some furniture for his apartment, so we have to decide what he should take. We want it to be nice for him there, and we want our new house to be nice for us."

"Why?" Sara said. They were parked in the driveway now. Louisa had already unbuckled and hopped out, and she was picking up pieces of the giant pinecones from the deodar cedar that had dropped and splintered in the driveway.

"Why what?" Ellen said.

"Why should it be nice at our new house? It's not really our house. *This* is our house." Sara nodded toward the yellow house, glowing in the late afternoon sun. "That other place is like a hotel, someplace we're going to stay but not to live."

"Oh, honey." Ellen didn't know what to say. She felt exactly the same way, only she was forty-four, not ten.

"C'mon, you can help Lulu get ready for whatever games you want to play with Cloud."

Sara frowned but allowed Ellen to lead her inside, where the girls collected every pillow in the house and piled them in the living room in preparation for hot lava. Louisa then went to work coloring an elaborate card for Cloud, with plenty of clouds and rainbows.

Ellen wandered through the house, trying to figure out what would fit into her new house and what would work for Sam. Did he want the upholstered yellow chair that he always sat in, usually with a girl or two on his lap, to watch baseball games on TV? Did he want the rocker in the girls' room that he'd spent countless hours in, shushing and rocking the colicky Sara? Did he want the pine coffee table, with the deep grooves where Sara and Emily had rolled their Matchbox cars over and over and over? Sam never seemed to care about his physical surroundings—if the furniture was even remotely clean and comfortable, he was happy.

I might as well do eeny, meeny, miney, moe, Ellen thought. I don't know what to give him, and I don't even want to think about arranging all these things in that other house. She made a halfhearted list on a piece of scratch paper and folded it away in the back pocket of her jeans. *Well, there,* she thought. *I'm done.*

She made dinner for the kids, welcomed Cloud and fixed a plate for him, too, and quickly brushed her hair and threw on a clean shirt. She had to hunt for Stella Blue Moon for Louisa, and Sara's favorite blue sweatshirt, which they finally figured out had been left in Sam's car. Ellen tried to call Sam on the way to the restaurant to remind him to bring it, only to realize that she'd left her cell phone at work. By the time she got to La Prima, Sam was there already, seated at a table in the corner, with a bottle of red wine and a basket of bread. Ellen was surprised. She was the prompt one; Sam was the late one. She sat down a little breathlessly, feeling rushed, apologetic, even though she was on time.

"Hey," he said. "I hope you don't mind, but I already ordered. I'm starving. You want to split the salmon?"

"Thanks," she said, turning to the waiter, who was already at her elbow. "The salmon would be perfect. And I guess I'll have some wine." She nodded at the bottle that was already uncorked in front of Sam.

"You look nice," he said, gazing at her shirt, a simple button-down in a rich, deep rose, and the plain silver cord that circled her neck.

"It's the lighting," Ellen said, nodding at the small oil lamp on the table. The walls were a rosy peach plaster, which also worked wonders on tired forty-something complexions. "This place would make Joan Rivers look great."

Sam smiled. "Right. Don't accept a compliment or anything. It might make it seem like you're going soft."

Ellen ignored the comment, fished around in her purse for her reading glasses, and put them on.

"So, I went through the house and thought about what you might need and wrote it all down." She pulled the hastily scrawled list out of her back pocket. "Of course, if there are other things you want that aren't here we can talk about that . . ." Her voice trailed off.

Sam refilled his wineglass. "As long as I've got a bed, a table, a chair, and some eating utensils, I'm pretty good," he said.

"But I thought you'd want some of the sentimental stuff," she said. "Those big framed portraits of the girls as babies, or the rocker. Or I thought maybe you'd want our bed. I guess there's no reason that I can't take the guest room bed and you could have our bed. You're the one who loves a big bed."

"You know, Ellen," Sam said, leaning forward across the table, "I really don't give a shit about the stuff. You're the one who cares about the stuff. What I care about is us, and the kids. Our family. That's what I want."

She sat perfectly still, silent.

He leaned closer. "I've made huge mistakes, and the house is gone. But, God, Ellie, I thought maybe, once it was over, and we got through the fact that we had to move, you'd think again about what you're throwing away here. I mean, I love you. I love the kids. I don't want us living in different places. I get it that you don't want to move, and I've signed on with a consulting firm here. I'm not moving anywhere to market new inventions anymore; that's done. I had high hopes for the baby beeper, but who knows? I can work on it in my spare time, and maybe Babies 'R' Us will call someday and I'll have a shot. No more moving; no more putting our own money into inventions. Really."

He looked at her expectantly.

Ellen was overwhelmed. It was just about the longest speech she'd ever heard Sam give.

"But you said you were tired of living in limbo and wanted to go ahead with the divorce," she said finally. "Just on Monday you said that!"

"Yeah, I know," he said, leaning back. He turned and looked toward the opposite wall, where glass bottles filled with olive oil stood in neat rows along the shelves. "And just on Monday I overheard that maybe you're interested in somebody else." He looked at her again. "So are you?"

Ellen's face grew hot; she could feel the warmth creep up her neck and her cheeks. She thought of Jeffrey, kissing her in the car, and she couldn't help it.

"No," she said. "No. I mean, we just split up a few months ago. I'm moving out of the house in two weeks. Sara is going crazy over the move and our separation, and to top it all off the house almost burned down last weekend. The *last* thing on my mind right now is getting into a relationship. Really, Sam."

He reached for the little jug of olive oil on their table and poured a small pool of the golden liquid onto his plate. He tore off a piece of bread from the basket and dipped it in the oil. "We never talked about that, Ellie," he said, "about dating other people while we were separated. I guess I wasn't planning to, so it never occurred to me that you would."

"Well, I'm not," she said and looked at him. And it was true. She certainly hadn't *planned* to run into Jeffrey and have lunch with him.

"All right," he said, picking up the bottle of wine and pouring more into her glass. "Okay. I trust you. But what about reconsidering about the divorce? If you think we should go back to counseling, I'll do it."

Ellen took a long sip from her wineglass and looked around the room. She felt completely blindsided. Here she was, in her clean shirt and pretty necklace, with a list in her pocket, prepared to have a civil discussion about dividing their earthly possessions, and now Sam was zooming off course. She had been so focused on *the house, the house, the house* that she hadn't really thought of her life after the house, her life as a divorced, single mother. It was all part of a nebulous future.

"I just don't know, Sam," she said finally. "I'm not ready to think about this."

The waiter appeared with their dinner. Ellen, grateful for the distraction, was happy to pick up her fork and break off a bite of the flaky salmon, to twirl spaghetti around in the bowl of her spoon. Did she want to stay married to Sam? Since the day they'd split up, in that bitter last fight over being forced to sell the house, Ellen had considered it final. The house was lost. Her marriage was over. They were both irretrievable. And since then, while she had considered many times how to get the house back, she had never considered trying to repair her marriage. It was the *house* that was important. She realized how ridiculous that seemed now, that the loss of timber and plaster and nails should mean more to her than the loss of Sam. They had gone to marriage counseling; they had hashed out her hyperresponsibility and Sam's reckless-ness. But she had never talked to the counselor about her passion for the house. She couldn't say in front of Sam that losing him was bearable but losing the house threatened her very sanity, could she? As she looked at him across the table, she did feel a horrible sense of loss and longing for Sam, for herself with Sam. *It's not the house,* she thought.

"I don't know," she said. "I just can't imagine that you're going to be happy doing consulting work. What's changed? You'll still want to be creating things and trying to market them. You'll stay settled until the next big idea comes along."

"I didn't say I was going to give up inventing," Sam said, lean-ing back in his chair while still looking at her. "But I don't have to move to do it. I want to be with you and the kids."

"I can't reconsider our whole relationship in the next ten days while I'm also going through this move," she said flatly. "I can't."

She looked at him defensively. "You just have to come and move out some furniture and keep things the way they are for now."

"All right, Ellen," he said. "I wish this was easier for you. The move, I mean. Giving up the house. I'm sorry that it's just so hard."

She poured herself another glass of wine. *Might as well drown my sorrows,* she thought. She slid the list across table. "Okay. So is this list of furniture all right with you?"

Sam picked it up, folded it without looking at it, and handed it back to her. "It's fine," he said. "I'll let you know when I can get a truck and stop by to get the stuff. I'm sure Pete will help me move anything heavy."

Ellen was quiet for a minute. "All right. So that's settled." *I can cross it off my list,* she thought, feeling angry with herself. *Split up with husband, check. Divide the furniture, check. What the hell do I want?*

She reached across the table for Sam's arm and looked at his watch.

"Oh, geez. I've gotta go," she said. She pulled her napkin off her lap and put it on the table, then rooted around in her purse for her keys. They paid the bill and walked out into the cool night air. Ellen hugged herself and jumped up and down on the sidewalk for a minute.

"Where did you park?" Sam asked. "I'll walk you to your car."

"Hang on," she said. "I have to stop in the shop and pick up my cell phone. I left it by the cash register."

Coffee@home was dark, the Closed sign in the window. Ellen unlocked the door and stepped inside with Sam behind her.

"You don't have to bother," she said, turning to him. "I can get it."

"No," he said. "I'll wait. You have any candy in here?" he asked. "We didn't get dessert."

"Sure. I think there are some Junior Mints over there on the counter."

"I hate Junior Mints," he said.

"Why?" Ellen said, feeling a little drunk and slightly silly. "Because they have the name 'Junior' in the title? Is it just too sissy a candy for you?"

Sam grinned. "That's it. Junior Mints are a threat to my masculinity."

Ellen laughed. She picked up her cell phone and came around to the middle of the room. "It takes a real man to like Junior Mints," she said. "Come on, let's go. Cloud's been stuck putting the kids to bed, and I have to work tomorrow."

"I know." They moved to the door. Out of habit, he bent to kiss her good-bye, and, out of habit, she turned her face to meet his. He kissed her gently, and then harder. She kissed him urgently, too, her lips meeting his, then the soft, insistent pressure of his tongue against hers, her arms around him, pressing him to her.

"Ellie—"

"Oh, God. Don't talk."

She kissed him again and again. He pulled away and kissed her face, her eyelids, her throat. She pushed him, kissing him the whole time, toward the storeroom in the back. They clattered through the door into the little room, lit only with the glow from the streetlamps shining through the small window up near the ceiling. Sam pushed her down onto a pile of braided rugs on the floor and lowered himself next to her. His hand slid inside her shirt, reached for her breast, expertly exploring her nipple, twirling it gently between his thumb and index finger. She was completely overcome with wanting him, needing to feel his weight on top of her and inside her. She sat up and pulled her shirt over

her head, unbuttoned her jeans and kicked them off. She reached
for Sam's shirt and helped him pull it off. The feel of his bare skin
against hers was electric. She rolled on top of him. He pulled
down the front of her bra so he could play with her nipples with
both hands while she rubbed herself against his hardness like a
teenager.

He rolled over so he was on top now and sat back to slide her
panties down over her ankles. He looked at her, then bent forward, kissed her stomach, and slowly traced a path of kisses
downward, his lips just grazing her skin. She lay, barely breathing,
as he traced a lazy circle of kisses inside her thighs, toward her
knees and back up again. She reached down with both hands and
pulled his head up. "I want you inside me," she said.

She guided him into her. Everything had changed; nothing had
changed. He rocked slowly, knowing exactly what she liked. She
wrapped her arms around him, holding him tightly against her
while she moved under him, feeling all of him around her and inside her. She ran her hands up and down against his back, thinking
of nothing but how wonderful it felt to have his weight on top of
her, his heat and hardness inside her. They moved together in a
rhythm honed in countless hours and years of lovemaking, like water running over rock, tracing a path always the same but always
changing, moving. *Like being rushed along in the water, like going over the
waterfall,* Ellen thought. She could think of absolutely nothing but
her own pleasure and how great it felt. She knew that Sam knew
she was close by the way she moved under him; she knew he'd wait
for her. She arched her back and moaned, gripping him so tightly
that he flung his head back and grimaced. He responded to her
with a more urgent rhythm of his own, finally collapsing on top
of her with a head-shaking groan. He lay there, covering her

completely with his body, then slowly rolled over, with one arm and leg still flung across her protectively.

"Wow, what was that?" Sam said finally.

"I don't know," Ellen said. For the first time in months she felt calm, relaxed—even sleepy. *It figures,* she thought. *I spend weeks not sleeping while I agonize over what to do with my life, and then as soon as I get laid I could sleep like a baby.* She smiled.

"What?" Sam said.

"Nothing," she said. "I just suddenly feel really sleepy."

He rubbed his hand absentmindedly against her arm, a familiar feather caress. "Ellen, really," he said softly. "Can we talk about this?"

No! she thought. *Please don't ask me about this. I want to just not think for a few minutes.*

"Maybe later," she said, as kindly as she could. "I just need time to think."

Sam's look was at once tender and cautious and confused. She put a hand up and ruffled his hair.

He studied her face, ran his fingers lightly over her stomach, bent his head to kiss her collarbone. "Okay," he said, getting up and rooting around in the dark for his clothes.

She got dressed slowly, then smoothed out the rug, making sure everything was in place. She walked Sam to the door of the shop and stood on tiptoe to kiss him gently on the cheek. He put an arm around her waist and held her to him, hugging her, then let her go.

"I'll see you tomorrow," he said.

Ellen picked up her coat and purse and carefully locked the door. She drove home, still feeling languorous and dreamy, half-asleep. She thought about their bed, with the carved pine headboard and the quilt, a blue and white drunkard's-path pattern, which she'd found on a family trip to Colorado. It was so cozy in that bed, lying back among the pillows and looking out the window toward the old orchard and the mountains in the distance.

At home she dropped her things by the back door, paid Cloud and said good night, then stuck her head in the girls' room and listened to their steady breathing. She walked across the hall to her room and slipped out of her clothes and into her nightgown. She climbed into bed without even brushing her teeth, feeling the cool softness of the sheets against her skin, already anticipating a blissful sleep.

She was just drifting off when she heard something. Was it one of the girls, wandering around downstairs? She listened again. No, it was a knock, at the seldom-used front door. Sam? Oh, God, she *really* didn't want to talk. Why was he suddenly going all touchy-feely on her now, when she least wanted to deal with it?

She pulled on the gray zip-front sweatshirt that hung on the bedpost and groped her way downstairs in the dark. The knock came again, soft but insistent.

Ellen opened the door. And there, standing on the front stoop in the moonlight, was Jeffrey Boyce.

CHAPTER FOURTEEN

JEFFREY STOOD THERE in jeans and a sweater, looking at her apologetically. Ellen stepped out onto the bricks. Under her sweatshirt she was wearing the nightgown Sam had given her three years ago, on their fifteenth wedding anniversary. It was pale purple, a clingy silk with spaghetti straps, and she was suddenly aware both that she was freezing and that she was not really decently dressed.

"Jeffrey! It's almost midnight."

"Ssh, Ellen, I know it's late. I just want to talk to you for a minute."

He looked at her, and she felt his eyes move over the hollow of her collarbone, the line of her hips beneath the gown.

Ellen looked down at the thin nightgown, and pulled her sweatshirt closer around her body. "I'm sorry. I thought it was Sam, so I didn't put on my robe."

"I'm actually here in a completely platonic capacity," he said, blushing a little. He cleared his throat and looked at her. "Ellen, I haven't been able to stop thinking about everything since we talked on Monday. It's like being in high school again. I can't think about anything else."

"Jeffrey, it was a wonderful day. I had a great time, too. But it didn't—"

"Ellen, I know it didn't mean anything," he said, finishing her sentence for her. "At least, it didn't mean anything significant. And I'm not here to make a pass at you. I really just wanted to talk."

Sleep, Ellen thought. *I need to sleep.* But Jeffrey was so earnest and sincere, and so gentlemanly. She felt inordinately fond of him, her kindred spirit in loss and frustration.

"We can't talk out here," she said. "It's freezing. Come on in. But if one of my kids wakes up, you better hide in the closet. I don't want to have to explain to anyone what you're doing here."

"Of course," Jeffrey said. "I don't mean to put you in an awkward position by coming by. I just knew we couldn't talk at the shop because you're always so busy, and there are so many people . . ."

Ellen turned and opened the front door and stepped into the hall, grateful for the warmth of the thick, round rug beneath her bare feet. "Come on into the kitchen," she said. "I'll make us some tea."

She padded quietly through the dark living room and dining room with Jeffrey behind her. She couldn't face the harshness of the overhead light, so she picked up two of the candles left over from her infamous party, lit them, and placed them on the counter. The brick floor was cold, and she slipped on her pink garden clogs from the shoe basket by the back door. *This is pretty sexy,* she thought. *The slinky nightgown with sweatshirt and garden clogs.*

"Have a seat," she said, nodding toward the step stool against the back wall. "Sorry it's such a small kitchen."

"I know," Jeffrey said. "I've seen the blueprints."

"I guess it will be bigger soon," she said, hating to be reminded.

It was so perfect now, this tiny, imperfect space in which she'd baked Christmas cookies and basted Thanksgiving turkeys and simmered chicken soup for sore throats.

She picked up the red kettle from the stovetop and filled it with cold water, then placed it back on the burner and lit the flame underneath.

"Do you drink tea?" she said, rummaging in the cupboard for the strainer and some kind of tea without caffeine.

"Sure. Anything's fine," Jeffrey said. He was sitting on the step stool, his hands in his lap, looking excited, almost eager.

"Ellen, I made an offer on the vineyard," he blurted.

She turned and faced him, amazed. "You *what?*"

"I know, I know. It seems crazy." He smiled. "And it's very unlike me, although not completely. I spent all this week researching it. The numbers are good; it's a solid business, with room for growth."

"What on earth did Jordan say?" Ellen stood across the room, the tea strainer in her hand.

"Well, that's the thing. Of course at first, she thought I was crazy—literally. But, after talking about it for the last few days, she's actually willing to consider it." Jeffrey put both hands on his knees and shook his head a little, as though he couldn't quite believe what he was saying. "I told her about it Monday, after I saw you. I believe we really could make a go of this. I explained we wouldn't necessarily have to move right away. I was thinking at first I could stay at the law firm and hire a manager to oversee it, just go down on weekends. It would be a chance for us to get our hands into it without the risk of moving the whole family down there. It's a beautiful place, with a nice house."

"And Jordan is okay with that?"

Jeffrey stood up and paced across the tiny kitchen. "Well, define *okay*. I mean, since she's known me the law has been my whole life, or almost my whole life. She signed on to be a lawyer's wife, knowing it would be a lot of long hours but also probably a lot of financial security. And that's exactly what our life has been."

He stopped pacing and leaned back against the counter, looking at Ellen. "I didn't want to tell her how trapped I've been feeling; I didn't want her to take it personally. It's not because of her. But then I began to think, *Why not? Why not just talk about it?*"

He smiled gently at her. "You were so sympathetic, Ellen," he said. "You made me think that maybe it wasn't totally crazy, some kind of nutty midlife crisis. It gave me the courage to really talk to Jordan. So I did."

"And she was sympathetic?"

"Oh, God, no, not at first. She really panicked once she understood I was serious. She's dead set against anything that involves leaving Portland—she does not want to go through moving again. But I kept thinking, *I want things, too.* And what I want isn't necessarily to be stuck behind a desk at Merrill Cole for another thirty years. I'd never make her move again if she didn't want to; I just wanted her to think about our future, about how it might look if I did something other than law."

Ellen stood across the room by the stove, the kettle beginning to hum behind her. *Oh, my God,* she thought. *It's an eleventh-hour reprieve. It's Dostoyevsky and the firing squad.*

"I'm just stunned that Jordan would consider this," she said slowly. "I mean, I obviously don't know her well, but from what you've said, and what she's said to me, she seemed very committed to moving in here, and getting the MAC club membership, and all the rest. This is such a huge step in another direction."

"I know," Jeffrey said. "I think she realizes how important this is to me, and how hard I've worked since we've been married so we can have all that we do now." He paused. "And I think she's known on some level that I haven't been truly happy lately. She thought it was *her;* that maybe I was sick of her complaining about Portland for so long, about wanting to move back East. She told me she leaped at buying your house because she thought it would convince me that she's okay with staying in Portland now, that she wants to be here long term."

Ellen remembered the night of the candle party, when Jordan had arrived after the fire, the uncertainty and fear in her eyes when Ellen had mentioned Jeffrey.

"And the kids are still little," Jeffrey said. "If it worked out and we wanted to move down there in a couple years, they'd still be young enough to adjust. And it's not going to happen overnight— it may be that after a year or two of managing it from a distance we decide it's too much work, or not the right lifestyle for us. But at least we'll have *tried* it, at least I'll know I gave it a shot."

Ellen was wide awake now, her heart pounding. She suddenly felt hyperaware of everything around her, the cool air on her bare legs, the sweet smell of the tea leaves in the open tin, the flickering shadows on the wall opposite the candles. She couldn't stand it any longer. "But does that mean you want to back out of the deal here, that you don't want to move into my house?"

"Yes," Jeffrey said, looking at her and smiling. "Yes, Ellen, that's exactly what it means. And Jordan agrees."

Yes! Ellen wanted to leap and pirouette in a ballet of joy. She wanted to run across the kitchen and kiss the beautiful sink where she'd bathed her babies. She wanted to throw her arms around Jeffrey and kiss him. But she did none of these things.

"Oh, Jeffrey," she said. "Oh, Jeffrey." And then she began to cry. She stood there in her nightgown and sweatshirt and garden clogs, her arms at her sides, weeping in a flood of relief and gratitude that felt completely overwhelming. Jeffrey watched her helplessly for a few seconds, then came over and wrapped his arms around her, letting her cry into the nubby wool of his brown sweater.

"I couldn't wait to tell you," he said. "That's why I came tonight. I'm glad it's all going to work out now, Ellen."

She let him hold her for a moment, then raised her wet face to look at him. She could feel the attraction and knew he felt it, too. His face, with the warm, bristly beard and full lips, was just inches away. He bent down and kissed her. She raised both arms and pulled his head closer, kissing him hard, too. Her tears salted their lips. He began to kiss the side of her jaw, near her ear, then her neck, then her clavicle. His hands slid around her waist, and he pulled her to him, pressing the fullness of his body against hers. But after having been with Sam just a few hours ago, it felt strange to her, foreign. She had a deep affection for Jeffrey, who was truly a sweet, good man. But the memory of Sam's lips on her body was too recent, too full with feeling for her even to know what she wanted right now. She couldn't complicate things even more.

She broke away and stumbled backward, until they were standing several feet apart, not touching. At almost the same moment the kettle began to whistle shrilly. Ellen turned automatically, picked it up off the burner, and turned off the flame.

"Ellen, I'm sorry," Jeffrey said, staggering back and sitting down hard on the step stool by the door. "Jesus! This has never happened to me before. I really did just come here to talk to you about the house."

Ellen pulled her sweatshirt jacket tight around her, conscious of her nipples sticking up through the thin fabric of her nightgown beneath.

"It's okay, Jeffrey," she said. "It's me, too. I get very emotional about the house, and you've been really understanding and supportive. I probably misinterpreted that. My God! You're married, and I'd never—"

"Neither would I," he said. "All appearances to the contrary."

He stood up and shook himself, as if to clear his head.

"I shouldn't stay here too long. Jordan and I went down to look over the vineyard yesterday and just made the offer this morning. They called tonight to let us know it's been accepted. Anyway, we can get in touch on Monday about whatever we need to do to sell the house back to you."

Ellen still felt suspended in disbelief. Her mug, filled with a tea strainer and a spoonful of chamomile leaves, sat forgotten on the counter, waiting for water. The kettle steamed on the stove. Her postsex languor had given way to an intense alertness.

"You're really sure?" she asked, looking directly into his eyes. "Jordan is really sure, too? I mean, we *have* been down this road before."

Jeffrey smiled. "I know. I know. I was wrong last time. This time, though, I'm completely confident. Jordan and I are really on the same page. It's actually been a great thing for our marriage—we haven't talked like that in a long time. If she does decide she wants to move down there eventually, she'll probably launch a new chapter of the Junior League and turn Dundee into the social center of the Willamette Valley."

Ellen's eyes searched his face.

"Please thank Jordan for me," she said. "This means so much, to my kids, too. I'm so grateful."

"Me, too," Jeffrey said. "Really, Ellen, if Jordan hadn't rushed into buying this house and I hadn't met you, I might just have plodded along on the same old path for another thirty years. I feel very lucky."

Ellen stood close to him, as she had that day at Dottie's bookstore, her head eye level with his chest, inhaling the slight aroma of cedar from his sweater. She had completely conflicted feelings about saying good-bye to him now. She was euphoric to think she might really be able to stay in the house, but she also felt a profound connection to Jeffrey, who understood why watching Louisa lick a wave was important, and why the house meant so much. He understood what she couldn't articulate about the ordinary things and moments that, taken together, made her life so extraordinary. She wanted the house; she wanted Jeffrey's friendship, too. *Can't I have both?*

"I'll miss you," she said. "I really will."

He turned his head, so as not to look at her. He seemed slightly uncomfortable. "Okay, then," he said.

"I'll walk you out," Ellen said. She followed him through the dark rooms and back into the front hallway, where Jeffrey stopped with his hand on the doorknob.

"Thank you," she said. "For everything." She stood on tiptoe and kissed his bearded cheek.

"I don't know if getting the house back will make a difference with whatever happens with you and Sam," he said finally. "But good luck."

He opened the door and walked down the brick path, through the little front gate, and out to his car, which was parked by the side of the road. Ellen stood for a moment looking after him, then turned her gaze up to the night sky, to Orion and the three stars of the hunter's belt glowing above the tips of the firs across the street. *Her* view. *Her* house. She couldn't believe it.

I have to call Jo, she thought. *And Sam. And tell the kids.* But not yet. She was definitely not going to tell the kids a thing until after all the papers were signed and it was absolutely, positively, once and forever her house again. She'd need to talk to her accountant about the money, and possibly selling off a share of the business. She'd need to talk to Sam. But right now, she was just going to savor this most happy, precious moment.

Ellen turned and walked into the darkened house and closed the door. Once inside she walked slowly through the house, in and out of every single room. *This is mine,* she thought, opening the door to the basement stairs. *This is mine,* twirling in the middle of the living room. She bestowed her silent benediction of thanks on every corner of every room. Finally, she extinguished the two candles in the kitchen, slipped quietly out of her clogs, and walked upstairs to bed, where she slept the deepest, soundest, most dreamless sleep of her life.

THE NEXT MORNING Ellen woke the girls by leaping on top of each of them and nuzzling their ears.

"Get up, get up, get up," she said. "It's a beautiful day." It was true. The sky outside the girls' bedroom window was a brilliant blue. A carpet of sweet woodruff covered the garden below with green and white, and the roses were blooming in creamy bursts of yellow and pink.

"Why are you so happy?" Sara asked, eyeing her suspiciously.

Ellen playfully smacked her bottom through the thick comforter. "What, I'm not allowed to be in a good mood?"

"You're allowed, you just usually aren't," Sara said matter-of-factly. "At least not lately."

"I'm in a good mood!" Louisa announced, rolling out from under her covers and standing up on the bed. "I'm in a great mood!" She began to jump vigorously on the bed.

"Are you in a good mood because you had dinner with Daddy?" Sara asked hopefully.

Oh, geez. Ellen winced. She hadn't even thought about that interpretation of her impossible-to-hide joy.

"Stop that, Lulu, you'll break the bed," she said automatically to the bouncing Louisa, while still keeping her eyes on Sara.

"We had a fine dinner, honey, but that really has nothing to do with my mood. I'm just happy today." She reached out and smoothed Sara's hair from her forehead, and tucked it behind her ears.

"You're weird," Sara said, shrugging Ellen's hand away.

"All right. Well, let's get dressed. If you hurry, we can stop and get pancakes on the way to school."

Pancake pandemonium broke out, with both girls gleefully rushing through brushing their hair and teeth and pulling on their clothes to make it on time. True to her word, Ellen drove them to the Original Pancake House for their favorite strawberry crepes on the way to school. She dropped them off and drove to work, humming all the way.

She felt translucent, airborne. There had never been a more perfect day in the history of Oregon, she thought. The sky was clear blue. Everywhere she looked Ellen saw color and light—the shining, glossy green of the rhododendrons, now in full bloom, with great mounds of pink and purple and white, the vivid, soft chartreuse of the leaves on the empress tree, the glowing white peak of Mount Hood to the east.

She moved through her day lightly, greeting every customer with a joyous smile that was instantly reflected back at her, a contagious happiness. She told endless corny jokes. At one point, in the midst of the midmorning crunch as they were both steaming lattes, Cloud looked at her and said, "So, you gonna tell me what's up, or are you just going to keep up this Cheshire cat thing all day?"

Ellen grinned. "I can't tell you—yet. But I will, Cloud. I promise."

She knew she needed to call Sam. But she was so happy, and so completely unable to conceal it, that she was afraid he'd think it was because she'd slept with him last night and leap to the conclusion that they were now reconciled—a conclusion she wasn't able to make. *Although on this day, feeling this way, I could love Sam again,* she thought. *I really could.*

She was standing at the espresso machine, tamping down the grounds for a shot of espresso, when the front door opened. She heard staccato footsteps across the floor and turned to greet the new customer. And there, looking uncharacteristically disheveled, was Jordan.

She didn't look like Jordan, at least not like the Jordan that Ellen knew. Her hair, usually shellacked into a perfect blond bob, was uncombed. She was dressed in a T-shirt and denim overalls, and her ubiquitous Tinker Bell sneakers. She carried her designer raincoat under one arm. It was the first time Ellen had seen her without makeup.

"Jordan—" Ellen began, smiling at her warmly.

Jordan cut her off. "I need to talk to you—privately," she said. "Now."

Ellen put down the cup in her hand. She felt her blood run cold, like in a novel, in a movie, a chill that penetrated her soul. "Okay," she said, passing the cup in her hand to Cloud. "Here, will you finish this drink for me? Regular latte, extra foam."

She turned to Jordan. "Come around here. We have a storeroom in the back where we can talk."

Jordan walked around the counter and brushed past Cloud. Ellen held open the swinging door that led to the back hall, and Jordan stalked through. Ellen followed her. Oh, God, what had happened? Ellen opened the door to the little storeroom and motioned for Jordan to go in. She followed and closed the door tightly. They stood face-to-face, next to the pile of braided rugs where Ellen and Sam had made love the night before.

"I really came here just because I wanted you to look me in the face, Ellen," Jordan said harshly. "I just wanted you to look at me."

"Jordan," Ellen said. "I'm not sure what's happened. Jeffrey—"

"Yes, Jeffrey," Jordan said. "Let's talk about Jeffrey. Let's talk about wanting a house so much that you seduce another woman's husband, *the father of three children,* so you can twist his mind to the point where he's willing to give your goddamn house back to you. I don't even know where to begin. I just can't imagine someone stooping so low, being so calculating and cruel—" Her voice broke.

"Oh, Jordan," Ellen said, taking a step back. "Oh, no. That's not what happened."

"Ellen, I'm not an idiot," Jordan said contemptuously. "Jeffrey told me everything. He told me about spending the day with you on the coast. He told me about kissing you!"

"It wasn't like that," Ellen said softly. "Please let me explain. It was all just so accidental. We ran into each other in the bookstore, and we were both going to Astoria, and—"

"And nothing," Jordan said. "From the minute you decided you wanted this house back, you've been scheming how to get it, no matter what the cost. So you encouraged this stupid thing about the vineyard, just to get him to back out of the house deal. How did you arrange it? Did you have some little network of spies who told you he was going to the coast, so you could 'happen' to bump into him? 'It was all so accidental,' I'm sure. And so very, very clever. And what did you do to get him to kiss you? Play on his sympathy? Cry? Flash a little cleavage?" Jordan looked contemptuously at Ellen's V-neck T-shirt.

Oh, God. All I wanted was the house, Ellen thought. *I didn't want to hurt anybody.* Why had Jeffrey told Jordan about the kiss? It seemed insane to Ellen. Thoughts ricocheted through her brain like pinballs. *He told her because he felt guilty. He told her because he thought she knew, she caught him coming home from my house late last night. He told her to protect himself, to make sure he'd never have another opportunity to kiss me again.* Ellen wanted to believe the best of Jeffrey. Maybe, she decided, he'd been so happy to find that Jordan was willing to hear him out, to consider the vineyard, to try to compromise, that he wanted to give something in return—his love, his honesty. He saw it as the start of a new chapter perhaps, and wanted nothing between them to mar it.

Only now it was a mess. Ellen was horrified to think that Jeffrey's marriage was in jeopardy because of a few shared moments of empathy and attraction. Looking at Jordan and imagining herself in Jordan's shoes (albeit ridiculous Tinker Bell shoes), Ellen realized that she would have been horribly hurt if Sam had kissed another woman. *Actually,* she thought, amazed that in the midst of this anguished discussion she could even think about Sam, *I don't want him kissing anyone else.*

She turned her attention back to Jordan. "You have to believe me," she said, looking directly into Jordan's red-rimmed eyes. "I didn't plan anything. I didn't seduce him. It was a kiss, and it didn't mean anything. He's very loyal to you, and he's so happy that you've been so understanding about the vineyard. Really, Jordan." Ellen tried to sound calm, reasonable, not pleading.

"So now you know everything Jeffrey thinks," Jordan said sharply.

"Of course not," Ellen said miserably. "Jordan, I'm sorry. I'm just so sorry." She stood helplessly, looking at her.

"Well, I just wanted to let you know; I'm moving with the kids into the house on Grace Lane, *my house*. You need to be out on May thirty-first, as the contract states. I don't really care what you do after that, although I hope it's not with *my* husband. You make me sick." Her voice was hard, brittle, contemptuous.

With one last bright-eyed stare, Jordan yanked open the door of the storeroom, stalked out, and left Ellen alone, standing amid the mismatched pottery and vintage snow globes and what seemed to Ellen to be the complete shambles of her so-called life.

CHAPTER FIFTEEN

"WHOA, WHOA, WHOA, start at the beginning," Jo commanded. Ellen was sitting miserably on the floor of Joanna's living room that evening, her back against the gray-green sofa, cradling a glass of wine in both hands. She was wearing jeans and her garden clogs and a pink button-down shirt, untucked and rumpled. Her hair was pulled into a loose ponytail.

"I missed about sixteen episodes here, I think," Jo said. She was sitting across from Ellen on the floor, leaning against the worn brown leather armchair that had been her grandfather's. A floor lamp next to the chair cast a circle of light on the pale green rug around her. Ellen could hear Pete in the kitchen humming as he washed the dinner dishes; the kids were downstairs watching a movie. Ellen wanted to just stretch out and bang her head against the floor, *thump, thump, thump, thump,* until she couldn't think anymore. Stupid, stupid, stupid, stupid.

"You never told me that you kissed Jeffrey Boyce," Jo said accusingly, taking a long sip of wine. "That's quite a detail to leave out of your little day at the coast."

"Oh, come on. We had just started talking about it the other day when Sam walked in," Ellen said tiredly. "What was I supposed to do, say, 'Hey, Sam, hang on while I tell Jo all about the guy I kissed today'? Really."

"Well, okay," Joanna said. "But you could have called me later."

"It just felt private to me," Ellen said. "We shared a moment; I knew it wasn't going anywhere. It just happened. I didn't want to gossip about it. I didn't think it was going to end up haunting me and ruining my life." She slid farther down on the floor, till she was almost prone, with just her head propped uncomfortably against the sofa. She held her wineglass by the stem and balanced it on her stomach.

"Well, you're not exactly Hester Prynne," Jo said drily. "Although I bet Jordan would love to carve a scarlet *A* into your little forehead with her Martha Stewart paring knife. Still, you don't need to martyr yourself over this. As you say, it was one impulsive moment. It's just unfortunate that it's the one thing you could have done to pretty much guarantee you never get the house back. Jordan is never going to believe you didn't plan the whole thing."

She looked at Ellen sympathetically. "I'm sorry, sweetie. *I* know you didn't plan to seduce Jeffrey to get the house back. But it does look bad." Joanna rummaged through the bowl of chocolate chips and nuts and dried fruit at her side, searching for little chunks of pineapple. She found one and popped it into her mouth. "So is Jordan leaving Jeffrey? Are you officially a home wrecker?"

Ellen closed her eyes. She was haunted by the thought of Jeffrey's kids. She hoped against hope that, although Jordan was furious, she'd get over it enough to stay married to Jeffrey. The house was lost to her forever; Ellen understood that now, even if she still found it hard to accept. But she remembered vividly the day she and Sam had told their own daughters that they were separating— the wide-eyed confusion on Louisa's round face, the raw, tight hurt that had clenched Sara's entire body. She didn't want to think of Jeffrey's children going through that because of one small thing they had done.

She remembered the story Jeffrey had told her that day at the Lazy Susan, about Lily standing in the garden, offering a drink of water to the full moon. It was an image of such innocence and generosity. What would Lily do if Jordan told her they were moving without Daddy?

"Oh, God, Jo!" Ellen closed her eyes and moaned. "I don't know! I'm afraid to call Jeffrey; I'm sure he's terrified to call me or try to see me. He's probably devastated. He was so *happy* about this, about everything working out for him with Jordan and the vineyard, and for me and my house. Why did he have to tell her about the stupid kiss?"

"Well, *that's* the million-dollar question," Jo said. "The compulsion to confess is beyond me, I have to admit. I mean I'm all for honesty in a marriage, but that doesn't mean you have to share *everything*. Hey, Pete!" Joanna leaned her head back and yelled. "Peter!"

Pete stuck his head in the living room doorway. His skin glowed with a slight sheen of sweat from the steamy kitchen, and his red hair curled around his forehead. His shirtsleeves were pushed above his elbows, and he wore Jo's Betty Boop apron, with a picture of Betty Boop in short shorts and a chef's hat above the statement "Some Like It Hot!"

"Yeah!" he said. "You called?"

"Yes," Jo said. "We need a male opinion. If you kissed another woman just once, and it didn't mean anything and you never planned to kiss her or any other woman again, would you feel compelled to tell me about it?"

Pete eyed her cautiously and then looked at Ellen. "Don't tell me Sam kissed some broad and 'fessed up," he said. "You guys *are* separated after all."

Ellen's stomach twisted; her shoulders went cold. "*Did* Sam kiss someone?" she asked lightly.

"That is not what this is about," Joanna said irritably. "Let's not get off track here. No, Sam didn't kiss anybody that we know of, although if you're privy to some information you want to share, Peter, feel free. This is just a hypothetical."

"Your hypotheticals are never just hypothetical," Pete said, leaning against the door frame. "But okay, if I had a moment of utter lunacy and kissed another woman one time, and it meant nothing to me or to her, I'd let sleeping dogs lie and not let the cat out of the bag." He grinned. "Brilliant and appropriate use of mixed animal metaphors, wouldn't you say?"

Joanna rolled her eyes. "Yes, brilliant. Good answer. That's what I'd expect a normal man to do." She smiled at him and blew him a kiss. Pete smiled back and turned toward the kitchen. "I'm not answering any more questions tonight, though, just so you know," he called over his shoulder.

"All right, so we've established that Jeffrey is not a normal man," Ellen said from the floor. "It doesn't change anything."

"Does Sam know?"

"No!" Ellen said. "What's to tell Sam? That Jeffrey and I hit it off and confessed our secret fantasies to each other, which consist of really racy stuff like gardening and home decorating? That I kissed Jeffrey once and now may have destroyed his marriage and definitely destroyed any prayer I had of getting the house back? I just don't see the point of telling Sam."

Ellen put her glass down on the floor and rolled into a sitting position. "Besides," she said, tracing a circle in the thick green plush of the rug with her finger. "Sam isn't making life any easier. I slept with him and he wants to get back together, although things didn't necessarily happen in that order."

Jo shook her head hard as if to shake water out of her ears. "What did you say?" she asked. "I could have sworn you said you slept with Sam."

"I did," Ellen said. "Last night."

"Last night?" Jo said, eyes wide. "Wow, I want to be you! One day you're making out with Jeffrey, a few days later you're having sex with Sam. I love this whole middle-aged siren thing!"

"Oh, please, Jo," Ellen said, rolling her eyes. "You sound like Jordan. She thinks I'm some conniving temptress, running around Oregon in my scarlet push-up bra and stilettos in search of a man to have my way with."

"Well, you did kiss her husband," Jo said.

"I know, and I feel guilty enough about it, believe me. He also kissed me, you know," Ellen said. "It wasn't exactly one-sided."

"Let's get back to the point," Joanna said, reaching up to set her empty wineglass on the little oak table next to the chair. "Does Sam really want to get back together? Would you consider it?"

Ellen was silent. "I don't know what I want," she said finally, lifting her head to look at her friend. "I know there's something wrong with me, Jo, but I feel such grief over losing the house that I almost can't think about anything else. It feels like losing a person I love, and I need to mourn it before I can move on to whatever is coming next." She looked at Jo with bright eyes.

"You are losing a person you love," Jo said. "Sam."

Ellen was silent.

"It's also the baby," Jo said. "I never thought you really let

yourself grieve enough after losing that boy, when you were pregnant before Louisa."

Ellen's eyes filled with tears. "Well, those are the simplistic an-
swers. I just can't believe that's *all* of it. I probably need years of
psychotherapy. The Woman Who Mistook Her House for a Life.
It feels like my whole life, everyone and everything I've ever loved
most, everything that I am, is represented by that house—*is* that
house. I don't know how to explain it."

Joanna looked at her, so sympathetically that Ellen could hardly
stand it. "Ellen, you are a fucking nutcase," she said. "And I love
you. We'll get through this."

"Thanks," Ellen said, standing up slowly. "I better get the kids
home and to bed. Please tell Pete not to tell Sam about all this."

Jo stood up, too, and came over and put an arm around Ellen.
"Of course. I think I'll jump his bones tonight and put him in
such a sex haze that he doesn't remember anything about this evening. How's that for a plan?"

Ellen laughed. "Let me pry the munchkins away from Emily."
She leaned forward and kissed Jo's cheek. "Thanks, sweetie. I'd be
lost without you."

⁓

ELLEN MOVED THROUGH the next two weeks in a fog. As each
day ticked off, Saturday, Sunday, Monday, Tuesday, Wednesday,
she had a growing sense of unreality. It couldn't be true that ten
days from this moment she'd be sitting in the middle of her other
living room, with the house on Grace Lane just a memory and a
photograph stuck on the mantel.

Sam stopped by on Thursday with a big powder blue pickup
truck he'd borrowed from a friend. It was the first time she'd seen

him since that night at the coffee shop. He had called once to see how she was doing and to set a day and time for picking up his furniture. He'd been cheerful and friendly; he wasn't pushing her at all, and she was grateful.

She had heard nothing from Jeffrey, and didn't expect to. She didn't know if Jordan had kicked him out, or if Jordan planned to allow him to move with her into the house. Ellen ached for him, poor Jeffrey, who had been so happy and hopeful the last time she'd seen him. Alexa had called to say that Jordan had scheduled the walk-through for 4:45 P.M. on the thirty-first, moving day. She requested that Sam be present and Ellen nowhere in sight.

"I honestly don't know what her issue is," Alexa told Ellen on the phone. "I know you never liked her, but she was always fine with me. She just seems incredibly uptight and pissed off right now."

"I'm sure." Ellen sighed. "But I can be in the house until she comes, right?"

"Yes," Alexa said. "That's fine."

So Ellen continued to go through drawers, clean out closets, take down pictures. On the top shelf of the linen closet she found the tiny cap that had covered Sara's head when they brought her home from the hospital, and the little hairbrush they'd used to try to tame her newborn curls. She found a pile of dead pill bugs in a box under the bunk beds in the girls' room, a leftover from the insect circus they'd tried to have one summer.

She did most of it when the girls were in school. She wanted the house to look as much like itself for as long as possible, to save the bare walls and empty shelves and empty rooms for the last possible moment, so the girls would always remember it as it had been for them, with the artwork taped to the kitchen walls and the papier-mâché duck hanging from the chandelier.

Thursday rolled into the weekend, and then the final week. The move was scheduled for the next day. Ellen lay awake for most of the night, not even tossing and turning, just still, silent, eyes open. She felt the house as a living, breathing presence around her, witness to all the most intimate and important moments of her life. She thought of the baby she had lost here, the little ghost spirit whose presence she alone knew. His entire being had been in this house, inside her body, in the things she'd imagined about him as she dug in the garden and folded the laundry on the big table by the dining room window. Would he come with her to the new house? She heard the wind brush the branches of the Douglas fir across the roof, heard the boards creak, and the rattle of the loose window in the bathroom. The house was a presence, with its own rhythms and voice and soul, and it was so tangled up with Ellen's soul that she didn't know how to extricate herself. Finally, she closed her eyes and slept.

She didn't wake up until after seven. She had wanted to wake early, to savor her last morning in the house, but she was so exhausted that she slept right through the early light. No time to think about last moments now. She climbed out of bed, zipped a sweatshirt over her nightgown, and went downstairs to make tea.

Sam had already arrived and was in the kitchen, rummaging through the drawers and putting anything he found into a cardboard box. He was wearing baggy cargo shorts and a maroon cotton sweater. The ends of his T-shirt stuck out from beneath the sweater.

"You're up late, for you," he said, looking at her carefully to try to read her mood.

"It's daylight saving time," she said, putting the kettle on to boil. "It doesn't get light until an hour later in the morning. I *hate* that."

Ellen opened the cupboard to get the one mug she'd left unpacked and punctuated her sentence with a slam of the door.

"I don't know why they have to mess with the natural order of things," she went on. "I think I'll start a movement to do away with daylight saving time forever. I bet a lot of people hate it. They'll probably name a new coin after me when it's finally abolished."

"Yeah," Sam said, giving her a strange look. "That'll be minted right after the Ted Kaczynski quarter."

Ellen smiled; she couldn't help it. "Right," she said. "Me and the Unabomber."

Sam eyed her tentatively. "Well. I know you're not in a great mood," he said, "but at least you can smile."

"Of course I'm not in a great mood," Ellen said, irritated now that he'd actually gotten her to smile on this terrible day. "What did you expect? Really, Sam."

She opened the door to the tea cupboard and found it completely bare. "Oh, shit. I remembered to leave out a mug and the kettle, but I packed all the tea. That's perfect."

"Do you want me to run to the shop and get you some?" Sam offered.

"No." Ellen sighed. "There's too much to do. I'll just drink hot water. Why don't you go wake the girls? If you drive them to school, I could start in on the cleaning."

"Want some of my latte?" Sam held out his giant cup, which was not, Ellen noted, from Starbucks. "You may have a better day if you get a little caffeine."

"No, thanks," she said.

Sam looked at her. Ellen could see the realization in his face that she was going to be unhappy and difficult no matter what he did, so he disappeared toward the stairs. In moments Ellen heard delighted squeals and laughter and thuds as the girls leaped out of bed and wrestled with their father. *How could they be happy today?* Ellen thought. *Have they forgotten?*

She poured cereal into their favorite bowls—blue for Sara, orange for Lulu—and got out the milk. *Our last breakfast here,* she thought. Then, *Stop it! You'll make yourself crazy.*

The girls came bounding into the kitchen within minutes, fully dressed, with hair uncombed. Louisa, who was wearing her favorite blue gingham dress again, held Stella Blue Moon by one leg. Sara was dressed in jeans and a green Tryon Creek Park T-shirt. They were both smiling over something Sam had done upstairs. Ellen felt a pang for their innocence and resilience.

"Hey, guys," she said, bending over to kiss the top of Louisa's head, then reaching for Sara. "Ready for cereal?"

"Yes!" Louisa grabbed her bowl and headed into the dining room. "Bring the milk please, Mommy," she yelled.

Sara picked up her bowl and gazed at Ellen. "Are you eating breakfast with us?" she asked.

Ellen looked at her, at her face, now serious, with traces of sleepy dust still in the corners of her eyes. She knew suddenly that a hurricane of emotion was roaring just beneath the surface of Sara's calm exterior and that she must somehow, in spite of her own despair, help her precious girl navigate this difficult day. She handed the carton of milk to Sam and crouched down in front of Sara.

"Hey, baby," she said, putting a hand up to caress Sara's cheek. "So I guess you remember this is moving day."

Sara nodded.

"Here's what's going to happen, okay? Daddy will drive you to school. Then he's going to come back and the movers are going to help us move all our furniture and boxes into the truck and drive them over to our new house. Then we're going to get our new place all fixed up. For a few days it will be like camping—maybe we can all sleep on the floor in my room until we get the beds set up. Emily and Jo will be over a lot to help us." Her eyes searched Sara's face. "If you want, I can bring you back here after school to say good-bye to the house. Or it may be that you want to go right to our new house and just remember this one the way it's always been for us."

"I want to come back," Sara said, fighting back tears. "After school. I want to come back and say good-bye to the house."

"Then that's what we'll do, sweetie," Ellen said. "We have the house until five today. We'll see if Daddy and Lulu want to come with us. Now eat your cereal."

"I want to go to my new house," Louisa said, sitting at the table with a mouthful of cereal.

Sara, who had wolfed down her own cereal, cast Louisa a look. "Maybe Lulu and me can say good-bye to the basement before we leave for school this morning," she said. "We need to make sure we packed all of our things from the Turtle Club."

"Okay," Ellen said. "Why don't you guys brush your teeth and comb your hair and say good-bye to the basement? Then Daddy will take you to school."

The girls ran toward the basement door.

"Teeth!" Ellen called. "And hair!"

"We'll do it after!" Sara shouted, already halfway down the basement stairs, with Louisa close behind her.

Ellen stared after them, listening to the clatter of their feet on the wooden steps, the murmur of their voices. She closed her eyes and put both hands over her face.

"Ellen? Are you all right?" Sam stood across from her.

She rubbed her eyes. *As if*, she wanted to say. *As if, Mr. Baby Beeper.*

She dropped her hands and looked at him. "Sara is really upset about this, you know."

"She seems fine."

"She's not fine, Sam. She's acting fine for you, because she doesn't want you to feel bad. But she's totally on edge."

"Well, I'm sure if that's what you expect from her, she'll oblige," he said with some exasperation. "Ellen, I know this is not what any of us wanted. But can't we just make the best of it now? Can't we just move on and assume things will be good again for all of us?" His voice was pleading.

Ellen was silent. She took the kettle off the stove and poured hot water into her mug. "I'm going to finish packing. You take the kids to school. The movers will be here at eight. Then we'll get everything loaded, and then I'll clean. I just have to get through today. I just have to focus on that."

"All right," Sam said. "I'm here, Ellen. Whatever you need." He went to the top of the basement stairs and whistled for the girls.

They raced back up the stairs, breathless. Ellen handed them their backpacks from the basket by the back door. "Have a good day, girls," she said, bending to kiss them. She put a hand on Sara's shoulder. "Daddy will pick you up after school and bring you back here, honey. You and I can say good-bye to the house while he and Lulu go and get things set up in our new house."

Sara nodded. "That's good." She looked at Ellen. "You have a good day, too, Mommy," she said. "Okay?"

Ellen smiled over the lump in her throat. "Yes, sweetie. I will. I'll see you after school."

The furniture and boxes were all loaded into the truck by one. What had seemed to be so many things, the accumulation of more than ten years of family life, looked pathetically small once it was all boxed and stacked inside the giant truck.

How can it be so simple? Ellen thought. One day you possess a place completely, with all your photos and sneakers and furniture and socks, and the next day it's all boxed and moved and the place is empty. It was so abrupt, so strange, that she could barely wrap her mind around it.

And now for the cleaning. No matter what Jordan was going to do to the house, Ellen planned to leave it spotless, with the floors scrubbed, the windows shining, the tile gleaming. She decided to start with the kitchen. She filled a bucket with hot, soapy water and grabbed a scrub brush from under the sink. The mover, an unbelievably tall and skinny thirty-something guy with a coarse black beard, stuck his head in the back door.

"We're going to grab lunch, then we'll take the truck over to your new address," he said. "We'll meet you there at three."

"That's great," Ellen said, kneeling on the floor. "Thanks."

She bent to work scrubbing the bricks. How many times had she done this? A thousand? Ten thousand? She should be able to figure it out, two times a week, for fifty-two weeks, for twelve years—a hundred and four times twelve . . .

Ellen was scrubbing, glad for the mindless task, and the distraction of the math she was doing in her head, when the screen door opened again. She looked up.

"Hello," Jordan said coldly. She was herself again, as Ellen knew her. Her hair was glossy and combed, and she was dressed in neat, pressed jeans and an orange sweatshirt with a giant white *V* across the chest. The Tinker Bell sneakers were gone, Ellen noted, replaced by sneakers with the same camel and black plaid as Jordan's raincoat. She carried a grocery bag from Zupan's Market.

"Scrubbing the floor isn't necessary, Ellen," she said. "We're going to be ripping it out."

Well, this is perfect, Ellen thought. *Here's Jordan, looking composed, and here I am, literally on my knees in front of her.*

"Do you need to drop something off?" Ellen was still trying to figure out what Jordan was doing here, four hours early, when she had made it so clear that she didn't even want to see Ellen.

Jordan put her bag on the counter.

"No. It turns out we need to get in early. The carpenter has to get started on the kids' rooms, and it's clear you've moved all your stuff out."

Ellen stood up, scrub brush in hand. "But we have until five, Jordan. That's what it says in the contract. I need these last few hours."

"Really?" Jordan arched one eyebrow. "You *need* these hours? Ellen, I think you're forgetting that this is my house. My guys need to get to work now. If you've got a problem with that, get a lawyer."

Jordan picked up her bag and opened the refrigerator. "I need to unload my groceries." She turned to look at Ellen one more time.

"And you, Ellen, need to leave."

CHAPTER SIXTEEN

"SHE'S NOT GOING to let us stay until five," Sam said, a few minutes later. He had walked into the kitchen in time to hear Jordan tell Ellen to go. He had pulled Ellen, who was in a state of silent shock, out to the deck and pushed her onto the bench under the cedar tree. Then he had gone back in the kitchen to talk to Jordan. Now he was standing opposite Ellen in the backyard, with his hands in the pockets of his baggy shorts, trying to explain the inexplicable.

"We have to go," Sam said. "She's giving us fifteen minutes while she and her workers unload their stuff. Okay?"

Ellen looked at him. "But the kids—"

"It's probably better for the kids to remember it the way it was, Ellie," Sam said. "Not to see it all empty like this."

"Okay." Ellen felt panicky, the prisoner finally about to face the firing squad after months of anticipation and dread. "Okay." She looked around helplessly.

Sam reached out a hand, and she took it, wordlessly, like a child. He pulled her up, and they walked together to the back door and into the kitchen. Ellen looked at the brick floor. Half of it was still wet, the other half unscrubbed. The bucket sat forlornly in the middle of the room, the scrub brush next to it. She felt the urge to get back down on her knees, pick up the brush, and resume her scrubbing, *swish, swish, scrub,* dip the brush in the bucket, *swish, swish, scrub.* The rhythm of it, the mindless monotony of it, seemed irresistibly appealing to her. If only she could hang in that moment forever, suspended like a cocoon dangling from a silk thread. She'd never have to move forward then, into the moment when she'd actually walk out the door of this house for the last time.

She and Sam walked into the living room, barren now, with faded rectangles on the walls where the pictures had hung, and holes in the plaster from the nails and hooks. The room looked smaller and dingier with everything gone. Only the bookcase, repaired since the fire, looked new and clean. Ellen's footsteps echoed against the hardwood floors, loud in the empty room. There was nothing to say. They walked through the hallway, into the small room that had been Ellen's office, then into the big guest bedroom with the view of the garden and the giant hydrangea outside the window.

They walked upstairs. Their bedroom had always been one of Ellen's favorite rooms. It was small but full of light from the huge double window across from the door. So much of what was important in their lives had been lived out here, sex and love and arguments and tears and sickness and the conception of children. The closet door stood open, and Ellen saw with a pang the erratic markings up and down the doorjamb—the record of the girls' growth, marked haphazardly over the last ten years, from the time Sam had held the newborn baby Sara upright so they could mark her twenty-one inches to last month, when Sara had proudly reached fifty-six inches. Ellen had meant to copy all the measurements down on a piece of paper so she could reproduce them in the new house, but she'd forgotten. There was no time now. She closed her eyes.

Finally, they walked across the hall into the girls' room. Ellen remembered when Sam had painted it, a surprise for her after she'd been gone for a week visiting her parents in Michigan with the new baby. He'd spent days asking her, "So if we did decide to paint the baby's room, what color would you paint it?"

"Cream," she had said. "With pale purple trim and a purple window."

He'd painted it a rich shade of cream while she'd been away, then she'd found the wallpaper border with the purple wisteria and shades of blue, and they'd put it up one day while the baby bounced in her saucer. Sam had matched the trim color to the shade of deepest lavender in the wisteria and painted the window and the baseboard. They'd hung an old crib quilt on the wall, tiny squares of yellow and blue and purple, and placed a mobile with tiny paper birds over the baby's changing table. Ellen could still see the hole in the slanted ceiling where the screw for the hook had been.

"This is the hardest room to leave," Sam said, looking around. "It's the room we brought our babies home to."

Ellen looked at him in surprise, stunned that he felt it, too. Then the tears pricked her eyes and she started to cry.

"Oh, Sam, please," she begged. "Don't make me do it. Don't make me go."

"Ellen . . . " He looked at her helplessly. "We have to go."

He came around behind her, put both hands on her shoulders, and pushed her gently toward the stairs. He walked her down the stairs, through the living room and dining room, and into the kitchen again.

"C'mon, Ellie."

Sam held her elbow gently and steered her out the back door. The screen door slammed behind them, the sound that had punctuated all of Ellen's days for thousands of days. Sam walked her into the backyard and up the walkway by the garage to the driveway. It was a beautiful day, Ellen noted. She could hear the crows in the tall fir tree by Alfred's house, and a robin in the big hydrangea in the garden.

Sam walked her to his car. "Get in. We'll go to your house and meet the movers and get all the stuff unloaded, then we'll pick the kids up at school and bring them to the new house. We can make it fun for them. It's an adventure. It's probably better this way, without a long good-bye, and without seeing you upset."

Ellen stopped and looked at his car, then back at the house.

"I can't," she sobbed. "I can't." She stood helplessly, all the loss of all the things at once washing over her in a wave of such grief that she felt drowned. Her marriage, her unborn baby, her history with her husband and children, her life as wife and mother, it was all there, in the house, and leaving it felt like leaving behind a leg or an arm or something even more, her brain, her heart, her lungs, something she literally couldn't live without. She leaned against the car and wept, not caring who saw her, not caring if she ever stopped. Sam came around and held her.

"Shhhh. Pull yourself together," he said, but not unkindly, and he wiped the tears from her cheeks with the sleeve of his sweater.

Ellen let him hold her, then open the door and push her into the passenger seat. She buckled her seat belt reflexively and leaned back, empty and bereft.

Sam got in and started the car and drove down the street, past the white picket fence that bordered the yellow house, past the great mounds of candytuft and phlox blooming along the rock wall out front, past the old orchard next door.

Ellen looked at it, one last time. Then Sam rounded the corner and turned onto Canyon Road, and Ellen's last view of the house was gone.

⁊

THE NEW HOUSE was white; a one-story 1940s bungalow with a pitched charcoal-gray roof and black shutters. The front door was weathered oak, with a tarnished brass knocker and two small glass panes near the top. A large plum tree was in bloom in the front yard.

The rest of that day seemed completely unreal to Ellen. She pulled herself together so they could pick up the kids at school, dealt with Sara's wild outburst when they had to tell her that she couldn't go back to say good-bye to the house, somehow oversaw the movers and told them where to place each piece of furniture. Sam ran out to get a pizza and a bottle of wine, and sodas, which were usually forbidden, for the girls. They ate around their table, the old Irish farm table made of thick white pine, in the new dining room. The whole thing seemed crazy to Ellen, as though they'd been beamed up from their rightful place in the world and suddenly deposited somewhere else, into a foreign country, a strange new land.

Louisa talked nonstop, about her day in school, about the closet she'd discovered in their new basement that she was going to claim for her "office," about could they get a puppy now that they didn't live next door to Emily, who was allergic. Ellen was grateful for her chatter, for any distraction to cover her own despair, and Sara's persistent silence.

Sam talked, too, maintaining an easy patter about the tree

house he'd build for the girls in the back, and reminiscences about the house he'd lived in as a boy, on Long Island. He sat next to Sara at dinner and kept one arm draped protectively across the back of her chair, reaching forward every now and then to ruffle her hair. He kept his eyes on Ellen, to make sure she wasn't going to break down again. Finally, after he'd helped unpack the sheets and make the beds, he came to Ellen, who was unpacking boxes in her new bedroom, and said, "I think I should go."

She felt completely spent, physically and emotionally.

"Did you tuck the kids in?" she asked.

"Yes," he said. "Lulu's asleep already. But Sara seems pretty wound up. I tried to talk to her . . ." He shrugged. "I really think she'll feel better in a few days, Ellie," he said, pleading. "Once the strangeness wears off."

"It feels like the strangeness will never wear off," Ellen said. She wasn't trying to guilt-trip him or be critical. It was a simple statement of fact.

"Do you want me to stay tonight?" he asked. "If Sara has a hard time, maybe I should be here, to help."

"I don't know," she said wearily, stacking T-shirts into a pile and placing them in a dresser drawer. "I don't want her to think we're back together or something, and you haven't spent the night since we split up in January."

"I'll sleep in the girls' room," he said. "On the floor between the beds. Maybe it will make tonight seem better."

"Fine," Ellen said. She was too tired to make decisions, or really to care about the outcome.

That night Ellen lay awake in bed, the curtains drawn. With her bedroom on the first floor, she had a view of the backyard, with its overgrown tangle of old rhodies and camellias, but she couldn't gaze out at the night sky as she had for so many years in the house on Grace Lane. Once she heard Sara sobbing but didn't trust herself to go to her, to comfort her without breaking down. She heard Sam mumbling reassurances, and a creak that she knew meant he had lain down in bed with Sara. It was a relief not to have to be the rock for one night.

OVER THE NEXT week the girls were busy with a million end-of-school-year activities, the class picnics and parties, the last spring soccer game, the soccer pizza party. Ellen drove them to their events, smiled, chatted, yet remained completely unconnected. She felt as though she were moving through Jell-O. Sam called or came over every day. He helped the girls unpack all the boxes in their bedroom and arrange the furniture and stuffed animals. He hung pictures on the walls. He showed them how to climb the giant camellia tree in the backyard and promised them a tree house by the end of the summer.

Ellen was a flag, waving stoutly in the wind, a model of resilience and flexibility and optimism; she had to be, for her daughters. But with every smile, every word of praise for the new house, every hug of encouragement she gave the girls, the lies grew thick on her, coating her skin and tongue like molasses until she felt like choking.

She *had* to talk to Jeffrey, just once more. She had to know what had compelled him to tell Jordan about their kiss, to detonate the bomb that had exploded their bright futures. Was he still in the house in Beaverton? Ellen looked up his address in the closing papers. But she was afraid to drive by in case Jordan and the kids were still living there while Jordan's army of workers reconfigured

Ellen's beloved house. She didn't know Jeffrey's cell phone number. Maybe she could call him at work. She racked her brain to remember the name of his firm. *It was two words,* she thought. *A big downtown firm. Miller Nash? No. Ball Janik? No. What was it?*

The following Sunday she was standing at the sink of her new kitchen, rinsing maple syrup off the breakfast dishes. She'd gotten up early, in what felt like a pathetic effort, and made pancakes for the girls. This kitchen, while not big, did have room for a small table and three chairs, right by the window that looked out over the front yard. Ellen had brought in a little round pine table from the shop and covered it with a tablecloth she'd found in the storeroom, bright blue with red cherries across it. She had three mismatched chairs from the old house, and a little lamp with a blue base that she set on top. She had to admit it was nice being able to eat in the kitchen, just the three of them, and it was also nice to look out on the front yard and the street when she was doing the dishes, as she was now. The girls were digging in the dirt by the root of the oak tree in the front yard.

The phone rang, and she wiped one soapy hand down the side of her sweatpants so she could pick it up.

"Hello?"

"Well, they still haven't moved in as far as I can tell," said Jo's voice. "There've been a lot of workers and trucks, but no moving van."

"Has Jeffrey been there?" Ellen couldn't help but ask. It was like an autopsy. The knowledge wouldn't resurrect the dead, but there was just the ineluctable urge to know what had happened.

"I've only seen your mystery date once, so I'm not sure if he's been there or not," Jo said. "Remember the time I almost bumped into him, back when he was Mr. Tall Vanilla Latte?"

"He's tall, thin, with short brown hair and a beard and mustache," Ellen said, ignoring the "mystery date" remark. "Remember? He's usually very neatly dressed—business suits, trench coats. He looks like a lawyer."

"Well, I've seen a lot of guys who look like former or current convicts, but no lawyers, so I guess he hasn't been around," Jo concluded. "I have seen Jordan and the kids."

"But they're not moved in?"

"No. Jordan's over all the time—I assume she's supervising whatever work they're doing inside. They've been doing a lot of work on the kitchen. And they've torn down the fence."

"The whole fence? All the way around?" Ellen tried to imagine the house without the white picket fence that had characterized it for all her tenure there—the small swinging gate opposite the front door, the pink climbing roses she had planted to cover the fence and bloom every June.

"Sshh, yes, sweetie, the whole damn thing," Jo said. "The house looks kind of naked and embarrassed, like Dick Cheney without his clothes on."

"Dick Cheney?" Ellen repeated, startled by the image.

"Well, I hate Dick Cheney. And I have to say I just hate the house now. Although to tell the truth, it's almost better that she ripped the fence down. Before, it was like seeing someone you knew and loved, like your mother, only it was just a mother mask and inside was some horrible alien out to destroy you."

Ellen laughed. "Oh, God, Jo, and Sam thinks *I'm* dramatic."

"You got nothing on me, kid," Jo said cheerfully. "I am a writer, after all. So when are you coming over?"

Ellen stiffened. "Not yet. I'm not ready to see it yet, Jo. For a while you guys are just going to have to keep coming here."

"Okay, fine," Jo said. "Be that way. No, seriously, I won't push you. But you can't stay away forever. And the kids need to get used to coming back here and seeing the house and being okay with that."

"I know, I know," Ellen said. "But it's only been a week. Give me a little more time. Hey," she said, changing subjects. "Is Stella Blue Moon at your house? I haven't been able to find her since we moved, and Louisa says she doesn't know where she is."

"No, she's not here," said Jo. "Is Louisa going crazy?"

"Strangely, no," Ellen said. "Usually she won't even go to sleep without Stella, and the one other time we lost her, she was just inconsolable. Maybe she's outgrowing sleeping with a doll. But still I'd hate to lose Stella. She's such a part of Louisa."

"I'll keep my eyes peeled," Jo promised. "So how's Sam? Any more late night romps in the hay?"

Ellen rolled her eyes. "Yeah, I've really been in the mood," she said. "No, no more romps. Sam has been great, I have to say. He's not pushing me at all, he's doing a lot of stuff with the kids. I'm just too depressed to make major life decisions right now."

"Fair enough," said Jo. "How about a minor one? Want to meet for lunch today and go shopping on Northwest Twenty-third? Can Sam take the kids? Or do you want to leave them with Pete?"

"No, Sam can do it," Ellen said, cradling the phone uncomfortably between her ear and shoulder so she could finish the dishes. "He was planning to come over at noon anyway. So yes, lunch and shopping would be a great distraction. I'll meet you at twelve-thirty. Kornblatt's? Mio Sushi?"

"Sushi," Jo said decidedly. "But I'll pick you up. No need to try to find parking spaces for two cars down there on a Sunday."

Ellen said good-bye, hung up, tried to stretch out the crick in her neck, and finished cleaning up the kitchen. Maybe shopping would revive her, she thought. She pushed open the window above the kitchen sink and yelled out to the girls that she'd be in the shower.

Ellen walked into her bedroom, still the messiest, least unpacked room in the house. She looked dispiritedly at the big boxes, piles of clothes, stacks of books. She had done practically nothing in here other than put sheets and a blanket on the bed. No pictures on the walls, no beloved objects carefully arranged on top of the dresser. The room was painted a bilious shade of green that Ellen couldn't stand. *I'll fix up the rest of the house for the kids,* she thought, in a wave of adolescentlike rebellion, *but this room will be the one that reflects how I really feel about living here.*

She peeled off her T-shirt and sweatpants, dropped them on the floor, and stepped into the bathroom. She looked in the mirror. She looked old to herself, and tired, and sad. She didn't remember looking like this last year, or even last month. Now the shadows under her eyes seemed to have deepened, and her skin looked dull, faded. If she could just look at herself in the mirror in the upstairs bathroom in the house on Grace Lane, she'd know if she was really the same Ellen. But here, in front of this strange mirror in this unfamiliar, pink-tiled bathroom, who was she?

The phone rang suddenly, and Ellen darted into the bedroom, only to realize that it was her cell phone ringing. She followed the ringing into the hall, where her purse sat on the floor. She scrambled inside it for the phone.

"Hello?" she said a little breathlessly. "It's Ellen."

"It's Jordan."

Ellen actually winced. She waited. She had nothing to say.

"I was going to call Alexa about this but decided it's better just to deal with you directly. The notes, I'll have you know, are *not* funny.

I'll tell you, if I could prosecute you for harassment, I would. So the message is this: We've found all your petty little notes, your joke is acknowledged, and I want you to stay away from me and my family in the future, is that clear?"

Notes? Ellen racked her brain. "Jordan, I don't know what you're talking about. Did someone mail you something?"

Jordan made a disgusted noise deep in her throat. "Okay, Ellen, you don't know what I'm talking about. I'm sorry I called."

"Jordan, wait! Really, what are the notes?"

There was a long silence. Finally, Jordan said, "Well, as if you didn't know, someone has left little notes saying 'I'll be back' all over the house. We found them behind all the switch plates when we took them off to paint. They were stuffed in between the cracks in the floorboards in the attic, and inside the fuse box in the basement. We even found them behind the baseboards. It's just childish, Ellen. Ridiculous."

Of course it's childish, Ellen thought, *because a child did it.* She remembered the day Sam had been fixing the switch plate in the kitchen and Sara had wanted the screwdriver. That was the same day, Ellen recalled, that Sara had asked for paper and scissors and pens to "play post office."

"I'm sorry, Jordan," she said. "I didn't know about the notes. The girls must have done it." *Why do I spend my life apologizing to Jordan?* she thought. *It feels as though I end up saying "I'm sorry" every time we speak.*

"I hope this is the end of it," Jordan said abruptly. She hung up.

Aaaargh. Ellen snapped the phone closed. *Reminder to self,* she thought. *Stop answering the phone unless you check out who's calling first.* She'd have to talk to Sara later about the notes. Had she enlisted

Lulu and Emily to help? *I have to give her credit, though,* Ellen thought. *That's a creative thing to do.*

She showered, dressed, said hi to Sam, and finally sank gratefully into the front seat of Joanna's car, happy to be getting away from the new house. They drove into the city on Highway 26, past the towering firs of Washington Park and the zoo, through the tunnel that snaked under Portland Heights and into Northwest.

"Lunch first? Shopping first?" Jo asked, steering slowly up Twenty-third Avenue.

"I don't care," Ellen said. She was staring out the passenger-side window. It was raining, as it always did in early June, and the pavement glistened. Everything was green and blooming. The sidewalks were crowded; Northwest Twenty-third was a destination shopping-eating-walking neighborhood, and with tourists in town for the annual Rose Festival, there were even more people than usual on the streets. Ellen could spot the tourists easily; they were the only ones carrying umbrellas. Oregonians just pulled up their hoods or got wet.

They were stopped at the light at Everett and Twenty-third. Ellen was idly counting tourists in the crowd of people waiting to cross when she saw a familiar face.

"Oh, my God!" she said. "Jo, let me out! Jeffrey Boyce is standing right there on the corner." And with that she scrambled to unlock the car door, finally pushed it open, and hopped out into the rain.

CHAPTER SEVENTEEN

ELLEN LEAPED OVER the puddle in the street next to the curb. Was he alone? She scanned the crowd but didn't see anyone resembling Jordan. She saw only Jeffrey, in the forest green parka he'd worn that day at the coast, standing with his back to her as he waited to cross Everett Street. She didn't want to call his name out loud. She pushed forward through the people on the sidewalk, her head bumping into umbrellas, until she stood behind him.

"Jeffrey," she said quietly, reaching out to touch his elbow.

He turned just as the light changed. The crowd surged, moved forward. He jumped, completely startled, when he saw her, then stood rooted, his eyes on hers.

"Oh, Jesus, Ellen," he said.

They stood on the southeast corner of the intersection, in front of a brick apartment building, under a row of sweet gum trees that lined the edge of the sidewalk. The rain was a fine mist, caught in droplets in Jeffrey's short hair, glazing the leaves of the sweet gum in brilliant green.

"I just have to know *why*," she said, without preamble. "I mean, it's over now. I'm out of the house. I'll never get it back. I just don't understand why you told her."

Jeffrey let out a long, deep breath. "We shouldn't be standing here," he said. "Ellen, I'm just so sorry. But I'm trying to salvage my marriage, and I can't risk having anyone see me talking to you."

She grabbed his arm and pulled him down Everett Street, away from the crowds and cars. She pulled him past the apartment building, behind a laurel hedge that separated the apartments from the two-story yellow brick house next door and shielded them from the busy intersection.

"That kiss was such a small thing," she said, still grasping the sleeve of his parka. She looked up at him. The rain coated her face, clung to her eyebrows and lashes. "Why did you tell her?" She was pleading.

Jeffrey took a step back from her, so she let go of his sleeve. His arms hung helplessly at his sides. "Ellen—" he began, then stopped and looked down at the pavement.

"What? What?" she asked. "It just seemed that we were so close to having everything we wanted, my house, your winery. I just don't understand."

He lifted his head to look at her, his eyes dark. "It wasn't that simple," he said.

"Jeffrey, just *talk* to me," she begged. "I need to know."

"I didn't plan to tell Jordan," he said. He ran a hand through his hair, scattering raindrops.

"Okay." Ellen looked at him expectantly. He was silent. "So—?" she prompted.

"So after I saw you that night and told you about the house, I went home. Jordan was still up—she thought I'd been at the office. I felt—I don't know, *confused*. I was happy about the winery; I couldn't believe Jordan was willing to consider it. I really thought

I'd just tell you about the house and go home, and that would be that. Happy endings all around." He stopped and shrugged.

"And?" Ellen wanted to just throw a fishing line down Jeffrey's throat and pull the words out, inch by inch.

"To be totally honest, Ellen, I'm very attracted to you," he said finally, looking away from her, down the street toward the stone tower of Trinity Cathedral. "That day we spent together really threw me; it wasn't just kissing you, it was talking to you, and laughing about our kids and everything. We seem to see the world the same way. Then seeing you so happy that night at your house, and touching you again . . ." His voice faded. He cleared his throat.

"And then there I was at home with Jordan, who is doing this huge thing for me in giving up your house and considering the winery—I just felt so disloyal. I feel a real connection to you. I can't *do* anything about it, but there it is."

Ellen stepped back. *Of course,* she thought. *I feel the same way. But I don't know what to do with that, either. I don't know what to do about Sam. I don't know anything and I'm forty-four. My life is not supposed to be like this.*

Now it was Jeffrey's turn to stand silently, waiting for the words to come from Ellen. She was mute.

He smiled, a thin smile that didn't reach his eyes. "I guess you don't have to say anything. The point is really not whether you feel the same way," he said. "Anyway, Jordan and I had a few glasses of wine after I got home that night, and I mentioned how well everything was working out for all of us, and how happy you were about getting your house back. Stupid! She jumped right on me and wanted to know how you knew about getting the house back already, so I had to tell her that I'd stopped by. She was really upset about that. Then I really put my foot in it. I was trying to explain, so I told her that you'd been very encouraging about the winery, that I went over to tell you about it because it was something we'd talked about. She got kind of hard and quiet and wanted to know *when* I'd talked to you about it, so then I had to explain about running into you in Manning, and having lunch together.

"She completely freaked out. Couldn't believe I'd discussed it with you before I'd discussed it with her. Couldn't believe I'd spent a day with you and not mentioned it to her. Couldn't believe I'd run over to your house so late at night. She was crying; I felt awful."

Jeffrey lifted his hands helplessly, as if in supplication, and dropped them again. "I really don't even want to talk about it anymore. It was the worst night of my life," he said.

Ellen didn't know what to say. Knowing *why* Jeffrey had told Jordan didn't change anything, didn't bring back her house or heal the brittle, aching grief she felt.

"God," she said. "*Then* you told her you kissed me?" She wouldn't have believed it possible, but she actually felt sorry for Jordan.

"It was a train wreck," Jeffrey said simply. "I could see it coming, I just couldn't stop it. Once I started telling her, I felt I needed to tell her everything. It was totally selfish; it was just to ease my conscience. I was probably a little drunk by then, too."

He stopped and squeezed his eyes shut, dug his hands deeply into the pockets of his parka.

"Jordan was so furious that she called and withdrew the offer on the winery first thing the next morning," he said. "It wasn't even twenty-four hours later. We'll lose our deposit, but—" He stopped and shook his head. His face was a portrait of misery, his eyes drawn down at the corners in sadness, the lids heavy. Ellen had always loved the laugh lines at the corners of his eyes, but even those seemed faded, weighted down.

"So the winery is off," she said. "But are you moving into my house, too, or—"

"No," he said, shaking his head. "No. Jordan has made that clear. She and the kids will move in once the remodeling is done; right now they're staying at a friend's house in Lake Oswego, and I'm still at our house in Beaverton."

"Oh, Jeffrey." Ellen ached for him. She pictured him there, in his house with the climbing hydrangea he had planted out front and the playhouse with the tower he'd built for his children, all of it empty, all the noise and mess and life drained out of it now that his family was gone. *Jeffrey's got his house but not his family,* she thought, *and I've got my family but not my house.*

A dark green garbage truck clattered down the street, leaving glistening tracks on the wet pavement. Jeffrey shook his head and said, "I'm sorry. I've screwed everything up—for you, for my family, for everyone. I don't know what else to say."

Ellen brushed her damp hair off her forehead and pulled up the hood of her red parka.

"You don't think there's any hope with Jordan?" she asked. "Your kids are so little still."

Jeffrey closed his eyes. "Right. Jordan is just— It's like the spice jars. She knew one day she'd be married and have a perfectly organized pantry, so when she was seventeen she made all the labels for the spice jars. She has always had a clear vision of what her life was going to be. That's why it was so amazing that she was willing to consider the winery; it was a real left turn. But her vision of life definitely does not include a philandering husband."

"One kiss isn't exactly the definition of philandering," she said. He turned his head away. "You and I know it wasn't just one kiss, Ellen," he said. "And it's not just that. She thinks you planned it all, that you somehow figured out my schedule so you could catch me alone at the coast and— Oh, never mind. But she thinks you did it all to get the house back. Then she found those 'I'll be back' notes, and they just seemed to confirm it for her. She thinks if I'm dumb enough to fall into a trap like that—"

"Sara wrote those!" Ellen said indignantly. "Really, I'm forty-four years old; I'm a little beyond hiding notes in the baseboards."

He sighed. "I figured Sara wrote them," he said. "But Jordan doesn't believe it. She doesn't think a ten-year-old could unscrew the switch plates, or be so clever about hiding them. She thinks you were behind it all."

"So she can hate *me*," Ellen said, putting a hand up to her neck to hold her parka closed as it began to rain harder. "But I don't see why she can't forgive you."

Jeffrey looked at her and smiled, a small, sad smile. "I don't know," he said. "You're getting divorced; why can't you forgive Sam?"

Ellen felt a shock shudder through her, an injection of ice water into her veins. *I don't know,* she thought. *Don't ask me that.* She stared at Jeffrey, her mouth open, her breath shallow and quick.

"It's not the same thing," she said finally. "What happened with Sam and me is completely different. He did something truly selfish that jeopardized our family's security. I—"

"I'm sorry," Jeffrey interrupted. "I shouldn't have said that. I didn't mean it to be cruel. You're right; it's different. I just think I want to try to get Jordan to reconsider."

Ellen looked at him. "Oh, Jeffrey," she said, as kindly as she could. "If you really want her back, you've got to do better than 'I think I want to try.'"

He was silent a long time now, his hands still in his pockets, the rain plastering down the hair above his ears. "I can't," he said finally. "Jordan was right to be upset; I was falling for you. I don't know what to do."

Ellen's cell phone rang, startling them both. "It's probably Jo," she said, scrambling to unzip her bag. "I jumped out of her car in the middle of the intersection, and she's probably wondering what the hell happened."

"I've got to go," Jeffrey said. "I'm sorry, Ellen. I can't be around you." He turned and shoved his hands into the pockets of his parka. "I really have to go. We've been talking too long. Someone might see us."

Ellen stopped searching for the phone and let it ring. The rain had suddenly stopped and the sun was breaking through the clouds, turning the wet pavement into a river of sparkling shards of light. The sun warmed her face, lit improbable diamonds in the raindrops caught in Jeffrey's hair. She wanted to hug him and tell him it would all be all right, but the words wouldn't come because she knew they might not be true. And touching him was too loaded, for both of them.

"I think about Lily giving a drink of water to the moon all the time," she blurted unexpectedly. "I hope you get them back, all of them, if that's what you really want, and you're happy."

Jeffrey's eyes filled with tears. "Thanks," he said and cleared his throat. "Good luck." He put his head down, walking quickly back toward Twenty-third Avenue. Ellen watched him until he crossed Everett and disappeared on the other side of the big Pottery Barn store on the corner. Her phone rang again.

"Okay, so if I'm interrupting something important, just hang up," Jo said. "I'll find you later."

"No, no, it's fine," Ellen said. "Where are you?"

"At Elephant's Deli, on Twenty-second. I couldn't find parking near Twenty-third."

"I'll walk over and meet you there."

Ellen snapped the phone shut and stood there in the sun, staring blankly at a carved King Tut figure on the art deco building across the street. She heard Jeffrey's voice in her head: *Why can't you forgive Sam?* She thought of Jeffrey, alone now in the house he loved, the one he'd tended and nurtured just as she had cared for her house on Grace Lane. Only what did the house hold for Jeffrey now that his family had moved out? Would she want the yellow house on Grace Lane without Sara and Louisa—without Sam? She thought of the bond that she felt with Jeffrey and that he clearly felt with her. Had she gotten so far away from Sam now that a relationship with another man was something she could really consider?

A sudden gust of wind blew through the branches of the giant oak tree in the yard next to where Ellen stood, sending a shower of water down on her head. She shook herself off like a dog and began to walk east. She wished she could help Jeffrey somehow, persuade Jordan to reconsider, but of course there was no way she could get involved.

God, what a mess. She and Sam and Jordan and Jeffrey and all their children spun around and around in Ellen's brain, coming together and breaking apart like the bits of colored glass in a kaleidoscope. She made her way to Elephant's Deli, a Portland institution that had recently moved into a soaring new building on Twenty-second Avenue just north of Burnside Street. Jo was waiting for her at a wooden table inside the front door, with a giant sandwich and a bowl of tomato-orange soup. Ellen sat down, too dispirited to eat, and recounted her conversation with Jeffrey.

Jo listened sympathetically, munching on her sandwich and offering bites to Ellen, who shook her head.

"So that's it," Ellen said. "Jeffrey's lost his family, I've lost the house. There's nothing else for it."

"I can just hear Mick Jagger and the London Bach Choir in the background," said Jo, whistling the first few bars of "You Can't Always Get What You Want."

"It's too much Unbearable Heaviness of Being for me," she continued, blowing gently on a spoonful of soup to cool it off. "In my humble opinion, you need to figure out what you want and stop dragging Sam along on a leash if you're not going to stay married to him. Jeffrey likes you; do you really want to be in a relationship with him? And while I'm dishing out opinions, Jeffrey needs to get a backbone and push Jordan into marital counseling, if nothing else. Furthermore, Jordan needs to smoke just a little marijuana once a day to take the edge off and make her friendlier to the whole human race.

"Come to think of it," Jo said, putting down her spoon, "a little toke now and then wouldn't hurt you, either. Sweetie, your life isn't *over*, not by a long shot. You've got a couple of brilliant little girls, a husband you're attracted to who actually wants to be married to you, as well as a pretty fun job—not to mention fabulous friends. Sure, I wish you still lived next door, and I get it about the house, but only up to a point. You're so hung up on the house you can't see what's going on with your life." Jo finished her speech and wiped her mouth with a paper napkin.

Ellen smiled at her wanly. "You're right, Jo, of course you're right," she said. "Only I don't know how I feel about Jeffrey; I don't know what I want to do about Sam. It was as though as long as we stayed in the house I didn't have to decide. I could pretend everything was the way it's always been. I didn't have to *do* anything. I didn't have to choose."

"Nice try," Jo replied. "Too bad life doesn't work that way." She grinned. "Okay. I know you're not going to take my advice and get stoned. So let's go shopping instead. You can bury your troubles in a pile of material goods and credit card debt, all right?"

Ellen nodded and stood up. She picked up the one remaining crust of Jo's sandwich from the plate, put it in her mouth, and chewed on it slowly as they made their way out. But she couldn't taste it at all.

෨

LATER THAT EVENING, Ellen lay in bed in the still-strange bedroom in her new house, staring at the plaster ceiling. Shadows moved back and forth as the wind blew through the branches of the giant rhododendron next to the window. *Why can't I forgive Sam?* she thought. *Because the house was our security blanket, the thing that grounded us. Wasn't it?*

She heard the bedroom door open and the soft padding of bare feet on the wood floor. She sat up to see Louisa, in her pink flowered nightgown, standing there twirling her curls with one hand.

"What is it, sweetie pie? Bad dream?" Ellen lifted the covers and held them open invitingly.

"No." Louisa came over and climbed into the bed, nestling against Ellen's side. Ellen pulled the sheet and quilt over both of them and hugged her.

"Mommy, I miss Stella Blue Moon! I can't sleep without her. I want her back!"

"Do you know where she is?" Ellen wrapped both arms around her girl, buried her face deep in Louisa's neck to inhale her warm, soft scent. "I haven't seen her since the move. She's probably in a box or a drawer we haven't opened yet."

Louisa pushed her face against Ellen's shoulder. "No, she isn't," she said, her breath warm on Ellen's skin. "She's at our house."

"Our old house? No, darling, we packed everything up, and Daddy and I checked all the closets and cubbies before we left. She's got to be in a box somewhere."

"No, she's at our house," Louisa persisted. "I hid her there when Sara and Emily hid the notes. They said we'd be back, so I thought I'd get her back."

"You hid her there?"

"Don't be mad." Louisa pulled back to look at Ellen in the half-dark. "Are you mad, Mommy?"

"No, I'm not mad. I'm surprised. Where did you hide her?"

"In the basement. In a secret place. Can we go get her?"

Ellen was thinking hard. She could never call Jordan and ask to get into the house to retrieve Stella Blue Moon. Maybe Sam could go.

"We can't go now, honey. We'll call tomorrow, and Daddy can go over to get her back, okay?"

"Okay." Louisa snuggled close again, her head on Ellen's shoulder, her small arm thrown across Ellen's stomach. Within moments her breathing slowed and came in small, regular whispers. She was asleep. Ellen held her but couldn't sleep herself. She couldn't stop thinking about Jeffrey. What would happen if she didn't get back together with Sam, if she stayed single? Would she date? Would she want to be with Jeffrey if his marriage was truly over? She gently slid her arm out from underneath Louisa and rolled over. She tried to picture being with Jeffrey, snuggling against him in bed, talking to him across the dinner table, making love with him. She imagined Jeffrey with her children, his serious but kind manner, carefully constructing gardens and playhouses for them. But as soon as she thought of the kids, she thought of Sam, and then she could only picture Sam, making love to her, his lips on her breast—

Oh, God, it's hopeless, she thought. *I'll be attracted to Sam until I die. Biology is destiny.*

ॐ

THE NEXT MORNING Ellen called Sam to explain about the missing Stella.

"Hey, cookie," he said when he heard her voice on the phone.

"Cookie?" Ellen asked. "You never call me cookie. Were you expecting someone else?"

He laughed. "Nope. I knew it was you. I'm just in a good mood today."

Ellen was silent for a minute. *What was going on?*

"Any particular reason?" she asked finally.

"Well, yeah," he said provocatively. "I got well-laid a couple weeks ago after a long dry spell, and it's put me in an excellent mood. How are you?"

"Sam—"

"Oh, relax," he said. "I'm not pressuring you, Ellen. I'm just kidding around. What's up?"

"Louisa seems to have hidden Stella Blue Moon somewhere in the house on Grace Lane, and she wants her back. I don't want to call Jordan to ask if we can go get her, so I was hoping you'd do it."

"Call the dragon lady? And enter her lair? My God, Ellen, is this like a quest? If I perform the task faithfully, will I win you back?"

"Oh, shut up," Ellen said. She was in no mood for giddy flirtatiousness. "If it wasn't eight A.M., I'd swear you were drunk. Will you call Jordan and see if she's found Stella or if she'd let you go in later today to look for her?"

"All right," Sam said. "I'll call you right back." She heard the click of the receiver.

Over breakfast, Ellen grilled Sara and Louisa about the notes and Stella.

"They were just notes, Mommy," Sara said. "I didn't think it would hurt anybody."

"It didn't exactly hurt somebody," Ellen said. She mixed together some cinnamon and sugar in a small blue bowl so it would be ready for Louisa's toast. "It's just—" *What?* she thought. *What? It's just that the woman who bought our house thinks I put the notes there and that it was all part of a devious plot to seduce her husband and get the house back.* "It's just the lady who bought the house was a little upset, that's all. Now where did you hide Stella?"

Sara looked at Louisa and frowned.

"In the basement," Sara said.

"I know," Ellen said. "But where in the basement?" Ellen silently wondered if Stella had been found and discarded by the workers doing the remodeling. She didn't know if they were working on the basement or not, but surely they'd been down there for the fuse box or the water shutoff.

"We hid her in a place I can't really describe," Sara said. "It's safe. I don't think anybody would find her for a hundred years."

"Well, you're going to have to describe it so Daddy can find Stella and bring her home," Ellen said with some exasperation. She picked up the toast as it popped up and put it on Louisa's favorite orange plate. She buttered it carefully and sprinkled a light powdering of cinnamon sugar over it.

"There," she said, putting the plate down in front of Louisa. "Did you eat all your yogurt? No toast until your yogurt is gone."

"I need more cinnamon sugar, Mommy!" Louisa said. "And I don't want Stella to be hiding for a hundred years. She's in a big box."

A big box? Had Louisa hidden her in one of the moving boxes? Maybe Stella really was here in the new house, buried beneath a jumble of extension cords and old flashlights and other detritus from the basement.

"You mean a cardboard box?"

"No, a *big* box," Louisa said, cheerfully munching her toast.

Sam called back.

"So I talked to Jordan, and she said I can go over this afternoon, around four-thirty, quarter of five," he said. "No one will be there; she has something going on at her kids' school or something, but she said she hasn't changed the locks yet so I can use my old key." He paused.

"That's great," Ellen said. "Except I'm not clear on exactly *where* Stella is. Louisa couldn't seem to explain it."

"Jordan sounded really weird," he said. "Not snotty, although you've always thought she was worse than I did. Her voice was really tight, and she seemed to want to keep me on the phone forever."

Ellen's stomach lurched. *To tell him about Jeffrey?*

"Well, maybe I'll pick the girls up at school and bring them with me," Sam said. "Unless you think that's going to traumatize them or something."

"I don't know," Ellen said. "I think it's too soon. I'll talk to Sara some more on the way to school. I actually planned to go to Jo's this afternoon. Maybe you could pick the kids up after school and drop them at Jo's, then go in the house and find Stella."

"Fine," he said. "I'll see you around five."

Ellen dropped the girls off at school. She drove over to Coffee-@home, trying to imagine where, in an empty basement, three children could possibly have hidden a doll that was almost sixteen inches long. She was slightly surprised that Jordan had agreed so readily to let Sam into the house. *But then,* she thought, *she probably sees him as her partner in cuckoldom, betrayed by his spouse or about-to-be-ex-spouse or whatever I am.* She wondered if Jordan would tell Sam about her day with Jeffrey, and the kiss. God, it would hurt him, particularly if he stopped to think that she'd been kissing Jeffrey just a day or two before she'd slept with him. Ellen's mind was whirring.

The shop was crazy, with Rose Festival tourists buying coffees and regulars seeking refuge from the rain and the moms' group that met every Monday morning chasing after their toddlers. Then one woman bought sixteen Harlequin plates and eight wine goblets that she wanted shipped to Virginia that day so they'd be there when she arrived home. The wrapping and packing occupied much of Ellen's afternoon while Cloud manned the espresso machine.

At five she suddenly realized that she was supposed to be at Jo's. She ripped off her apron, tossed a hurried good-bye to Cloud over her shoulder, and got into her car. It was cold, and still raining. She didn't even think, until she turned onto Grace Lane, that this would be the first time since they had bought the house that she would drive onto this street and not pull into her own driveway. She drove slowly up the street. She was shocked at the sight of the house without the white picket fence. It did look naked and embarrassed, as Jo had said. Mostly it looked unreal, foreign, a stranger you tap on the shoulder because you think it's someone you know, only to find when she turns that there's barely a resemblance to the person you thought she was.

She pulled up across the street from the yellow house and parked in front of Alfred's. She sat inside the car and studied her house hungrily, the way you study pictures of someone you haven't seen in a long time, searching for every change, every nuance. She was amazed at how much landscaping Jordan's army of workers had gotten done in just a week. The fence was gone. The climbing roses were gone. The great unruly masses of phlox and lamb's ear and candytuft were now carefully manicured into neat round mounds. The foxglove, which had grown in crazy stalks of pink and white and purple in front of the fence, had all been removed. The entire garden was mulched and neat. The rain had dyed the beds dark brown. Rocks had been placed in careful rows along the edge of each bed, and along the grass next to the curb, so no one would make the mistake of driving over the grass.

It's all contained, Ellen thought. *Everything in its place, and everything held back, pulled in, cut down. It's all arranged, like the spice jars in the pantry.* She got out of her car and started to walk up the street. Her feet made splattering sounds on the wet pavement. She walked around the corner, up the hill along the side of the yellow house and toward the low-slung black roof of Joanna's brick house just beyond. She could not take her eyes off the yellow house. Was the purple wisteria wallpaper border in the girls' room gone already? Was the living room chocolate brown? It was like staring at a bloody operation on one of those medical shows on TV; she didn't want to look; she couldn't turn away. She saw Sam's car in the driveway.

Jordan wasn't around; she'd told Sam to use his old key to get in. *Maybe I could just peek in the back door to see the kitchen,* Ellen thought. *Maybe if I see it all changed, it won't seem like mine anymore. Maybe that will make it easier.*

She walked down the driveway and put out a hand reflexively to push open the gate until she realized that the gate and fence were gone. She smiled at herself, at her hand reaching out for the phantom fence. She made her way up the walkway to the new back door in the new mudroom. She pushed on it tentatively; it was unlocked. She opened the door, stepped in, and then drew back, coughing.

The house was filled with smoke.

CHAPTER EIGHTEEN

ELLEN STOOD FOR a second outside the door, her heart and mind racing. Was Sam in there? Oh, God, oh, God, oh, God.

She turned to run to the car, to her cell phone, but then turned back to the house. What if Sam had brought the kids with him? Could they be in there, too?

The kitchen phone is closest, Ellen thought. She ran into the kitchen, coughing. Her eyes stung as the smoke hit them.

"Sam!"

She felt for the counter, for the sink. *What am I supposed to do? Stop, drop, and roll. No, I'm not on fire. I'm supposed to get a wet cloth and hold it over my mouth and nose.* The smoke seared her lungs. She ripped off her sweater to hold it under the faucet, but the sink was no longer there, taken out in Jordan's remodeling. She dropped the sweater on the floor. The phone, she had to get to the phone. *Get down.* She dropped to her hands and knees, and felt her way across the floor to the wall by the dining room door where the phone was mounted, but it was gone, too.

"Sam!" She called his name even as the smoke choked her, even as she was blinded by the sting of it. What if he was unconscious and couldn't hear her? What if the girls were with him? She'd find them, because of course she knew this house so well she could make her way through it blind, find her way around every corner and into every closet or nook or cubby where two small children might hide.

"Sam! Sara! Lulu!"

"Ellen!"

The voice came from below, from the basement.

"Sam! Where are the girls?"

"They're here with me. But I can't get up the stairs."

Ellen turned and crawled toward the basement. She could see the floor beneath her but nothing in front of her, around her. She tried to breathe through her nose, but with each breath the smoke made her cough. The air was hot, choking. Her heart was beating so rapidly that for a moment she thought she'd pass out, right there on the kitchen floor. *No!* she thought, willing her body to move forward. *I have to get the kids and get them out.* It became the only thought in her brain, primal, instinctive, like the urge to shoot to the surface for air after staying underwater a moment too long. *I have to get them I have to get them I have to get them.* She kept crawling, coughing, her heart hammering away. She felt the brick of the kitchen floor beneath her hands and knees, then the smooth wood of the back hallway.

She reached the basement door. It was open, and the doorway was filled with smoke so thick and black it was impenetrable, impossible. And on the basement stairs, flames. Oh, God, they were in the basement and there was no other way out and they would die there, trapped like rats in a hole, her babies and Sam. She could not even imagine it. She could hear the girls crying now. And if they were going to die there, so was she. Because there would be nothing left of her if this fire leaped through the glossy brown curls on Louisa's head, melted the smooth skin on Sara's sweet face— Ellen slammed a door on the images in her mind and started down the stairs.

"I'm coming!" she called.

"No!" Sam's voice was sharp, urgent. "Get out! Call 911! I've got them as far from the fire as possible. We just need help fast!"

"Get in the crawl space! The crawl space under the dining room!"

The voice was right next to Ellen's ear, but Ellen couldn't see her, although she felt the rough denim of Jordan's overalls brush against her arm.

"We started digging yesterday to expand the foundation for the dining room," Jordan said. "There may be a space where they can get out." The basement was a square, with cinder-block walls and two small windows in the southwest corner. Along the south wall, the top of the cinder-block wall opened onto a space about four feet high with a dirt floor. The cement foundation surrounded it on the other three sides, with small vents cut into the cement every six feet or so.

Ellen was in a panic. "Get them out! Get them out! They have to get out!"

She felt Jordan grab her arm, grip so tightly that it hurt, her neatly trimmed fingernails cutting into Ellen's skin.

"They'll get out," Jordan said. "I called 911. They'll be safe in the crawl space and can breathe through the vents there if they can't fit through the opening. Now you have to get out."

"No, no, no." Ellen was shaking her head and moaning, kneeling on the floor. The heat was incredible. She was drenched in sweat and panting, breathless. *If I just leap,* she thought, crouched at the top of the basement stairs, *I can get through the flames and get to them*. It didn't matter if the fire tore through her clothes, singed her hair, blistered her skin. She had to get to her children. Jordan stood next to her, still holding Ellen's arm. She began to drag her, pulling her away from the flames on the basement stairs and toward the back door.

"No!" Ellen cried, stretching away from Jordan. "My kids! My kids are there!"

Jordan continued to drag her, both hands wrapped around Ellen's forearm, pulling her along the bumpy brick of the kitchen floor. She was surprisingly strong.

"Sam will get them to the fresh air," Jordan said. "He'll get them out. It doesn't help anyone to have you in here."

"My kids are in there," Ellen sobbed. She repeated it over and over. "My kids are in there."

With a heave, Jordan dragged Ellen across the threshold of the back door and pulled her out onto the concrete, into the fresh air. Ellen felt the damp, cold pavement under her legs, felt the mist on her face. She could hear sirens now, and see the dim flash of lights beyond the smoke that was pouring out the back door. Two firemen in full gear materialized in the smoke, faces obscured by masks.

"There's a man and two children in the basement!" Jordan shouted. "You can't get down the stairs. They're in the crawl space under the dining room, here." She held the arm of one of the men and ran around toward the side of the house where the dining room was.

Ellen stood up. She started to run back in the door, back to her babies and Sam, but the other firefighter grabbed her and pulled her up the driveway. There were fire trucks everywhere.

"My kids are in there!" Ellen screamed. She pulled and fought.

The firefighter wrapped both arms around her and held her back. "We're getting them out," he said. "You can't go in there."

"No, no, no, no, no," Ellen said, shaking her head and finally collapsing into sobs.

The fireman pulled her across the street. "Stay here," he said. "We'll get them out and bring them here." He nodded to another firefighter standing by the truck. He came over and held Ellen's arm, and the first fireman disappeared.

"No!" Ellen said. "No."

The fireman led her to an ambulance parked by the curb. He pushed her down onto the grass. A paramedic clipped a small black probe to the end of her finger. "I'm checking the level of oxygen in your blood," he said, "to make sure you didn't inhale too much smoke."

Ellen raised an anguished face to the paramedic. "My kids are in there," she choked out. "And my husband."

He lifted his eyes from the probe to look her full in the face. His skin was tanned brown and freckled, with lines carved across his forehead and more lines etched from his nose to his mouth. His eyes were a brilliant blue. "Our guys are the best," he said evenly. "They'll get them out. They will do everything to get them out."

His eyes and voice calmed her for a moment, and she tried to stop sobbing, to slow down her breathing so she could take a full, deep breath.

"I tried to get to them," she said. "I wanted to get to them."

"That's how most people die in fires," the paramedic said. "Let the pros get them out. Your blood oxygen level is fine," he said. "You must not have been in there too long."

Then why did she feel starved for air? The rain-scented air

cooled her skin, but she felt as though her lungs couldn't pull it in fast enough.

"Try to take slow, deep breaths," the paramedic said. "You're hyperventilating."

Jordan appeared now, with yet another firefighter. Her skin was dark with dirt and soot. Little rivers of sweat carved clean pink pathways down the sides of her face. Her blond hair was covered with a fine layer of dust, too. She looked at Ellen. "It's going to be all right," she said. "They're going to get them out."

Another EMT turned to Jordan and began to check her out, asking her how long she'd been in the house and how much smoke she'd inhaled.

Suddenly four firefighters jogged into the yard in oxygen masks, their heavy coats filthy. They moved cumbersomely in their big boots. Two of them carried bundles in their arms, bundles with brown hair. Ellen jumped up, yanked the probe from her finger, and ran to the men, who carefully put down a dirty, sobbing Louisa and an equally dirty, silent Sara. Ellen, shaking and weeping, gathered them into her arms.

"It's all right, it's all right, it's all right," she murmured over and over, rocking them, feeling the glorious living, breathing warmth of them. She held both the girls, shushing them, murmuring into their hair. Sam fell onto the grass next to her, coughing. His face was black, and his eyebrows were gone, singed off. *Everything could have been gone*, Ellen thought. *My entire family could have vanished in a few seconds, gone forever.* She felt bile rise in her throat, then pushed the girls toward Sam and crawled over to the bushes and vomited, spewing out all the smoke and terror, and the awful images that still crowded her mind. There was nothing to say.

She heard a high-pitched voice screaming across the street. "Let me go! Where are they? Where are they?"

Joanna tore into Alfred's front yard, barefoot, in a sweatshirt and jeans. She stopped short when she saw the four of them huddled on the grass. Her eyes were wide, terrified. She looked at Ellen, at Sara, at Louisa, at Sam. Ellen could see her counting them in her mind. Then she fell to her knees and burst into tears, sobbing helplessly with relief. Pete was right behind her and knelt down, gathering her in his arms, murmuring that everyone was okay.

Ellen looked at them, then at Sam, sitting on the grass with the girls clutched against his chest, and burst into tears again in a flood of relief.

Sam rolled his eyes in mock exasperation. "Oh, great," he said. "Everybody's crying. Now *that* really helps."

"I'm not crying, Daddy!" Louisa said brightly, wiping her eyes.

"That's because you're too dumb to cry," said Sara.

"I am not dumb!" Louisa wailed, releasing fresh tears. "Mommy!"

Ellen gathered Louisa into her arms and held her. "I know, sweetie. You're a big, brave girl and I'm so proud of you." She reached out for Sara, locked her eyes on her face. "You did great, Sara. You listened to Daddy, you didn't panic, you did everything right. You're so brave, and so smart."

Sara's eyes welled up. "It blew up. Everything blew up and then the fire got so big so fast."

"Shhh. It's over now. It's all right."

Ellen looked at Sam over the top of Louisa's head.

"They hid Stella Blue Moon inside the furnace," he said. "I guess the furnace hasn't been on. But then it came on while we were down there. I heard the click, like you always do when the pilot is lighting, then the gas, then there was a big poof of fire and then something under the stairs just exploded. I grabbed the kids and ran to the far corner—the stairs were on fire. I thought I could get them out the little window there, but it was jammed. I smashed it with my fists"—he held up his arms, which were bloodied from elbow to palm—"but I couldn't get the glass out. And the air came in and the fire just roared."

Ellen had never seen Sam afraid before—truly afraid. She saw now in his face what those moments must have been like, trapped with the kids, with the smoke and flames and heat, clawing at the shards of glass in the window frame so he could clear a space big enough to squeeze through a small child. He would never have fit through the tiny basement window himself.

He would have saved the kids, Ellen realized, and then he would have died there. She had a momentary vision of her world without Sam in it, with him gone forever. *It would leave a hole in the center of my life that would never get filled again,* she thought. *I couldn't bear it.* She felt a rush of love for him that overwhelmed her, that froze her in place, silencing the loud voices and sirens and activity around her. She closed her eyes.

"You did good, Sam. Thank you. If the girls—" Her eyes filled and she stopped.

He looked at her, and then his eyes filled, too. He immediately squeezed his eyes shut and shook his head, hard. He struggled to compose himself so he could talk.

"I didn't want the flames to get them," he said finally. "I couldn't let that happen. It just happened so fast. I always imagined if there was a fire I'd be able to run through it to save the kids, but I couldn't get up the stairs with them. The heat was so intense. And

I didn't know if whatever exploded under the stairs was going to keep exploding, maybe while we were trying to get up."

"You did everything right, Sam," she said, wanting to calm him. "You did. They're fine."

"Jesus, think of the nightmares they're going to have," he said.

"They can sleep in our room for a while," Ellen said. "For reassurance."

"God, yeah," he said. "They'll have to. Or I'll have to sleep in their room for a while, for reassurance."

Ellen stood up. Now that she was standing, she could see the house. Smoke billowed from the back in thick, black clouds, completely obscuring the tall Doug firs in the backyard. Three fire trucks were arrayed around the house, one in front and two on the side. They had driven right over the rocks Jordan had placed so carefully to keep cars off the lawn. The neatly mulched flower bed along the west side of the house was trampled into oblivion. Ellen noticed Jordan standing about ten yards away, next to a firefighter who had his hand on her shoulder. They were both watching the fire, faces transfixed. Ellen walked over to them.

"Jordan?" She touched her other arm.

Jordan turned to look at her. "Are your kids all right?"

Ellen felt tears rise again. "Yes, God, yes. They're going to be fine." She tried to swallow her tears so she could speak.

"I need to thank you," she said finally. "I would have run down there after them. I couldn't think. You saved me, and you saved them. I owe you everything."

Jordan looked at her. "I don't know what happened," she said. "I was going to stop in to make sure your husband found whatever he was looking for, and then I saw the smoke—" She stopped.

"We had painters in today, but they weren't using blowtorches or anything."

"It was the furnace," Ellen said. "Sam was in the basement with the girls and the furnace came on."

Jordan furrowed her forehead, drawing black lines in the soot on her face. "We had the furnace inspected just last month," she said, "before we signed the papers. I haven't had it on since you moved out, but then the guys painted inside today, and it was so damp they thought it would take forever to dry." She closed her eyes and put a hand to her head, as though mentally running through everything she'd done that day. "I set the thermostat for the furnace to go on at five. I thought I could run it all night and it might help keep it warm enough inside to dry the paint."

"Sam said he heard the furnace go on," Ellen said. "But then something exploded under the stairs."

Jordan opened her eyes. "The paint. We've been storing all the paint and cleaning supplies, everything, under the basement stairs. I just can't believe that having the furnace go on would ignite it."

It was Stella Blue Moon, Ellen realized. The pilot light went on, and Stella, made of cotton jersey and cotton batting, with her brown yarn hair and red felt boots, must have burst into flames. And maybe the flames were big enough to ignite the paint, or the fumes, that were there just a foot or two away.

Ellen was silent. "It was Louisa's doll," she said finally. "The one Sam was in the house looking for. I think she hid it in the furnace. Oh, my God. I'm so sorry."

Jordan laughed, with a sound like a dry cough. "It just figures," she said, staring at Ellen and then looking away, her eyes rimmed with tears.

Ellen didn't know what to say. She was afraid that if she said more she'd make Jordan angry, or seem somehow fawning, pathetic. She was genuinely overwhelmed with gratitude. She did owe Jordan everything. Her gratitude was enormous, incomprehensible, inexpressible. She would be connected to Jordan for the rest of her life now, even if she never saw her again, even if Jordan hated her. Every day she would know that each silly laugh of Louisa's, each warm hug from Sara, each moment with Sam, would exist only because of what Jordan had done.

There were shouts coming from the direction of the house. Ellen peered around the truck. The smoke was thicker now, blacker, but it couldn't hide the bright orange glow of the flames that lit up every window of the beloved yellow house. Flame licked at the window in the girls' upstairs bedroom, shone brilliantly from the living room, roared and crackled through the dining room.

It's burning, Ellen thought. *Everything. The doorjamb with the kids' measurements, the brick floor in the kitchen, the closet under the eaves—it's all burning.*

The fireman turned to Ellen and Jordan. "One of you owns that house, right?"

Ellen looked at Jordan. "She does," she said, nodding. "It's her house."

The fireman turned to Jordan and put an arm around her shoulders. "I'm sorry, ma'am," he said. "We did everything we could. It's gone."

CHAPTER NINETEEN

ELLEN LEANED AGAINST the blue Formica counter in the kitchen of her house, staring at the photo she held. It showed the yellow house last Christmas. Snow covered the roof, dusted the steps leading up to the front gate, and coated the rock garden in powdery white. The big deodar cedar and Doug firs loomed over the roofline, black against the white sky. Swags of cedar boughs were looped across the picket fence, with bright red bows on every fence post, and a wreath of noble fir adorned the gate. The yellow house looked brave and cheery in contrast to the gray sky, the white snow, and the green-black trees. It was like looking at a photo of one of her babies at age three months or six months, with their enormous dark eyes, the delicate shell-like curve of each ear, the plump, dimpled fingers. It always made Ellen ache for the baby who was gone, even while she loved the child who was here. It was like that now looking at the photo of the house. She loved it with all her heart; she'd never see it again.

Even then, I knew it was our last Christmas in the house, Ellen thought. *I just didn't know it was the house's last Christmas, too.*

The shock of the day before was still fresh. Indeed, at noon Ellen still had not slept. After riding to the hospital, they'd all come home to Ellen's new house. Sam had stitches in his right arm and hand where he'd been cut by the window glass, and minor burns. The girls were fine. Ellen and Sam had taken turns showering, then helped the girls bathe, washing the soot out of their hair, scrubbing the ash from their skin. The water swirled in a murky gray circle down the drain. Next Ellen had wrapped the girls in fluffy towels and their soft cotton pajamas. She laid them down to sleep in her big bed, with herself and Sam wrapped around them, afraid to let go. Sam, completely exhausted, had fallen asleep instantly, curled on his side, his body spooning Sara's small form. The girls were asleep quickly, too. The soft, even sound of their breathing soothed Ellen, even as she had lain awake, staring at the ceiling, trying not to replay all the what-ifs in her mind.

But she hadn't been able to shut them out. What if the kids had been killed? What if they'd gotten out but Sam had died? What if all three of them had died? *It was so fast. One minute I was thinking about Jordan's compulsively organized garden, and five minutes later everything I loved most in the world could have been gone forever.* She'd stared at Sam, at the girls, and at the shadows on the ceiling until the pale, rosy glow of early morning suffused the room. Then she'd simply gotten up, pulled on a sweatshirt, and gone to the kitchen to make tea.

Sam was up now, whistling in the shower. He always showered to wake up. Ellen fingered the photo of the yellow house. She wished with all her heart she could be more like him, able to let things go. He had slept for almost twelve hours straight, barely even moving. She'd watched him much of the night. His thick, dark eyelashes hadn't twitched, and his arm had remained around Sara protectively, even in sleep. *I love you*, Ellen had thought. *You drive me crazy and probably always will, but I love you.*

She didn't know how to tell him. Now, even after a sleepless night, the fact of the four of them, the *need* for the four of them to be together, seemed indisputable. She saw a core of steadiness and strength in Sam that flowed like lava underneath the surface of things. Yes, he'd always have the love of risk that led him to ski off cliffs or—God forbid—mortgage the house for his latest invention. But he had hardened this year, in a good way, like the trees in the Petrified Forest. The vague sense of mistrust she'd always had—*he's irresponsible, you must be vigilant in case he fucks up*—was gone. *I don't need to be married to someone even more vigilant than I am, like Jeffrey does. I just need someone who's vigilant enough.*

She heard the shower stop, heard more whistling as Sam dried himself off—*probably with* my *towel*, she thought with a smile. The girls were watching a movie in the family room in the basement, tucked under the old red and white "couch quilt." They'd wanted the comfort and security of familiar things this morning—cereal in the blue and orange bowls, the sound of Ellen's kettle whistling on the stove, a video they'd seen a hundred times before.

Sam walked into the kitchen, his hair damp and sticking up in a million directions. He had a towel around his waist and wore one of his old sweatshirts that Ellen had kept.

"I don't suppose my pants are wearable," he said. "They must reek of smoke. I couldn't even find 'em."

"I threw them in the wash this morning," she said. "But they may be a lost cause. I might have some sweatpants that fit you."

He arched what would have been an eyebrow but was only singed stubble. "I doubt it," he said. "You're a midget. Don't you have any of my clothes here?"

"I don't think so, but I'll look," she said, heading to the bedroom.

"I guess I should be glad that your house isn't full of men's pants," he called after her.

"I don't let men leave their pants here unless they're staying for good," she called back.

She could hear him rummage through the cupboard above the sink. "Does the Coffee@home queen actually have coffee at home? Man, do I need coffee."

Ellen emerged from her bedroom carrying a pair of paint-splattered jeans. They had been Sam's originally, and then she'd adopted them for painting and gardening because she could slip them on over her own pants.

"Here," she said. "These are yours. They should fit."

"Great." He took the pants and pulled them on under his towel, then tossed the towel over the back of one of the kitchen chairs. "And the coffee?"

Ellen winced. "I hate to tell you this, but I don't have any. I'm sorry."

"Well then, I'm outta here," he said. "I've got to go to Starbucks and get coffee."

"Very funny," Ellen said. "I'll run to the shop and get some beans. I need to talk to Cloud anyway."

"I hope it's a short conversation," Sam said. "Bring me a latte, too, will you? Where are the girls?"

"In the den, watching a video."

"Good. They seem okay?"

Ellen picked up her keys from the counter. "Yes. I told them they could stay home from school today." She paused. "They're going to want to stick close to us for a while," she said. "Like little barnacles."

"That's how I feel about them," he said. His eyes moved to the photo on the counter. He looked at it for a moment, then at Ellen.

"It was a good house," he said.

"It *was* a good house," she said, leaning in to look at it again. "I thought I loved it more than anything."

"I know what you thought," he said, looking at her intently.

"Sam—"

"Coffee first," he said. "Go get the coffee."

He waited a beat. "Then when you get back, I need to run out for a minute."

"For what?"

"Pants," he said with a smile. "I need to stop by my place and pick up some clean pants. That is, if you're ready to let me leave some pants here."

Ellen smiled back. "Bring 'em on," she said and reached up to kiss him.

She drove in a daze. She had a strange sense of unreality, as though she were sleepwalking. *Maybe I'm in shock*, she thought, standing for a moment outside the store. Everything was the same; the black and white Coffee@home logo sign hung in the window, just above the back of the blue couch, and the yellow umbrella stand with the bright red and blue parrots on it, just visible through the window. And everything was different; she would never walk through the world as carelessly again, knowing how much could have changed in an instant.

She pushed open the glass door, relishing the warmth and the heady, comforting smell of coffee and warm milk.

"Hey," Cloud greeted her with a smile. "It's after noon. You really must have slept in."

"You wouldn't believe the night I had," Ellen responded, reaching for a bag of coffee beans from the bookshelf on the far wall. She had stepped behind the counter and picked up a cup to make a latte for Sam when her cell phone rang.

"Ellen? Oh, my God, it's Alexa. I just heard. I can't believe the house is really gone. Are you all right? Are Sam and the kids okay?"

Ellen took a deep breath in and exhaled through pursed lips. It hurt; it just hurt to think of the house reduced to ash and cinder block and a few blackened bricks.

"We're all fine," she said, cradling the phone against her chin while she poured milk into the metal pitcher for steaming.

"I just got off the phone with Jordan Boyce," Alexa continued. "She's going to sell the lot; just wants nothing to do with it anymore. Actually, that was one reason I was calling, to see if you'd be interested."

Ellen's mind reeled. Buy back the lot? The little plot of earth with her beloved children's goldfish buried in the backyard and the wind singing in the firs at night . . . They could build a new house. Not an exact replica of the yellow house, but with all its most-beloved characteristics. They'd still be next door to Jo.

"I don't know, Alexa," she said finally. "I haven't really slept; I can't think straight yet."

"Of course," Alexa said. "I don't need an answer now. Just wanted to let you know."

"What's Jordan going to do?" Ellen needed to know. She truly wanted Jordan to be happy. She wanted Jeffrey to be happy, whatever that might mean for both of them.

"I'm not sure. She'll get insurance money from the fire. What a freak thing! She said they had paint stored under the stairs, and it just exploded. She mentioned that she and her husband were thinking about buying a winery in Dundee, but she wasn't sure."

The winery! Maybe now Jordan, too, saw how tissue-thin the strands were that connected everything. Maybe the yearning for something different that Jeffrey and Ellen had shared seemed truly minor now compared with the enormity of all that they could have lost.

"I'll talk to Sam and call you about the lot, Alexa," Ellen said. "If you talk to Jordan or Jeffrey again, please tell them I said 'Thank you.' For everything."

Ellen clicked off the phone and finished making an enormous triple-shot latte for Sam. She told Cloud she'd call him later; she needed to be at home all day.

Back at the house, she washed all their clothes again and again, to get the smoke and soot out. They watched videos, the four of them tucked together under the couch quilt. She made comfort food, thick smoothies with fruit and yogurt, mashed potatoes, roast chicken and gravy. Finally, after dinner, she felt herself begin to relax, felt her shoulders drop a little, her breath come more slowly and evenly.

She and Sam agreed, in little more than a look exchanged over the children's heads, that the girls would sleep in their room again. Ellen, finally ready to sleep, made up beds for them on the floor, with thick comforters and quilts piled in a stack underneath sleeping bags. "Like the princess and the pea," she told them. "You have twenty layers here."

Ellen tucked them in and kissed them both, then lifted the quilt and climbed into bed beside Sam. She slid over next to him and laid her head on his chest. He slipped his arm around her and ran his fingers lightly up and down over her forearm.

"Hey, so we haven't talked about the baby beeper," he said softly.

"Oh, Sam, please. The baby beeper is what got us into trouble in the first place. Can we leave it alone?"

"I really worked a long time on that transmitter, you know?" he said. It was the same tone he used when he was explaining some complicated football play on TV that he wanted her to understand. He knew she really wasn't that interested, but it was so compelling to him that he just *had* to share it. "I wanted it to be tiny enough that you could stitch it inside baby clothes without noticing it, but it still had to be loud enough that you could hear it from half a block away. And it needed a strong battery, so it wouldn't go dead too soon."

"Mmm-hmm." Ellen closed her eyes. She finally felt as if she could sleep, after all the hours and all that had happened.

"The problem was that when you stitched it into a onesie, then you had to take it out to wash the onesie. The thing just went dead when it got wet. So I fixed that problem."

Ellen was almost asleep now, her cheek pressed against his chest, feeling the warm hum of his voice. "So the baby beeper is waterproof now?"

"Nope," Sam said. "Water kills it every time. But I managed to sell it anyway."

"You sold it anyway," Ellen murmured. "You sold the baby beeper. To Babies 'R' Us?"

"No, Ellie. To Staples, and Office Depot, and Target, and Wal-Mart. I put a little adhesive on it. You can stick one on your glasses, your car keys, your wallet, your coffee mug—anything you have trouble keeping track of. It means never losing anything again. God, they paid me a shitload of money for it."

Ellen opened her eyes and sat up. "Really?"

He grinned, gazing up at her. "Really."

"When? Why didn't you tell me?"

"I just got word about a week ago." He put both hands behind his head and leaned back, looking up at her, enjoying her surprise.

"And then, I don't know. I wanted to be sure you didn't love me just for my money."

She was speechless.

"It's certainly enough to let me tinker around with inventing for a long time. Or we could put some into expanding Coffee@home. Or a new house."

She didn't know what to say. Ellen slid back down in the bed and lay next to him, her head nestled against his side. She was too tired to figure this out now.

"I just wanted you to know," he said. He stroked her hair.

A new house? A rebuilt version of the yellow house? *No*, Ellen thought. *I don't need it. I don't even want it anymore.* In the half-light, she could just make out the familiar shape of the pine armoire against the far wall, the outline of the painting of the Columbia River Gorge on the other wall, next to where the girls slept on the floor. She snuggled closer to Sam, under the warmth of the blue and white quilt. She could hear Louisa's deep, steady breathing across the room, and Sara's gentle snore.

And the thought came, and ran through her head again and again, a prayer and a prayer answered, a blessing, a fulfillment:

I am home, I am home, I am home.

1. Places, from Ellen's house to Portland itself, play a key role in the book, and almost seem like actual characters. Was Ellen's love for the house understandable, or did she put too much importance into the meaning of a place? What do you really give up when you leave a place you love, whether it's a house or a town or a neighborhood? Why do we invest so much in our physical environment?

2. Ellen's definition of "home" changes by the end of the novel. What really makes a house a home?

3. To what extent do people have to give up their dreams once they're married? Whether owning a winery, inventing a new product, or living in one's dream house/home, each of the characters in this book struggled to articulate their own dream and live it, while still trying to consider the needs of spouses and children. Which characters achieved their dreams by the end? Were the sacrifices involved fair, or too much?

4. Ellen is a very self-sufficient character. Is there anything "out of balance" in Ellen's relationships with her friends and/or family members?

5. What is the definition of being heroic? Who was the hero in this book?

6. Some people love the idea of a fresh start and feel the need to move every few years. Why is Jordan's approach to her own move so different from Ellen's? Whose approach is more realistic? More common? Why?

7. Being vulnerable can open one up to relationships (or even just the thought of relationships) that otherwise might be unthinkable when our reserves are stronger. Why are Ellen and Jeffrey drawn to each other? Is their mutual attraction based only on their situations? Why or why not?

8. Could Jordan and the heroine ever have been friends if they had met under different circumstances?

9. Given that Ellen seems to be a woman who "has it all" in so many respects, what is it that is really driving her to divorce?

10. Where do you think Ellen gets her strength? Why would a woman like Ellen engage in risky behaviors such as attempted arson and romance with a married man?

11. Have you ever gone back to a home you loved and left? Was it what you expected?

12. Ellen has trouble understanding Jordan's fascination with where she went to college. Are there real regional differences like this across the United States? Or was Jordan's attitude more a function of her own personality than her East Coast upbringing?